THE LAST TAXPAYER
AT KING HENRY'S FAIRE

BILL SCANNELL

Black Rose Writing | Texas

First printing

This is a work of fiction. Names, characters, businesses, places, events, and incidents are either the products of the author's imagination or used in a fictitious manner. Any resemblance to actual persons, living or dead, or actual events is purely coincidental.

ISBN: 978-1-68433-884-9
PUBLISHED BY BLACK ROSE WRITING
www.blackrosewriting.com

Printed in the United States of America
Suggested Retail Price (SRP) $20.95

The Last Taxpayer at King Henry's Faire is printed in Garamond

*As a planet-friendly publisher, Black Rose Writing does its best to eliminate unnecessary waste to reduce paper usage and energy costs, while never compromising the reading experience. As a result, the final word count vs. page count may not meet common expectations.

This book is dedicated to my father, **William F. Scannell**
February 12, 1925 - April 19, 2012 He served in the Pacific Theatre during WWII, was an excellent trial lawyer in Massachusetts, the best Father to his children, and a fine and compassionate Judge. He was a wise, wonderful man and we all miss him greatly.

This book is dedicated to my father, William P. Scannell

February 12, 1926–April 10, 2012. He served in the Pacific Theater during WWII, was an excellent trial lawyer in Massachusetts, the best Father to his children, and a fine and compassionate judge. He was a wise, wonderful man and we all miss him greatly.

THE LAST TAXPAYER
AT KING HENRY'S FAIRE

1

Nix was at her squaricle, short skirt hiked to her high thigh, long summer legs thrown across the desk, one foot resting on the keyboard, the other bouncing on the former's ankle. She was staring at her cracked and broken pedicure, scrolling through the early morning emails.

"Fuck me in the ass on a Monday morning," she mumbled, "that little prick Buffum is going to regret this."

Reaching for the phone, she banged in a four-digit extension, "Steiger?"

"Hey Nix, how was the wee..."

"Check your inbox. I'll be right over."

"Why?"

"Check your inbox."

Nix tapped Steiger on the shoulder, who turned and said, "What's this all about?" Steiger turned back to finish the email, "It's August twenty-eighth, Nix. Why's Buffum assigning a case at the end of August? This put me over limit. The IRS wasn't like this when I started. I'm going to have to write an Efficiency."

"We're going to have to write Efficiencies, you selfish douche. Despite the shame of it, we're partners."

"So, it puts us both over. What's he trying to pull?"

"Open the attachment."

"What the fuck is King Henry's Faire? Failure to file thirty million in taxes?"

"Thirty-two million, actually, which is an estimate, read on."

"It's a ten-year delinquency, Nix, and we're only just getting it. It says here the last known taxpayer has been dead for ten years. No one recoups on ten-year old delinquencies when the taxpayer is alive. This is the kiss of death. My stomach is roiling, Nix, turning cartwheels."

"Does baby need a burp?"

"No, but it hurts and this is going to put us over max for the rest of the year and into next. There goes the bonus again. This is total fuckery, Nix. Think we ought to go to the Union?"

"Why?" she was calm, "I think we better see Buffum. That's who gave this to us."

"About that, Nix, you know, maybe I ought to see Buffum."

"As in you and not me?"

"Yeah, don't you think?"

"No. You can see him if you want. I'll take care of me."

"I didn't mean anything, Nix. It's just, you know, you and Buffum. You know....

"No, I don't, Steiger, what's wrong with me seeing Buffum?" Nix got up and began walking to their supervisor's door, Steiger close at her heels.

"Oh, Nix, come on. You, ahhh, when it comes to Buffum, you know, you're a little, that is, he thinks you're a little abrasive."

"Abrasive?" Nix kept walking, "I'm not abrasive. He hasn't seen abrasive. Maybe if I dry fuck the little weasel he'll feel how abrasive I can be."

"Okay, Nix, let's stop for a minute and think this through. There are rules, actual laws to consider."

"Don't give me that social contract bullshit, Steiger. I'll cover my dick with crazy glue and pour sand on it. Then let's see if he thinks I'm a little abrasive."

"Please, Nix, let me talk to him."

"Do what you want, come or stay, but you don't speak for me."

"Let's first get a coffee in the break room. C'mon, Nix. Think this through. It affects me too."

Nix rapped on Buffum's door. All she heard was a tinny echo through the hollow modern door. She rapped again, harder, louder, longer.

"Hi Nix," a curly white head followed by a pleasant face popped back from the squaricle next to Buffum's door, coasters locking as the chair jerked to a stop, "Buffum's not in this week."

"Hi Marge. He's not?"

"He took an unscheduled vacation. Won't be back 'til after Labor day. But he said if you were looking for him to tell you that everyone gets old cases. They resurface now and then and you just have to do the necessary. He said he's more concerned with closure than collection. He said to say that twice."

"Thanks, Marge, like your hair."

"Thanks, Nix, at my age I figure, hey, why can't I go natural? Besides here and the market, the only place I go is the bowling alley where all they see is my ass."

"Good point, Marge. I like you so I'm not going to leave a message."

"Thanks, Nix. You're saving me seven hours on the phone. I baked some banana bread. It's in the kitchen."

II

Squinting my way down Central Boulevard, all the way through the trailer park to the State Highway, the powdery sand has been resting all night. There's a convenience store on the far side of the intersection. Damn, that sun's in my eyes. Not a car, not a person, not even a dog has left a track. The sooty fine sand has laid pure and undisturbed until my footfalls create tiny dust devils that spit and spat before falling apart for the first time of the day. It sure is going to be a hot one for late summer, dust devils this close to fall.

I'm the Fool but my private name is Rodrigo, which it ain't, but until I get a couple warrants straightened out or some new documents, it is. The King's been staying in my trailer for a week. Seems longer because it has me sleeping on the floor. I got a sore neck and now my head's cocked all the time. That ain't the worst of it. His Majesty doesn't believe he has to wear anything except a bathrobe. He calls it his ceremonial garb but I was with him when he got it at the Walmart. It's a polyester leopard print thing you wouldn't wear if someone gave it to you. Makes me itch to look at it and the stitching's cheap. The seam split up the back. Now there's nothing to cover his church bells.

I get four Red Bulls and drink one right there. I'm still drunk and sniffly, but now I'm wide awake. I buy an empty cup from the Slurpee machine so I can sit on the curb and get some water from the hose now and then so that Red Bull don't sneak back up. It's going to be a long walk back to the trailer. I hope the King ain't there, but I know he will be. That's why I got the two extra Red Bulls. Save me from making the trip again.

The King got into it with the Queen. Word around the park is there's trouble in paradise. Nothing more than that except for people taking note that the Blacksmith ain't around, mostly when the Queen's away. I'm not saying a word. The Queen is as bad as the King, maybe worse. She's smarter than he is, but that's a low bar. And the Queen has long memory. That gives her more ammunition than the King, who can't remember anything except his hurt feelings. When she does show up she's all, 'La de dah, look what I picked up at the secondhand store for half nothing. Don't the leaves look pretty when they start to turn?' Sends the King into a rage.

We open next weekend and nobody is ready, as usual. Every year there's the panic of the weekend before. I've been the Fool for the last seven years. For three years before that I was a weaver and assistant potter, and before that, well, forget before that. You see, I'm not worried about myself. Playing the Fool comes naturally. I ain't worried about the Queen either. She's a pro and can turn it on and off. I am worried about the King.

He's down to about a hundred and thirty pounds and when you're six two, that's willowy. Looks like a bag of bones about to have a baby. He's bug eyed and hollow faced most of the time, muttering under his breath and can't seem to hold a thought, like my cousin Gordy Hole after a brain aneurysm laid him low. Now Gordy sits at a window. I hate to say it, regret thinking it, but sometimes I wish it was the King sitting at a window.

The King is my barometer of fucked-upness. I see the pressure falling and I slow up. But that don't mean I don't get pissed. I do, for sure, but I'm not wetting my pants or shitting the wall or waking up with a needle hanging out of my arm or a joint burned to my lips. So, if I want this season to start out right, I'm going to have to get our cut rate King on the other side of fucked up for some part of the next few days.

And honestly, I'll have to straighten out myself a bit to do it. Not straight up straighten out, of course, more moderately straight, even keeled but gently rocking. What I'm trying to say is I could have a RBnV right now and that would be fine. There's nothing wrong with a morning snoot to chase away the chill and the ill. But a second one right after, that's a mistake. It's prudent to wait until noon, late morning, anyway, or thereabouts. It's about pacing. That's what his Majesty says, but he don't practice what he preaches.

There is an all you can eat joint a mile and a half up the State Highway called Ye Olde Country Buffet. I have some money in my sock drawer that the King don't know about. I decide to fatten him up and give him something other than booze to digest so I pay my neighbor, Alfred, a double amputee on disability, to drive us up there. But the King won't go until I tell him the place has a bar and a happy hour, then we can't get there fast enough. Alfred waits in the car because he has to while the King and I find a booth with the kind of view the King likes.

To me the back of one booth looks the same as the back of another, but what do I know?

The King orders a Manhattan and gets a plate of food six inches high, but that's fair. Buffet rules. But what's not is that before he even takes a bite, he lights up a cigarette, right there in the booth. Well, King or not, no one smokes inside a restaurant and I think that includes buffets. But the King seems ignorant of this rule. Someone comes over and then someone else and before you know it we're getting the bum's rush.

Only before they throw us out, they tell us to pay for the food and drink. The King digs in his heels at this. He tells them they're going to have to throw me in jail before we'll pay a nickel. I try to clear this up and tell them there's no need to call the po-po, but the King won't back down. He's threatening to sue them and says if he bothered to eat the food he's sure he'd get sick. Then he makes sick noises. I try to pull the King aside to let him know my ID is sketchy but he's not listening. He's pointing at the manager and calling him names and his mother worse. The whole Country Buffet is staring at us now, so I grab the King and run him outside and push him into Alfred's car and we get out of there fast. Like most Kings, this one is great for starting trouble but worthless when it comes to dealing with it.

The King is still mad by the time we get back but when he sees the Queen's car and the Blacksmith's truck parked next to it, he gets quiet, which is a bad sign. It's true that our King is full of awfulness. But as long as that awfulness is coming out of him, even if it's just in dribs and drabs, everyone is okay. When he gets quiet, though, and that awfulness stays put, watch the fuck out. Behind the big talk the King is just a little boy. He's a scared little boy with mental problems and addictions. He's an angry boy with whisky dick and venereal diseases. He's a crazy boy that thinks he's a king. And I know this for certain when the King tells Alfred to drive to the gun store. This is the quiet King, the King at his worst.

I'm worried the situation is spinning out of control. I suggest we stop at a mom & pop liquor store I see up ahead, thinking I might be able to distract the King with a quart of Comfort. I still have the money I was going to use at Ye Olde Country Buffet. But once we get inside, I see this store has a side business selling nightcrawlers, guns and ammo and the King is asking, "Well, why don't you carry hollow points?"

Alfred is in the car, of course, and I step out on the porch and signal him to drive away, but he can't understand me. I'm making gestures and then I just start yelling at him to go but he just cups his ear and squints for some goddamn reason. While this is going on the bell on the door behind me dings and the King walks out, takes my wallet off the chain, and goes back inside. He comes out again with a bottle of Comfort, a thirty rack of Bud Light, a box of ammunition and a new nickel-plated revolver with a stained wood grip stuck in his pants.

"Oh no," I say.

"Can't wait to warm this bad boy up," mumbles the King, unsmiling.

We get back in the car and I'm worried the King has stumbled into dangerous territory.

Alfred says, "Where to?"

I give him a 'what the fuck is wrong with you' look?'

So, Alfred asks, "What's wrong?"

I shake my head and the King cracks a beer, saying, "Back to the park."

Humming to himself, Alfred turns the car around and heads back to the trailer park where he must not realize there is about to be a bloodbath. The three of us are in the front seat because no one wants to sit in the back with Alfred's dog, 'Rescue'. Rescue reminds me of Alfred because his back legs don't work, but he also reminds me of the King because he barks all the time, is always in a bad mood, and tries to fuck everything but can't.

Alfred is driving slowly, what would be a crawl to most. I ask him why he drives this way and he looks me in the eyes and says, "I can see just fine and I think fine too. But my reaction time suffers. I hesitate, so I go nice and slow."

Just as I was about to ask how you figure that, a truck with a load of frozen beef clips the rear of Alfred's slow-moving Buick, tearing off the bumper and spinning us in circles. Alfred lets go of the wheel so he can reach over the seat and rescue Rescue. Pilotless, the car straightens out, bouncing down the road faster than Alfred ever drove. We can hear the engine racing. Standing on his stumps, still facing backwards on the seat, Alfred shouts, "The accelerator is stuck," before turning his attention back to his dog.

Not remembering that the controls are on the steering column, I reach down with both hands to try and free a stuck accelerator pedal that ain't there. While I'm down there the car jumps the road and careens over some rocks, grazes boulders and picks up speed. After one such jounce the King's new gun goes off, firing a round that grazes the head of his penis and enters the backs of my hands. From there, it severs the fuel line.

The car slows down but now it's on fire and headed for a low stone wall that may be too high and probably too solid. It stops us dead but the fire gets worse. Legless Alfred is now in the backseat trying to get himself and Rescue out of the car. Good luck with that. The King and I are trying to get the front doors open but we can't because the passenger door got jammed when we hit the wall and I can't work the driver's door because my hands are shot up.

It looks like we're screwed but then the King turns and kicks out his window, climbs through and yanks the door open from the outside. He pulls me out and then runs to the rear driver side door and pulls out Alfred and then Rescue. The car explodes, but we're okay, only a little singed, except for my hands and the King, who has half his royal mane burned off and a bullet grazed penis bleeding all over his pants.

For a second, I forget everything I know about the King. In that moment, standing on the grass with Alfred's car engulfed in flames and Alfred crying into Rescue's spotty fur, the King looks like a hero. I never thought of him that way. There never was a reason. That I hadn't made me wonder. Was he who I knew he was or had he somehow changed?

Soon enough an ambulance shows up and then two more and we get fussed over and taken to St. Tillo's Hospital where I get these giant bandages on my hands. The King is calling me Jesus and when he's not, he's saying they only put those bandages on to keep me from jerking off. Which is funny because he's got a giant bandage on his wiener with a catheter snaking out of it, but I don't say a word.

We all laugh hard and genuinely because it's over and nobody is dead. Alfred, though, is sad as could be. He still hasn't got any legs and now his car is gone, but at least he has Rescue. We're all in one big room so I tell the King and Alfred that we have to figure out a way to get some insurance money from somebody so Alfred can get another car.

The King says, "I got it. You and me sue Alfred for not having legs to help stop the car and, let's see, we ought to throw in speeding, reckless driving, and putting the life of his dog ahead of you and me. Sound right to you, Alfred?"

Glassy eyed, sniffling, and kissing on Rescue, Alfred mumbles, "Yup."

"Okay the King continues, "Did anybody get the number of that truck? There was a truck, wasn't there? Anyway, whatever we get, the three of us split equal. But if Alfred needs a little extra from you and me so he can buy a good car, that's okay too."

Everyone agreed, and while we were each thinking about what exactly makes a car good, who strolls in but the Queen. You could tell she'd been crying or wanted us to think so. Alfred and I turn to each other so they can have some privacy, but it's a hospital and we're in one room so there isn't much of that.

The Queen says she's sorry and the King says he's sorry too and before long she's sitting on his bed and lifts up the covers and sees the giant bandage on his wiener and starts to laugh. The Queen has one of those laughs that other women hate. She says he has quite the Royal Scepter and the King starts laughing too and so do me and Alfred, though Alfred doesn't have a fuckin' clue what a Royal Scepter is. He's mostly thinking about his next car and how good it's going to be.

We get released after a couple of days and the Faire goes off on time and without a hitch, except I still have these giant bandages on my hands. But everyone thinks it's part of my costume as the Fool, so they laugh and make fun of me as always. The King and Queen are getting along great and the Blacksmith is staying in his shop. We dodged a bullet this time, even though I didn't.

III

Walking to the Bellingham Square T station, Sava Prochuk munched a sticky bun. He wasn't far from his rooming house in Chelsea, still he shivered under the thin windbreaker he wore in the cool misty rain and complained to himself, 'I should have gotten espresso. What is wrong with me, catching chill in balmy weather. Back in Ural I go bare chested on this day. Am going soft at sea level, I am, with many sweets to consume. Must toughen up for to keep in shape and ready'.

Sava was on his way to meet his parole officer. There had been a terrible misunderstanding and somehow he ended up in court with a criminal charge of indecent assault and battery on a child under sixteen. Sava tried to explain his innocence to everyone, including the judge, but it was like he was speaking Russian, which he spoke as a first language, but that wasn't it. They simply chose not to understand him, Sava knew, and that was especially true of his parole officer, Hakeem Joseph.

"Good morning, Mr. Hakeem Joseph, Sava Prochuk here."

"Yes, Mr. Prochuk, good afternoon. Have a seat. I'll be with you shortly. I still have someone with me."

Several minutes later he led an attractive young woman from his office, saying, "I'll see you again in thirty days. And don't forget, you promised me a coin. There may be a drug screen, I'm not certain. Good work. Come on in, Mr. Prochuk."

"Hello Mr. Hakeem Joseph."

"Mr. Joseph is fine."

"I am glad. I have beginning of head cold."

"No, I didn't mean that. I meant that you may call me Mr. Joseph. We agreed to this last month."

"I am sorry, my English is de... delinquent, no, no, defective."

"Deficient, Mr. Prochuk."

"Da, Mr. Joseph, deficient is my English, but I have something to say. I have practiced so to get it right."

"I think I know what you have to say, Mr. Prochuk. You told me last month."

"I have try to tell you but words run from me. I have practiced this time."

"Mr. Prochuk, you have been found guilty of indecent assault and battery on a child under sixteen. That's been decided, no matter what you tell me. You went to prison and you were paroled by the Board. You have no other matters in corrections or the courts. You are a free man, under certain conditions. You should be looking to the future now, getting your life in order, moving on."

"Like a cinder in my eye or stone in my shoe, this so-called crime is no such thing. I am engaged to Dushka, who is eighteen, and older sister to Anna, who is almost sixteen. They are from village on other side of the mountain from my village back in Ural, so I know. Mr. and Mrs. Grinka, with Dushka and Anna, come to America to Boston. Somehow at Immigration the papers for Dushka and Anna get mixed up. Now Dushka is fourteen and Anna sixteen. Is big mistake."

"Mr. Prochuk, it may not be as much of a mistake as you think, even if she is sixteen, but I don't want to talk about this. My time is valuable. There are people waiting."

"I have more, Mr. Hakeem Joseph. We were engaged in Orthodox Church. We slept in room with her parents, on a mattress on the floor with heavy board between us and that old woman's evil eye on me all night. I wouldn't touch myself, let alone Dushka."

"Listen, Mr. Prochuk, I understand you're troubled, but this is a new country. Things are different."

"It's a crazy place if you want to know."

"It seems that way, I'm sure. But the thing about America is this. When bad things happen, even just unfortunate things, people say they're sorry, they learned their lesson, and they won't do it again. Maybe they did it, maybe they didn't. Who knows? It doesn't matter. As a society we want it to go that way so everyone can move on. That's what we do in America, we move on. You don't have to like it, you just have to move on, like everyone else. Now, are you still employed with the...."

"Cleaning Professional Assignments Staffing Company, sir."

"Yes, and you are assigned to, ahhh, the IRS, let's see, on Cambridge Street, so that's......"

"Is up the hill over there. My Supervisor is Mr. Buffum, extension 1442."

"If I called Mr. Buffum right now, Mr. Prochuk, what would he say?"

"About what?"

"About you."

"I know who he is and he knows who I am. That is all. He works in the daytime and I work after he goes home or wherever."

"What else?"

"I am on time or early. I see Mr. Buffum one time a week. I am on time for that too. I know my job and I do it. I am meek like mouse."

"All right, Mr. Prochuk, that is how we move on. We're making progress. I can tell this man you work for has had a positive effect on you."

"He has effect on me."

"Seems like a good man. He trusts you to do your job and you do it. Am I right, Mr. Prochuk?"

"If you say so."

"From what you say, Mr. Prochuk, he sounds like the kind of man who gives a person the chance to succeed. Do you admire him?"

"I am a broom, Mr. Hakeem Joseph. Mr. Buffum doesn't see me. No one does. There is little to say about what I do. Only if I don't do will I hear from anyone. I do the same things in the same way in the same order every night. No one cares about the broom unless he is not there. I have to go to work now or I am late."

"Here's a thirty-day date. See you then, Mr. Prochuk."

"Goodbye, Mr. Hakeem Joseph. Thank you for listening."

IV

I looked up from wrapping my hands. A dark colored Ford Five Hundred rolls into the Faire, rumbling across the parking lots and stopping about twenty feet from us. It's only eight in the morning. After a minute or so a man and a woman step out. They look so po-po they could be TV po-po. She's wearing dark glasses and shoulder length black hair, which she brushes away with her right hand, flicking her head as it falls forward so we can see the disgust on her face.

We are sprawled on wet grass around a picnic table, booze sick and drug itchy, waiting for one of the King's morning meetings before we can get back to bed. She turns her head to scan the trailer park, litter covered Faire grounds, and the trash strewn parking lots.

"Steiger," she says.

"Yeah?"

"Which one of us is Buffum trying to fuck in the ass," she says, not looking at who must be Steiger, but still at us, through those dark glasses.

"It's you for sure, Nix. He hates you more than he'll ever hate me."

"C'mon, Steiger, me more hated than you?"

"Your ex-husband got custody of your baby. What is she, a year old? Larry ain't even a good guy."

"She's more than a year and what can I say, they bonded. You can't account for those things, but I never got banned from the kitchen and had to wear a sign around my neck saying, 'I'm a thief'.

"I was wrongly accused."

"Damn, Steiger, have you taken a close look at these, ah, what's the collective for shit bums?"

"I think shit bums is the collective, but I'm not sure. The better question is what's their median blood alcohol level?" Steiger waved at the blood sucking insects, "C'mon, Nix, can't we just get down to business and get back to civilization?"

"I'd say it's about a point one three, maybe a one two, only because it's morning and no one I know can drink in his sleep. We have a sad little group here, Steiger, and from a collections standpoint I'd have to say it ain't going to be worth the trouble. This place is such a cluster that maybe Buffum is trying to fuck us both."

Steiger slapped at a green head and asked, "You sure this is the place?"

"Didn't we see half a dozen billboards on the way down here? Recognize the skinny drunken pervert laying on the grass in the bathrobe? Think there are two of them this side of the Sexually Dangerous Wing at Souza-Baranowski? That's the King, Steiger. Of course, this is the place."

"Yeah, but these guys don't look like they got two nickels to rub."

"Maybe that's why they haven't filed taxes, Steiger. Ever think of that? Maybe I better go find out."

The woman cop was wearing nice shoes, designer, half heel with an open toe. After she got through the tall grass they weren't as nice.

"Who's in charge?" Nix asked.

"Who are you," asked the Queen, "and what do you want? The Faire is fucking closed. Come back Thursday at noon."

"How charming, I'm Agent Nix."

"And I'm Marie of Romania," replied the Queen. "We're still closed."

"And this is Agent Steiger. Say hello, Agent Steiger."

"Hello," he said.

"This is my badge and here are my credentials," Nix continued, "We're with the Internal Revenue Service. Are you in charge?"

"No, I...

Turning away, Nix asked, "Who is? We've been calling and writing for months and finally had to come down here because no one answers the goddamn phone or signs for registered mail."

"Did you call the 800 number?" the Queen asked.

"I don't know," Nix looked at Steiger, who shrugged his shoulders, "probably. We called some numbers. Maybe that was one of them."

"Well, you have to call the 800 number if you want to get anywhere. There's a menu..."

"Well, we're here now, aren't we?"

"Don't get pissy with missy because you called the wrong number," the Queen rolled her eyes, "Some bitches are bitches."

Still laying on the grass, the King stuck his arm up in the air for me to pull him upright. Steadying himself against the thinner air, the King said, "Thank you, Fool," He tied his bathrobe tight, cleared his throat and said, "Fair lady, would you pleasure me with your company?"

"Would I what? Are you in charge?"

"I am their liege but I can't answer that question. We are free spirited and unbroken to the wheel of your so-called civilized world. Rise and approach, fair traveler."

"Rise and...? The fuck are you saying, mister? Why are you talking like that and who are you? Let's see some ID."

"I am Henry, Lord of this realm, ruler of all you survey. I am the liege of this court and those who call it home. Blessed be our Kingdom, Lord, and Savior. Blessed be all who live and travel here."

"Blessed be," some of us mumbled, hoping it would speed things up so we could get back to sleep.

Hands on her hips, shaking her head, Nix called over her shoulder, "Steiger, don't you want to handle this?"

"You're doing great, Nix."

She sighed, "Listen, fella, I'm going to need your full name and some ID."

"Tudor."

"House or school?"

"House," answered his Highness, "now may I provide you with a libation, Agent, aah?"

"It's Agent Nix."

"Nix, that's right. There is some very fine coffee brewing but it's far better once we liven it up. Wench!"

A young woman, still in pajamas, busily texting, replied distractedly, "Yes, my liege, your pleasure?"

"A cup for our visitors and fortify hers."

"You mean cream and sugar?"

"Just get it, will you? And bring the bottle of Fireball from my trailer. You know the way, of course."

"Oh really, Your Majesty, you say I know the way? It ain't ten feet from where you're standing, but I ain't never been in there and don't say otherwise."

"Impudent cow."

"Fuckin' drunk."

"Stop it, you two," Nix interrupted. "We don't want coffee. We want answers. For starters, who owns this business? And please, right now, let's see some ID."

"We have no IDs here," the King frowned, arms open at his sides, "IDs are tools of repression and exclusion. I know my subjects and they know me. That and God's good will is all we need on earth."

"Hurry up, Nix," Steiger slapped at himself, "the greenies are biting the shit out of me."

"Okay, so, King Tu...?

"King Henry. We are the house of Tudor."

"You aren't making this any easier. Can we go someplace and talk? That trailer over there. I never thought standing on grass could hurt so much."

"That's my trailer," smiled the King. "Come with me, please. I'll find you a chair."

The Queen popped up at this, "It's my trailer too."

Ignoring her and taking Agent Nix by the arm the King asked, "You are new to our realm, are you not?"

"You people are different, King. You know, right, different being a euphemism for peculiar?"

"To you, I'm sure," the King was at his most charming, "but isn't that why they make chocolate and vanilla ice cream?"

"Not a fan of ice cream, sir. It can't hold its shape, temperature, or consistency. It's weak, conformist, and suggestible."

"I never thought of ice cream that way. Could you write that down, Agent Nix, so I can add it to the list of what I say? Oh, I'm afraid it's a mess in here," the King stepped over a pile of dirty laundry, "Careful, the light's out and the Queen doesn't pick up after herself."

"Probably a Queen thing."

"You're catching on. Let me hit this switch."

They sat at a drop-down trailer table that seemed to have six carefully cut lines of cocaine on it. With the heel of one hand the King swept the lines onto the still shiny cover of September's Guns & Ammo, stashing it all in the bathroom and locking the door.

Laughing, the King explained, "Some of my subjects pay their tithe in powdered rhinoceros horn."

"Yeah, right," Nix slipped off her shoes and rubbed her feet. "We sent an easy fifty letters to this place for failure to file income tax returns. Returns haven't been filed for ten years. That's when the last known taxpayer died."

"Died?"

"Yes, Stanley Zimochowski."

"Stan died?"

"Ten years ago. You didn't know?" Nix arched her brow.

The King looked thoughtful, "Seems like I saw him just yesterday."

"Yesterday, you say?"

"Seems like."

"Was it?" Nix pressed.

"Seems like it is all I said."

"Could it have been earlier than yesterday when you last saw Stanley Zimochowski?"

"Sure."

"Could it have been ten years since you last saw him?"

"Anything is possible, Agent Nix. Black hole time travel is theoretically possible right now."

Nix paused, sizing up the King, "Stanley Zimochowski was your employer, wasn't he?"

The King's smile shrank and tightened, "That's not any of your business, Agent Nix."

"Actually, it is my business. Where the taxpayer is difficult to ascertain it is my responsibility to establish the relationships of the people at the business with the former taxpayer and with the business itself. If I don't ask these questions, I'm not doing my job."

"I have a suggestion for you, Agent Nix. Don't ask no questions and you'll live a longer, happier life. It's good advice. You ought to take it.

"Was that a threat, sir?"

"Just a piece of advice you should consider. Now where were we, let's see. You were saying something about your sheriff not being able to collect some taxes. What a shame. A good sheriff is hard to find, most of them always with their hand out."

"What I was saying is there hasn't been an income tax filing in ten years, sir. Filing and collections are different things. But while we were waiting for you or whomever to file, we weren't just sitting on our hands. We have projected your annual returns, calculated the money due and, with penalties and interest, we estimate that you owe the federal government thirty-two million, seven hundred and fifty-two thousand dollars. I'm rounding the estimate favorable to the taxpayer. How would you like to work that out, sir?"

"I may be King but I don't bother with details. You'll have to pester someone else about that, perhaps my Chamberlain or Lord of the Exchequer, if we have one. But as King, I command you and that itchy fellow with the evil eye to leave. You have no jurisdiction here. And even if you did, I'm going to issue a pardon for Stan, nunc pro tunc."

"What does that mean?"

"It's one of the things I say. But what I do know is that you have no power in this kingdom. There's such a thing as sovereign immunity and I do know what that means. It means the king can do no wrong, and I'm the King. It means we don't owe no stinking taxes."

"You, sir, are right off your nut."

"And you're a frigid bitch. Get off the premises before I have you thrown off."

"The last guy who said something like that to me lost three teeth and had his jaw wired shut for three months. Keep it up and you'll be envying him."

"Away with you, harlot. To a nunnery!"

"Have it your way, King . I'll be back with a subpoena."

"We'll burn you at the stake, witch."

"Sir, threatening an IRS agent is a ten-year felony that you serve in a federal penitentiary. A skinny little pussy like you wouldn't last a week."

"I am nearer God than thee. Away, slut. Begone, vile creature, before I roast thee!"

V

"Fool," called the King, laying on the picnic table, eyes closed, waiting for everyone to show for another meeting, "did you hear that po-po bitch say Stan never paid his taxes and then he up and died? What killed Stan anyway? With this tax nightmare it was probably suicide."

Unwinding the bandage on my left hand because I had to go to the can, I had to stop what I was doing because my hands started shaking. I took a deep breath and wanted to say, 'Stan paid his taxes until he was too dead to pay 'em. He died of cerebral hypoxia. (I memorized this from the death certificate they gave me, notarized). That's lack of oxygen to the brain. That's what happens when someone wipes peanut butter on the centrifuge of the World's Largest Cotton Candy Machine and turns it on with Stan, a man with a peanut allergy, locked inside. Locked inside! Stan died a gruesome death, clawing at his throat for air.'

But I don't say any of this. Frozen in one spot, I look at the ground, waiting for the moment to pass, but it drags on. The King's not helping by staying quiet. Now I have to say something. If I say nothing, it'll sound louder than anything I might have said. I search for something to say and finally blurt out, "It was no suicide. He had a peanut allergy."

"Peanut allergy," the King repeats this a couple of times, like he's just learned the words and is only now tasting them, "how gruesome and unexpected."

Shaking my head and stuffing the bandage in my pocket, I walk over to the portable toilets and almost call over my shoulder, 'Unexpected by Stan, for sure, but not by the person who killed him. Stan was locked in that cotton candy machine after someone put Skippy in the centrifuge. That same someone turned it on; the same person that had a big fight with Stan just before Stan died.'

But I don't, of course. Of course, I don't. I can't. There are consequences to messing with the clockworks, especially going back in time. I'm part of the clockworks, tick, tock. I'm an after-thought or a speck of dust that blew in, but still, I'm part of it. Not the part that figures out what begets what and what is to be borne by whom. That stuff is for other people. It's beyond me.

Still on the picnic table, scratching himself, the King found the early morning sun and sighed, soaking it up. He yelled over to me at the potties, "We could talk ourselves sick over Stan's death, Fool. The fact is that the investigation didn't come up with nothing. Who knows how and why shit happens? Stan must have smoked twelve cigars a day. He inhaled 'em. Maybe it was lung cancer or mouth and throat cancer that killed him. Who knows?"

I had just gotten comfortable in my favorite potty when the King said that. Maybe it was the cocoon of hard plastic that made me feel safe enough to shout, really yell back at him through the screening, "He never had the chance to die of something else."

I was mad and breathing heavy. I really said it this time, shouted it. It wasn't in my head and it wasn't under my breath.

"Really?" the King shouted back, adding a moment or two later, and without real enthusiasm, "Still, it makes you wonder."

"Yeah," I yelled back, shaking with anger as I kicked open the hard plastic Port-A-Potty door and held it open with my feet so the King was sure to hear me, "Makes you wonder what? Why would you wonder? Why you?"

"Just wonder, Fool, just wonder."

Yawning and complaining, the players straggled over. The Queen dragged a lawn chair next to the King and sat heavily. She was wearing a modest tiara and talking on her phone to a seer from the Psychic Hotline. She held up a hand for the King to be quiet.

"So, what do we do, Doris?" the Queen asked, chewing on a nail. She ah-huh-ed a bit and then said, "Really? Fight them? This is for real, Doris. It's the government. You know, Standing Rock and Waco. They're getting a subpoena. Ah-huh. Ah-huh. Ah-huh. You're sure about this? Well, yeah, on paper, I guess, but.... I'll tell him. Siege warfare, yeah, I got it. That's what I'll tell him. Okay, talk to you in about a week, I hope. Because these calls cost a frickin' fortune, that's why. Yeah, bye. You too, love to the kids."

"Hey, Ronnie," the Queen slid the phone into her bra holster, "you got to hear what the psychic had to say."

"About the horses?" asked the King.

"Horses? What about horses?"

"Today's sheet, Santa Anita and Churchill Downs," the King spread out his hands, exasperated, "'Sa'matter with you, Diane?"

"You mean the races? Why would I ask her about the races? I called her about that IRS bitch and what we got to do."

"Oh yeah, that's right, what'd she say?" the King put on his thoughtful face.

"She says we got to dig a moat and some tiger traps and strengthen this place for a siege," said the Queen, a little unsure of herself.

"She said what?"

"I know, right? She said we got to wage siege warfare. That's what she said."

"That's the stupidest thing I ever heard."

"I know, right? But here's what she also said. She said we got to call the news media. I say to her, really Doris, how do we call the news media? And she goes, it's just the newspapers, radio stations, laundromat bulletin boards, and shit local TV. She even said we ought to put something in the church bulletin. Can you imagine? The walls would come tumbling down. She also said to go to the nearest college and put posters up about how the government is picking on us."

"Okay, why?"

"Doncha see? As long as the reporters, students and cameras are around they'll be afraid to bother us because we'll look like victims and they'll look like bullies."

"We are victims and they are bullies."

"I know, right?"

"Can you stop saying that Diane?"

"Saying what?"

"I know, right?"

"You know what?"

"I know right. You say it all the time. It's bothering me."

"Oh, it bothers you? Hmm, I didn't know we were going there. Let me go get your list of faults out of my delicates' drawer and we can hash this out."

"Okay, Diane, forget it, but can you not say that all the time?"

"I know, right? Is that what you mean? I know, right?"

"Yes, that's what I mean. It's annoying."

"I know, right? Ooops. I've got an idea, Honey. Why don't I just substitute one phrase for another. Train myself to say something else whenever I want to say, 'I know, right?' I know what I can say. I'll say, 'The King is the thirty-first best lover I ever had' whenever I really want to say, 'I know, right?' Problem solved."

"Thirty-first?"

"Middle of the pack. Now, the psychic also says that we have to dress up in our work outfits and fight with swords and catapults and rocks. We got to ye and thee and thou and stay in character. She says they'll eat it up on TV news and business is going to be better than ever. The way she talks, it's free advertising. I'll have one of my ladies in waiting make up a Facebook page and this time I'll have her use spell check. We'll call it King Henry's Renunciation. That's the psychic's suggestion."

"I don't know what it means but it's got a ring to it, Di. It's kind of important sounding. That psychic is on the ball."

"Yes, she is and she said we can't use guns 'cause nobody likes them anymore. We might be able to use Greek fire, whatever the fuck that is, or a cannon. She wasn't sure if cannons were around back then."

"Back when?" asked the King.

"Whatever the time is that we're pretending we're in, I guess. Your time, King."

"My time?"

"The time in which the Faire is set when England was a country. She also said we got to pitch a campaign tent and wear armor and gowns while we mill about theeing and thouing and making threats and promises on people's heads. It could be fun. I'd like to be on TV."

"Hmmmm, why not?" the King was wearing his 'I'm not as fucked up as you think face', "At least we know how to do that. But first, we have to stock up on drugs and alcohol."

The Queen scowled.

"For medicinal purposes, Diane, not just fun. How about explosives?"

"We'd only blow ourselves up, Worship," the Queen wound her fingers through the King's, "We're best at pretending, aren't we?"

"My Queen, my beauty and my brains!"

"I know, right?"

VI

Nix walked into Steiger's squaricle, "Wake up, Steiger."

"No, Nix, I just got to sleep. Come back in twenty."

"Get up. We're on TV."

"I'll have to call Mother."

"Not for this you won't. That King at the Faire said you were an imbecile, an imbecile and a jackbooted Nazi. He said you were staring them down and I threatened him."

"Did you?"

"We encourage people to cooperate. That's what we do."

"You're never happy unless you see a pee spot."

"You should try liking your work a little more, Steiger. Come on, we have to see Buffum in five minutes."

"Is he pissed?"

"I don't know. Fuck nuts told me to get you and get to Buffum's office."

"Doyle?"

"Yeah, he went on about it. I'm sure Buffum's not happy. He never is when one of us is in the news."

"Fuck me, I was looking forward to an easy day. Think he's going to make us write reports?"

"We'll find out. Wipe the drool off your chin. Look like you've been awake."

"What a way to start the day," Steiger got to his feet.

Buffum is the Northeast Regional Supervisor for the IRS. He has a large territory and runs it from the Boston office. He isn't fond of Nix. Everyone knows this, but Nix acts like they're pals. And she talks back, which he never appreciates, and laughs at him ceaselessly. There is another reason he doesn't care for Nix. At last year's holiday party, she had too much to drink and asked Buffum to dance.

He should have known better. In the middle of a slow dance Nix stepped back, slapped Buffum hard across the face and accused him of getting aroused.

Of course, Buffum denied this vociferously, but Nix said this wasn't her first dance and she knew what those things felt like better than he did. She stubbornly maintained that even though his was of inferior size and oddly spongy, it was definitely a member of the species at attention. When asked specifically whether Buffum's penis was in a discernible state of arousal, Nix said it was ha...difficult to determine. When pressed she offered that rather than angry, it seemed a bit peckish, bordering on annoyed more than anything else. Everyone had fun with this except Buffum, who never acknowledged that anything happened. Now, however, whenever he has to meet with Nix he has a witness.

Nix rapped on the door and asked if Buffum was decent. He said, "A moment, please, we're waiting on Doyle."

Turning the knob and smiling at Steiger, Nix said, "It's me and Steiger. We'll wait with you."

"No, no, you can wait out there. He'll be right along. Hold on a minute."

"Coming in," she said and as they did Buffum stood up, banging his knee on his desk drawer, knocking over a tape recorder, batteries spilling all over the floor. He reached for the phone to get Doyle.

Nix said, "Steiger will help you chase down those batteries, Mr. B."

Steiger looked at her, saying, "My back's been acting up. My doctor told me to keep from bending or stooping."

Nix held Steiger's gaze, "Did he tell you to stop whining and complaining?"

"He's a she, Nix. She told me no bending or stooping."

"But you can grovel?"

"Sure, but only upright or seated."

"Why does a man get a woman doctor, Steiger, and how is your mother?"

Buffum was sweating and annoyed, "Please, you two, just sit quietly while we wait for Doyle."

"Nice chairs," Steiger added, "can I get one of these for my back? It'd really help."

"Send a request to HR," Buffum wiped his face with an over large handkerchief.

"Ahh, Mr. Buffum, sir, following up on that. Can I cc you so it looks like you're in the loop?" Steiger asked, rotating his index fingers around one-another, and finishing with a shoulder shrug.

"Ah, Doyle, come on in," Buffum wiped the back of his neck, "You both know Doyle, of course. Here's a pad, Doyle. Take notes."

"Okay, but..."

"The tape recorder isn't working."

"Fix the tape recorder, Steiger." Nix commanded, "Don't be a pussy."

Buffum shook his head at this and Steiger said, "Why don't you fix it, Nix. I'm sure you know how to put batteries in electronic devices better and faster than I do. Look, Nix, there's a battery under Mr. Buffum's desk, right between his legs. Crawl under there and get it."

"Stop worrying about the tape recorder you two," barked Buffum.

Steiger looked hurt, "We were only trying to help."

"Tell me about this Renaissance Faire."

Nix stretched her legs out. She had on a short skirt and seemed pleased that Buffum was looking everywhere but at her. Now checking her nails, she answered, "I wouldn't call it a Renaissance Faire. Maybe it is, but it's supposed to be about King Henry Tudor from England. That's what their King told me."

"Their King?" Buffum turned to face Nix, so she fiddled with her blouse button until he looked away.

"Yeah, they have a king," Nix continued, "He seems to think he has sovereign immunity and can't be sued and he can issue pardons to anyone we go after."

"That's crazy, Nix," Buffum seemed genuinely disturbed, "this is the United States of America."

"I told him that, sir, but he didn't seem to care."

"Well, care or not, it is the United States of America."

"Don't tell me, tell him."

"Besides that, what's his beef?"

"He didn't say, but if I had to guess, I suppose it's that he doesn't want to file or pay his taxes."

"Oh, fiddlesticks," sighed Buffum, "did you bring up an Offer in Compromise?"

"He doesn't acknowledge that he owes anything. That doesn't leave much room for compromise."

"Is this King the taxpayer?"

"We don't know. He wouldn't tell us. We left and I told him we'd be back with a subpoena."

"You mean a warrant?" asked Buffum.

"Yeah, a search warrant for the records," answered Nix, "You know search warrant, subpoena, same thing."

"Well, Nix, not to be critical..."

"Then don't be."

"Not to be critical but there's a difference between the two."

Nix shook this off, "He doesn't know that."

"Whether he does or doesn't, there's a difference. Check page 820, I think it is, of your manual. Are you sure you said subpoena?"

"No, I said warrant."

"Are you sure?"

"I said warrant. I said search warrant and subpoena."

"Well, have you issued a subpoena or applied for a warrant?"

Turning to Steiger, Nix asked, "Have you issued a subpoena or applied for a warrant?"

"Ahhh, me?" Steiger looked sheepish.

"Yes, you," Nix fired back.

"This morning," Steiger lied.

"Good work, Steiger." Buffum stuck a finger in his collar to let out some air. "You too, Nix. But what about the threats that the newscaster reported? I know that taxpayers get scared and will say anything. When I was in the field we always worried about that."

Nix sat up, "You were a field agent?"

"Way back."

"Must have been. I've been here seven years and you've been sitting in that chair, in this office, the whole time."

"It wasn't, that is, I wasn't a field agent for long."

"Hey Steiger," Nix turned to him, "how long have you been here?"

"Let's see, my pension vests in seven years so, hmmm, I've been here, ah, thirteen."

"Take a breather, Steiger," Nix suggested, "don't use all your oxygen on small talk, but do you remember Mr. Buf... "

"Forget about that, Nix," interrupted Mr. Buffum, "It was a long time ago."

"Must have been," Nix wasn't giving up, "I mean, Steiger is old and you were here before he was. I didn't think you were that old."

"He was old when I got here," Steiger popped off, "and bald too, right Mr. Buffum? I think you look better with the hairpiece but bald heads are in now. Even guys who aren't bald are going bald."

"Back to business, please. Strike that last comment, Doyle, from field agent to now. When do you follow up with these carnival people, Nix?"

"In a couple of weeks, no more than three."

"Don't you have a calendar?" Buffum asked, brows raised.

"In the meantime," Nix continued, "Steiger and I are going down there to run the vehicular traffic and get an idea what this kind of seasonal business draws. We'll note vendors, subs, if any, day or contract laborers and follow up. Once we get the raw numbers we'll run them through Accounting and they'll tell us what else they need for attribution. Then, Steiger's going to send out keeper depositions to the vendors. By the time we're done we'll have a good idea what the take is. It's not always houses, spouses, and boats that undo a tax cheat, Mr. B. Sometimes it's a hot dog bun."

"Fine," said Buffum, "but, and this is important, can you two please be polite and not ruffle any feathers. This King knows our weak points. Whenever we're in the news it's negative."

"Be polite? That fucking King called me a frigid bitch. He called me a harlot and a slut too. I should have pistol whipped him on the spot."

"Come on, Nix, that's not funny, or legal." Buffum squirmed, "Scratch all that out, Doyle. Try and take the high road. Nix. You're the professional. While I'm loathe to do this, Nix, if I approve your vacation request and pay that outstanding expense report that, frankly, I shouldn't, can you please go easy. The Service doesn't even have an open file on that casino and that hotel isn't on our list."

"I told you, Mr. Buffum, it wasn't the casino. It was the taxpayer at the casino and the hotel that was adjacent to the casino. The taxpayer went..."

"Okay, Nix, not now. But is it possible that you will behave in a professional and courteous manner if I approve the expense report? It's budget time, Nix, and you don't want to be responsible for any shortfalls, budget cuts, or lost jobs, do you?"

"I'm always professional, Mr. Buffum, and I'm working on being courteous."

"Okay, okay, I'm approving it. Just promise you'll be nice."

"I can't promise anything, Mr. Buffum, but I'll try."

"Can you give me a little more than that, Nix?"

"No, but can you expediate the expense check? I'm a little short this month. My baby needs braces."

VII

The King told me I was getting a promotion. He said I wasn't going to be no Fool dummy no more. Instead, he says I'm going to be a Fool target dummy. That's because a fellow came by that has a dojo off the State Highway. He's a drunk and calls himself Sensei and said he saw the King on TV and thought he needed help acting tough because he looked scared and weak. Sensei said his rates were reasonable but once he met the Wenches he became volunteer. Now we can't get him to leave.

The King wants me to put my hands in these big catcher's mitts and let his subjects punch and kick them while Sensei is teaching them martial arts. I told him it was a bad idea because both my hands are broke already from getting shot and I haven't even started physical therapy. The King has it figured differently. He tells me he's looking down the line like a risk manager. He says that since my hands are broke already there's less risk of loss in a new injury. It's a head scratcher, for sure, but maybe that's why he's the King. Otherwise, he's just a mean, lying, waste of booze, drugs and sexual failure, but I don't say so. This King has memory when it comes to grudges.

I stuffed them mitts with newspaper, but I didn't even need that. No one except Musclebound Stable Boy came within a foot of connecting. We ain't martial arts Carnies, I can tell you that. But the Queen took notice when Musclebound Stable Boy kicked and punched near my hands. She clapped her hands like a girl at a birthday party.

This morning I woke up to the sound of someone banging the angle iron. The King had taken to doing this lately. Everyone rolled out of their tents and trailers and staggered over to the picnic tables, angry and wanting to know what the commotion was about. It's sad to see the performers hung over and in their robes and jammies. The Blacksmith stumbled over with one of the Wenches on his arm. I think her name is Clara. It's Clara now.

"Where's the fuckin' fire," asked the Blacksmith loudly.

The King ignored him, but the Queen didn't. She seemed put out with Clara holding on to the Blacksmith's thick arm, especially since Clara was only wearing a short, mostly see-through teddy with one of the Blacksmith's shirts over it. I don't know why she bothered. It was a warm morning and the shirt wasn't buttoned so it didn't cover nothing but her fanny. The Queen didn't say a word but she crossed her arms and scowled. Everyone else shuffled over in twos and threes, yawning and grumpy, obviously wishing they were back in bed.

The King said, "I'm sorry to get y'all up so early but we're going to dig a moat around the trailer park today and dig some tiger traps too so we got to get an early start. Doreen's friend Belinda...."

"She goes by Coach," offered Doreen. "Don't call her Belinda. She doesn't like it."

The King stared Doreen down. He doesn't like getting interrupted and hates being corrected even more. Also, his memory isn't reliable and when he gets interrupted he can lose his train of thought, which can cost him his patience, "Well, thank you Doreen. Anything else?"

"Just don't call her Belinda or she'll get mad."

"Did everyone hear Doreen? Okay, now where was I before, ahh, that thing about whatshername, oh yeah, Belinda. Belinda has a backhoe. She's coming over this morning to dig a moat around the park, so we got to make sure the kids don't get in her way. Also, she'll be digging up the access road. The Farrier, the Blacksmith, and Musclebound Stable Boy are going to be laying a steel reinforced two-lane plank drawbridge but they ain't going to start until she's done digging so if you got to go out today make sure you get out early. And park in the parking lot when you get back. I'm going out for supplies in a little while. If you need anything, let me know and soon. We could be stuck here for a while if the Feds show up."

"Where are you going?" someone shouted.

"Different stores, let's see, there's the Walmart and Home Depot and I got to go to Shusta's to get gas to run the generators in case the Feds cut the 'lectricity and propane for cooking and Hamm's for food and vodka and the gun store."

The Queen popped off at this, saying that the psychic told her no guns and that if we start shooting, the po-po and the state and federal po-po and who knows what other po-po are going to have every excuse they need to move in and disarm us. That is, if they don't start shooting from the-get-go. "Guns cross the line," she crossed her arms as she told His Majesty.

The King said, "We're just getting prepared, is all. Who said anything about shooting?"

The Queen turned her back and said, "I know you and if you got a gun in your hand it's likely going off. Just like it did when you crashed Alfred's car and shot the Fool and your useless willy. All we can shoot is a cannon or Greek fire. That's what the psychic said. If you have to fire something, fire a cannon."

The King laughed, "A cannon is way worse than a gun. A cannon is a weapon of mass destruction."

The Blacksmith laughed at this, "Why don't you go down the road to the state college. They got a cannon they shoot off at half-time."

Everyone laughed and so even though he was a blacksmith of few words, he felt encouraged to add, "We got guns enough, and ammo too. At least I do. If you don't have enough guns or ammo, buy for yourself but don't go using none of our money."

There were cheers at this and the Blacksmith beamed. Clara held him tighter. The King got red in the face and his right hand worked its way down to where his right front pants pocket would have been if he hadn't been wearing just his bathrobe. The Blacksmith smiled and everyone else laughed. Even the Queen hid a grin.

"I'm going to the liquor store too," added the King, "and I'm going to pick up some drugs. Should I only get enough for me?"

"NO!" shouted everyone, including the Blacksmith.

"Okay then. We have to start stringing razor wire around the camp. Potter and Mason?"

"Right here," one of them answered.

"While I'm gone you're going to gather the kids and start stringing razor wire."

"The kids?"

"Sure, I've got plans for everyone else."

"Yeah, but...the kids?"

"Don't worry, kids heal faster than people."

"They do?"

"It's scientific," the King answered as though everyone knew. "The last thing I want to say is we're on a war footing and that means..."

"A what?" asked the crowd, astonished.

"A war footing, you know, preparing for war."

"Are you fuckin' nuts?" asked the Blacksmith, trying to regain some of the high ground he'd ceded, "They'll squash us. There'll just be a hole in the ground where we once were. Fun and games is fun and games, but I'm not going to war with the government, not with you, not with anyone. You got a screw loose."

"Oh, I got a screw loose? Okay, you tell me how you're going to pay that IRS cop thirty-two, almost thirty-three million dollars?"

"Installments?"

"Not likely. The only way we're going to get this monkey off our backs is to embarrass them into backing off."

The Blacksmith stood up straight, hands on his hips, and laughed, "Embarrass them? That's your plan? That's the stupidest thing that ever came out of your stupid mouth."

"Really?" the King stood up straight as he could, "Well, it's not my plan. It's a psychic's plan, okay? A psychic from the Psychic Hotline came up with the plan. Doesn't anybody ever listen to what I say?"

"No shit," buckled the Blacksmith. There were 'ooows' and 'ahhhs' throughout the crowd.

"Yeah, this is a plan from the Psychic Motherfucking Hotline. You think they're going to give us a plan that doesn't work? They know what's going to happen. This plan is a guarantee if there ever was one."

There was no arguing this. Still, the Blacksmith had reservations, "Things are different then, okay, I see, but the truth is I got a little record and did some time in Shirley back in the day and there might be one or two other things, you know, floating around, so I don't want no one looking too close. If it's war, even if we win, I lose."

The Farrier and Farmer 7 stood up and said they were in pretty much the same boat and so was I, truth be told, but I didn't stand up or say anything. I suspect there were more of us in this pickle.

The King was exasperated. He said to the Blacksmith, so all could hear, "The way you keep finding fault with everything I say makes me wonder if you're just looking to start a 'cootie tah'."

Puzzled looks were exchanged. Someone asked, "Just what in the heck is a cootie jar?"

"It's cootie TAH," corrected the King, "and the Blacksmith has got ideas about one."

"What I got ideas about?" asked the Blacksmith. "I don't got ideas. I don't got cooties. I'm worried you're going to get me in trouble, is all."

"You want a cootie tah, is what you want."

The Blacksmith shrugged his shoulders, "I don't even know what you're saying."

"A cootie tah," the King was red in the face by now, "is when you try to take something that don't belong to you. It belongs to someone else."

All you could hear were flies buzzing and traffic from the distant highway. It got more uneasy when the bullfrogs at the dry lake started in. Then the King said, "Like my Kingdom," and everyone let out their breath and color came back to the Queen's face.

The Blacksmith said, "I don't want that. Who wants a Kingdom that owes almost thirty-three million dollars? Why don't we all just leave?"

The King was ready for this, "Yeah, why don't we just leave? So, Blacksmith, you leave and where do you go? You got a record and you ain't been to school. You got open cases, probably warrants. You did time in Shirley. No one is going to hire you anywhere that ain't a kitchen with a stack of dishes. How does that sound for the rest of your life? How does it sound to the rest of you?"

There was shuffling and nodding but no one said a thing, so the King added, "How about this. Everyone who has a problem with the po-po or probation or parole or immigration or anything else will dress in the same clothes as everyone else. We'll wear camo and bandanas, except for the knights, who have faceplates. We'll tuck our hair into hats or scarves, except for the knights and maidens, you know why. We'll be like old style ninja's. No one will be able to tell one from the other. How about that?"

"Hooray," they cheered.

VIII

"Awwwh, Nix, crack your window and lower the back ones. You reek of booze. It's leaching through your pores."

"Shut up, Steiger."

"My Uncle Herman was a rummy. When I was a kid he sat on the curb in front of our house with his rummy friends. One of them always had a load in his pants. Do you know my Uncle Herman?"

"Please."

"I'm just saying, Nix, you've got that same piquant scent, Eau de Crap."

"Don't talk, Steiger."

"You ought to be in a hospital on IV fluids."

"Steiger, please."

"Wanna tell me?"

"No, it's like the last thing I want but I know you won't stop until I do, so here goes. I got my expense check and I got an overnight sitter and took my ex out. We went to the casino."

"You know Baby Daddy Larry has a gambling problem to beat the band. Are you trying to ruin him, Nix?"

"No, I wanted to make him happy and I needed to get laid and Larry always does it for me."

"What'd you lose?"

"Everything, and Larry's mortgage payment."

"Oh damn, you fucked poor Larry on your way to Fuck Me Town."

"Yup, but what's worse is about four AM Larry tried to pimp me out so we could get back in the game. That's what he said, so we could get back in the game," Nix wiped away a tear.

"What happened to your knuckles, Nix?"

"Oh, I put Larry in the hospital. Broke some teeth, broke his left arm, and wrecked the cartilage in one knee. He'll recover but I'm guessing he'll lose his job, pussy that he is. I'm going to find myself back in court and I haven't even paid my lawyer for the last time. On the bright side, that guy that Larry tried to pimp me out to saw the whole thing. Made him rock, he said, so when I was done he went over and took the money out of Larry's pocket, added another hundred or two and pushed the wad into my hands. So, tell me, Steiger, is it weird..."

"Of course, it's weird. Weird doesn't do it justice."

"I haven't even told you what I think might have been weird."

"I thought. I mean, ahh... you were asking me if I thought it was weird that you took money from a guy your ex-husband was trying to pimp you out to, right?"

"Steiger, this guy admired how I took Larry down, the methodical way I went about it and, I think, the focused pain I applied. He's a pain aficionado. That's what the money was for."

"Oh, sorry, for a minute there I thought that you and that guy went off and..."

"Of course, we did. I told you I wanted to get laid. But what I was going to ask you is if you think it's weird to have the neck of a bottle of vodka shoved in your ass and emptied? It's called boufing."

"So, Nix, I'm writing this down for later but my first impression is, why would anyone do that?"

"It gets you drunk faster."

"I'll bet it does. I'll bet it can kill you too."

"Yeah, Steiger, I bet it can. I feel like last night it might have killed me for a few minutes."

"Maybe that's why you smell so bad; you're starting to decay."

"Think so?"

"It happens fast. Get out of the sun and stay away from apples."

"The uncircumcised cock guy Larry tried to sell me to is from Belarus. He says everyone over there does it."

"Yeah, we ain't in Belarus, Nix, are we?"

"No, I'm fuckin' here, Steiger, on my way to that olden time English Faire and I'm drunk and tired and shaky and in a wretched mood. I hope we don't run into that King. I'm not in the mood for his bullshit. I might have to light him on fire."

"Why don't you sleep, Nix, and I'll count the cars. Don't think about fire or that shitty King."

Nix slept in the back seat of the Five Hundred and only got up to use the Port-A-Potty. Steiger set up on a folding chair under a tree near the main gate about a quarter mile away, facing the sun. He had a little counter in his hand like umpires use at baseball games. He counted the cars, nodding off now and again, so he didn't notice when the King and the Fool drove through the gate in a van full of supplies and parked next to the Five Hundred.

The King got out of the van and checked out Nix, snoring open mouthed on the back seat and said, "Well, well, well, what have we got here, Cinderella?"

Also staring at Nix, the Fool said, "You mean Sleeping Beauty, don't you, Majesty?"

The King pulled out his phone and took a series of pictures of Nix snoozing. The flash got one of her eyes to flutter.

"Damn, what happened to you, Agent Nix? You look like you've been run over and then backed over to make certain," the King was smiling ear to ear.

"If you know what's good for you, King, you'll turn around and leave right now."

"Excuse me, but this is my domain, not yours. I ought to be the one telling you to leave. What are you doing here, loitering?"

"Move along, Your Grace. Not today."

"We want to know what you're doing here. Are you spying on us?"

"Get going, King. I mean it."

"I have to take a few more pictures first. Not saying where they'll end up but where's your office?"

"You've been warned."

"We're so scared. When did what we do on our property become any business of yours?"

"Your Majesty," the Fool interrupted, "I think we ought to get over to the park. Some of these groceries got to get in the fridge and some in the freezer. And this lady seems like she's in a bad mood. Let's just go. It's what you ought to do."

"Awww, I think this poor po-po had too much to drink last night, my Fool. I can smell it from here. She's drunk on the job. Did you have a bad night? Was someone mean to you? Were you sad and did you drink too much?"

Nix sat up, adjusted her clothes, opened the back door, and got out shakily.

"I'm videotaping you, Agent po-po, so no funny stuff. Oh drat, the battery...oh, fuck. Give me your phone, Fool."

"I don't have no phone. We oughta go now."

Nix shook her head, flexed, and bounced on her toes a couple of times before pointing to the Fool and saying, "You have five seconds to disappear, starting a second ago."

The Fool ran, sole flapping, arms swinging, and didn't look back. Nix told the King to give her his phone, which he did. Nix opened the door to a portable toilet and dropped the King's phone in a pile of wet poo. The King started to say something, but Nix shushed him, almost gently, saying, "Get in the Port-A- Potty with your phone, Your Majesty."

"We will not," the King replied.

"Last night I put my ex-husband, father of my baby, in the hospital and I like him, at times. I don't like you at all and never will. Now get in the Port-A-Potty or I'll put you there."

"You knave, you low cretin, I'll never."

"Fine, let me give you a hand."

"Okay, okay, I'm getting in. But what are you going to do to me? I have a weak stomach."

"Nothing. I'm just making sure you can't bother me for the rest of the day. Now sit quietly and don't say a word."

After the King got in the Port-A-Potty, Nix let herself in the driver's side, turned on the Five Hundred and backed up against the hard-plastic door of the portable toilet. Then she turned off the car and climbed into the back seat and fell back asleep until her phone rang.

"Yeah?"

"It's me, Nix."

"Yeah, me who?"

"Steiger, Nix, who else would it be?"

"Sorry, Steiger, I fell asleep in someone's car. What's up?"

"Look, Nix, it's almost four and the traffic has slowed to almost nothing. I can just guess about how many more cars might dribble in. It's mostly trucks, actually. I'm hungry. Come pick me up and let's get Korean."

"Roger that, Steiger. Be there in a minute."

Nix got back in the driver's seat, started the car, opened the windows all the way, adjusted the rear-view mirror, and slipped the Five Hundred into reverse. She didn't step on the gas, but neither did she step on the brake. Not until she heard the King scream and felt, more than saw, the Port-A-Potty tip over did she drop it into drive.

IX

Lying in bed, hands behind my head and still in bandages, I stare up at my dirty louvred trailer windows, imagining the stars above. The peepers start in and then an owl begins to hoot. It sure had been a busy day with all the construction and the King getting locked in the Port-A-Potty and then bathed in poo and blue poo water. Fortunately, His Majesty is so scurvy that neither the chemicals nor the poop itself caused him any long-lasting ill effects, except maybe the annoyance of getting asked if he had 'the blues' or 'another shitty day'.

But when we finally got him out of the Potty he'd grown quiet, which you know ain't good. So quiet that if Mark William Calaway, The Undertaker himself, was standing in front of him and the King had a loaded gun he'd likely have emptied it right in the wrestler's midsection. The King worshipped The Undertaker. He would have had twenty of his babies if he could. That was the measure of his despair.

It's a cool evening and, laying still, I hear the rustle of the breeze. Listening to the dawn of night, I let the cool vodka burn its way down my throat. This is the most wonderful time of year. We're all working steady and getting paid. The fruits and vegetables have been harvested from everyone's truck patch so there's no worry there. The hubbub of summer is past and dusk is growing earlier.

I like the softness of dusk. The light it provides ain't direct. It's a little awry and never too bright. Who needs to examine every flaw? Who has to see everything to know exactly what it is. Not me. Dusk is like being safe inside and looking out.

There's a scatter of conversation from some other trailer and then the soft patter of someone walking by. Distant laughter hangs in the air and I decide to take a stroll. I'm going to walk around the park, not through it, and maybe have a pee in a Port-A-Potty. The tank in my trailer is getting full and I'd like to wait until at least November before emptying it. Smells less.

Outside it's cooler and the sounds are distant, except for my footfalls. High dark clouds have moved in but snowy moonlight pokes through now and then. Even though the Port-A-Potties are there, I don't walk too close to the boundary of the parking lot because the moat's been dug and we had the firefighters from Horseshit Falls come by and fill it. It only cost us a six-person Premier Pac that the Horseshit Falls firefighters said they were going to raffle off for charity. What that means, though, is that the Chief is going to be here for the next couple of weekends, taking Viagra, fondling the Wenches, and drinking hard liquor. The clouds break up a bit and I can see someone about fifty yards distant, walking my way.

Even though it's dark now and he's far away, I think it might be the King. This man's head looks bandaged, he seems to be wearing a soft collar and he's using one crutch as he walks towards me. The King did talk about borrowing a neck brace. This guy even walked like the King, angry and unsure. But then he's gone, nowhere to be seen. I stop and squint but that doesn't do any good. I'm about to call out when I hear someone cry, "Help!" But this voice sounds muffled and far away and the King, or whoever, wasn't that far off. So, I start to walk fast towards where I last saw him and then I hear someone again and it still sounds far away, so I start to run, but then I stop and put two and two together and I come up with tiger traps. That's why the King can't be seen and sounds so far away. In the daylight I know where those tiger traps are but at night I don't have a blind man's guess where they might be. I walk real slow towards where I last saw that person and cup my hands over my mouth and yell, "King, where are you?"

And I can hear someone call back, faintly, "Get me the fuck out of this fuckin' hole."

So, I yell back, "King, keep talking so I can find you," so he says, "Fuck you in your fucking fuck hole you fucking fuck nuts. Come fucking get me out or I'll fuckin' kill you."

Only the King could pack so many fuck words in one fuckin' sentence. Soon enough I find the one the King fell in. Good thing we didn't bother with punji sticks. Chandler wanted to stake them in the bottom of the traps but some of us thought they posed a hazard so we wouldn't let him. He got sulky and went to his trailer and came back with an armful of snakes that he keeps as pets. He threw them in the tiger trap and said, "Try and stop them."

Well, I didn't want to panic the King. There was more than one tiger trap so who's to say the snakes are in the one the King is visiting? Not me, so I lay on the ground and carefully stick my head over the side of the hole he found and say, "King?"

"A knighthood for you, my splendid Fool. Get me out of this hole."

"Is there anything else down there with you, King?"

"Like what, Fool?"

"Like anything. Like any badgers or racoons or snakes?"

"Snakes? Why would there be snakes? Goddamn, it's cool tonight and nearly fall. Why would there be snakes?"

"I don't know. Some people keep them as pets."

"Like Chandler?"

"Yeah, like him."

"Are you saying that one of Chandler's snakes got away?"

"Yeah, that or Chandler threw all of them in a tiger trap because he was mad at us."

The King got quiet, which, again, you know. I was regretting leaving my trailer. The silence dragged on.

"King?"

"Fool, you get me out of this hole or I'll spend my last breath choking the life out of you. Get me out now!"

"I gotta go get some rope."

"Give me a stick first so I can hold off the snakes."

"Don't you have the crutch you been walking with?"

"I lost it in the fall. Now, get me a stick you fucking idiot!"

"Hold on, King. Here you go. I got a big one. That boa's grown. Damn, ain't this a bad dream?"

"Don't be long, Fool. This is the worst day of my life."

I didn't want the King getting down on himself. He's no good but he's the only King we got, so I said, "Cheer up, Majesty. You've had other bad days. You've even had worse ones and not that long ago."

"Hurry up or I'll strangle you when I get out."

X

Nix was nodding off in the ladies' room, nursing her hangover when Marge called her name from the door, "Hey Nix, Buffum just put out an APB for......Mother Goddamn, Nix, what is that smell?"

"Ever been to Belarus, Marge?"

"No, can't say that I have but you better clean up fast. Buffum is beside himself, screaming for you and your friend Steiger."

"What about?"

"Some king."

"Oh, no, he wants to see me?"

"Pronto."

"Got a mint, Marge?"

Fortunately, it wasn't news for Nix to be recovering from something while she was at work. She tapped on Buffum's door.

"Come in," she heard. It was Buffum, but this was a different Buffum. This was the gruff, sneaky, edgy, Buffum, a Buffum to be wary of.

"You were looking for me?" Nix let herself in and made for the chair next to Steiger.

"I got a call from News 10. They asked me to confirm or deny a story set for tonight at ten. I got a preview. Steiger, get up, don't say a word, and go back to your desk. Right now. Nix, stay seated."

"Should I have counsel?" Nix asked Buffum.

"You'd know that better than I, Nix."

"What is the purpose of this meeting?" Nix asked, politely enough.

"It's informational. I need information and you're going to give it to me. Is that understood, Nix?"

"No, it's not, Mr. Buffum. Tell me what this is about and if you are alleging that I've done something wrong, tell me what it is."

"Okay, Nix, since you persist in this charade of innocence...."

"Charade of innocence? Are we prejudging now? Tell me what you think I've done."

"You and that King Henry......"

"So that's it. What's he saying now?"

"You promised you'd be nice, Nix."

"I said I'd try."

"I've gotten one hundred and seven phone calls since this morning and an endless stream of e-mails. This is unacceptable," Buffum wiped down his face. "Nothing else is getting done. Washington called. What do I say to Washington?"

"You tell them you don't know what this is about and you stand by your agents. Tell them this King is a deluded scofflaw trying to create trouble to change policies as they pertain to him. That's all you have to say."

Not interested in her response, Buffum asked, "Did you do this, Nix? Tell me straight up, did you do anything even like what he's talking about?"

"Do what? I don't know what he's said but I had nothing to do with him so, no, of course not, Mr. Buffum. You shouldn't have to ask."

Ignoring this, Buffum persisted, "Were you at that Fairgrounds?"

"Steiger and I were there in order to count cars so we'd have some basis for our income attribution and won't look like we're whistling Dixie through our assholes when the taxpayer takes us to court or files for bankruptcy. We made no secret of being there but we never went further than the parking lot. Why are you even asking? Did he see us there and make something up?"

"Doyle, strike the whistling Dixie remark when you transcribe this."

"Yes, Mr. Buffum," Doyle wrote a note on his forearm.

"Now buzz Steiger and get him back in here."

Steiger knocked and let himself in, sitting down next to Nix.

Buffum pulled out his handkerchief and patted his cheeks dry. He cleared his throat and said, "Your stories line up but that doesn't mean this isn't serious, it is. This is a serious matter. I'm going to have Legal brief me on the consequences of all this, legal and otherwise, and maybe get some recommendations from counsel about where we take this."

Nix sat up straight, "We're sorry Mr. Buffum. The truth is this king is a drunk and a drug addict, drug user, anyway, and he's desperate and out of his mind. He'll say or do anything if he thinks it will mislead or discourage us."

Buffum tried to stare Nix down, "These TV news reports make the Agency look weak and poorly staffed."

Nix didn't blink until Buffum broke the stare. Calmly, she continued, "When I met this King, Mr. Buffum, he steered me into his disgusting trailer to talk things out and right there on the table, in plain sight, was a razor blade and six lines of what only a fool wouldn't recognize as cocaine."

"Well, Nix," Buffum straightened his tie and spoke to the tape recorder, "I don't think I'd recognize cocaine and I don't consider myself a fool."

"No two people agree on everything, Mr. Buffum, but my point is the King swept those lines onto a magazine cover and locked everything in the bathroom. Then he told me the stuff was powdered rhinoceros horn, which is illegal, and that his subjects gave it to him instead of taxes. Seriously, an aphrodisiac worth ten thousand dollars a gram in that fuckin' trailer park? I don't think so. He was fucking lying to a federal agent."

"Language, Nix! Doyle."

"This guy, Mr. Buffum, thinks he's a king, a real king. He told us he had sovereign immunity and we were powerless to collect taxes in his domain. No, wait, in his realm. He called the other losers who work there 'his subjects'. Oh, and he said he could pardon anyone he wanted, including himself. Are you getting this, Doyle?"

"Leave Doyle alone, Nix. He doesn't work for you."

Continuing as though Buffum said nothing, Nix added, "If you have to say anything about these ridiculous allegations, Mr. B, focus on the fact that this so-called King won't tell us his name. He won't show ID, though repeatedly asked, won't tell us who owns or runs King Henry's Faire, has refused to return numerous phone calls, refused to reply to repeated mailings, and refused to sign for any registered letters. He told me he's not going to show for a deposition that I scheduled for next Wednesday at two in the afternoon and he won't tell me why. This is a con man, Mr. Buffum, and a ten-year tax cheat. You can tell the media that we'd happily respond to any of the King's questions but he first has to tell us his name and the name of the taxpayer. In fact, until he does, it would be irresponsible to discuss this matter with anyone so, no further comment."

"He's not very patriotic, is he?" intoned Buffum.

"Hell no, Mr. Buffum," Nix agreed, "you're right about that, he is not patriotic. He set up his own little country. This is how the Civil War got started. Someone decided that he was going to play by his own rules instead of the ones everyone else was suffering through so, shazam, the Civil War."

"There's no room for kings in America, Nix."

"Amen, Mr. B. You should say that if you have to give a news conference about any of this. People love a tagline like that."

"It's not a tagline, Nix, I believe it."

"That's why it's such a good one."

Buffum paused, "Do you think I'll have to give a news conference?"

"The way things are going, yeah."

"Damn, I've got earned time I have to use. Do you think you and Steiger should continue with this case? I'm not so sure."

"I do, Mr. Buffum, and I'll tell you why. This guy is all about my rights and your wrongs. But he won't even tell us his name or what his interest is in this Faire. What's with that? The court of public opinion isn't going to look kindly on a one-way Charlie like him. This is a one-day news cycle, Mr. B, max. And finally, I don't know how to say this any other way except to say, I got my dick in this King's head."

"Oh, Nix."

"Really, Buffum, I do and I'm going to poke around in there a little and see what I turn up."

"Please don't talk that way, Nix. Doyle, make that sound less, I don't know, horrible."

"Yes, sir."

"Nix, why can't you be more like Doyle?"

"I just got through telling you, Mr. Buffum, I've got this dick."

XI

The King softly tapped on my trailer door, whispering. "It's me, your King, open up."

I only left him twenty minutes earlier. We had a breakfast meeting with the staff and the King went on and on. There must have been fifty Styrofoam breakfast sandwich containers and wrappers blowing around. I had to chase them all down. When I was done I stopped back at my trailer to soak my feet because a flapping right sole has altered my gait, making my back sore and my feet hurt.

"Let yourself in, Majesty. I'll be right with you."

"I would let myself in, Fool, but the door's locked. Why would you go and do something as suspicious as that? Are we keeping secrets?"

"Sorry, but at the meeting you said we have to be security conscious and that means..."

"Right, right, of course. Just testing, Fool. Glad you were paying attention. Open the door."

"I'm drying off my feet to do just that."

"Thank you, Fool. I hope you really were soaking your feet or pulling your pud or some such worthy activity and not trying to sneak off for a drink."

"What's that, Your Majesty?"

"I meant what I said this morning about being alert and prepared for the enemy. No more day drinking and moderate, strictly moderate drinking at night. I'll have you know that I haven't had a drink in seven hours if you can believe that."

This was technically true. It was also true that he'd only been awake for two.

"So, Fool, do you keep a bottle around for a guest or to jumpstart the morning?"

"Not anymore. You were pretty firm about waiting until nightfall before cracking the neck.'"

"I might have been too firm, I fear. I could have gotten carried away. That's the danger when you paint with too broad a brush. Circumstances are different for everyone. I should have been more aware and more considerate, Fool. I might be fine without a drink, as you can see, but you may need one for any number of reasons."

"My foot, back, and leg are sore because I've been walking funny."

"There you go, perfectly legitimate reason for a royal dispensation. Go ahead and have one."

"That's okay, Your Majesty. I soaked my feet instead. I'm feeling better."

"Go on, have a drink. Don't let me stop you. I've decreed it."

"I don't really need one now, but thanks, Highness."

"Fool, you've got me feeling bad and blue about this. It's eating away at me. I'd much prefer it if you'd take a snort or maybe two."

"Thank you, my liege but..."

"No buts about it. Now, have that drink. Have one now. Let me get the bottle for you."

"Well, Your Majesty, I might have something in the bathroom, behind the plunger, for emergencies."

"You sit there, Fool, and rub those sore feet. I'll get it for you. Don't move."

The King went into my bathroom and came out after a while. That vodka looked a little lighter than the last time I glanced its way.

"Ah, Fool, that's better."

"What's better?"

"Why knowing that you'll be having a drink, of course. Here you go. Tip that up and bend your elbow. Take a good long pull. There, even I feel better now, Fool, just knowing I didn't subject you to any half-thought cruelty about the drinkie."

"Thank you, Your Majesty."

"Let me put that bottle back,"

"Many thanks, Your Grace, but I'll hold onto it a moment."

"Right, well then, good morning, Fool. I'll be seeing you around and let's keep this between the two of us. Just saying, silence is a virtue, old friend."

After I found a new hiding place for that bottle I had a swallow and followed the King out the door. My back did feel a little better and so did my feet.

XII

"Hey, Nix?"

"What do you want, Steiger?"

"Take a ride with me."

"I'm kind of busy."

"Doing what?"

"Getting a handle on King Henry's Faire. I was going through the vendors' records you subpoenaed. This Faire does a good business and has every year for the past five, maybe longer. I haven't gone through everything but don't you wonder why a place like that stops filing taxes?"

"It's usually greed and people living beyond their means."

"I know that Steiger, but this is a cash business. Why not at least file and claim nothing? Not filing all but guarantees that we come knocking. And as far as living beyond their means, you'd be hard pressed to find a lower standard of living anywhere in this state than whatever it is in that trailer park."

"I know, it's confounding, Nix. That's why I want you to take a ride with me. Come on, I'll buy lunch. I got a friend, Leo, over in Chelsea. He's a private investigator. I got Buffum to take him on as contract labor."

"You got Buffum to agree to an outside investigator on one of our cases?"

"Yeah, on the King Henry's Faire non-filing. Buffum told us to do the necessary and I told him this was necessary."

"How so?"

"I said to him that if he was afraid of bad publicity he shouldn't use employees to do the dirty work. Instead, I told him, he ought to hire contract labor to serve as a buffer between the Agency and the King and he went for it."

Steiger's car was parked in an outdoor lot, one of a herd of crappers. They got in and Steiger drove up New Chardon, took a right onto Cambridge and hopped on Storrow where they joined a traffic jam.

"I don't eat lunch in Chelsea, Steiger. I won't even go to Dunks there."

"Don't know what you're missing, Nix. Chelsea's changed, but we'll go to Charlie's in Cambridge, if you want."

"But that's the other way. Why Cambridge?"

"'Cause I got to pick up my laundry in Somerville. My Mom won't do my laundry anymore. She says..."

"I don't want to know, Steiger, and we're not doing that. We'll go see your friend in Chelsea but after that we're going to the Casino. That's it. Loan me a hundred so I can make back some of the dough I dropped there and maybe make it to the end of the month."

"Deal."

Steiger's car smelled like it had been strip clubbed. The chalk outline of a rumpled suit lay on the back seat. Wrinkling her nose, Nix asked why it smelled so bad, reminding Steiger that if he still thought he was dropping off his laundry, he better think again.

"That's my club suit, Nix. It stays in the back unless I need it."

"Why would you need a smelly thing like that?"

"When's the last time you went to a strip club, Nix?"

"Larry took me to a place on Route One for my birthday last year. It was okay but why the suit?"

"Well, strippers aren't the most hygienic people. I mean, a lot of it's the job. They have to rub up against guys in the Champagne Room. Who knows what germs and bacteria are on them? And they have to smell the breath, body odor and greasy clothes of these guys, yuck, and worse, way worse. Those poles are filthy and the money in their G-strings lays right up against their pussies. Well, there's almost nothing filthier than money."

"Your mind is filthier than money."

"Maybe, Nix, but what are you going to catch from a filthy mind? A bad idea? Not the case with filthy pussy. Plus, strippers wear the worst kind of perfume. Maybe it's to cover up the stink of the customers, I don't know, but I like the smell of a woman."

"Oh, Steiger, you're turning my stomach. I better not see your nostrils quiver. I'll take an eye out."

"The smell of that perfume makes my Mother's stomach turn too. If I ever come home wearing the clothes I wore to the strip club she has an allergic reaction, which alone is bad enough. What's worse is she'll wheeze on endlessly about the sin of loose women and dirty touching and that sort of thing."

"TMI, Steiger."

"It's made her touchy and expectant. Now, if she smells anything, even if I wear my club suit, take it off and change back into my real clothes, she makes me strip buck naked and walk to the shower. The worst part of this is that if I'm coming home from a club then I've still got at least a blue veiner, if not a no-nonsense boner that I'm saving for later. Mom will tsk-tsk and chase me up the stairs with her broom, calling me a dirty bird and other hurtful things."

"Oh, Steiger, there's so much wrong with what you just said, I don't know where to begin. Let me process this but while I do can you answer a simple compound question?"

"If it would make you happy, Nix, sure, just don't make it too hard."

"Does your family not believe in using towels and bathrobes or is there some reason for you to be naked and aroused with your mother as she berates and prods you with a broomstick? On second thought, Steiger, don't answer. We're better off rewinding and wiping out this conversation. We'll have to set this one on fire and bury the ashes. Otherwise, I can never look at you again, not without thinking about it."

"In a good way, as a thoughtful person who takes precautions?"

"No, not in a good way, Steiger. Are you daft?"

"No, I'm just driving and honestly trying to answer your questions about my suit and trying to follow the conversation. If you're going to be nasty, don't ask me questions. What's your problem? It's just a human-interest story."

Nix nodded, "Oh, it is, Steiger? Like Oedipus Rex is a human-interest story? Have you ever heard that one?"

"Yeah, I'm pretty sure I have. I know Rex Oedipus. I mean, I know his work. Goes by the moniker Long Dong Motherfucker, as I recall. He was a wrestler before he got into porn. What's Long Dong got to do with any of this?"

"Forget I said a thing, Steiger, not a goddamn thing. But let me tell you that only a sicko like you could see your broom wielding Mommy scolding her naked and aroused adult son as a human-interest story. You are alone on the planet with that one."

"I don't think so, Nix. There are some people who like clams while others prefer mussels."

"What does that even mean?"

"Tony Curtis said it. I don't mean Tony Curtis the porn star. I'm talking about the real, old Hollywood guy. He meant it's a matter of taste. We have to agree to disagree, Nix."

"Or not, Steiger. Can you just drive? No more talking."

"But I have something to tell you. It's got nothing to do with strip clubs or laundry. It's about our case and it's for your benefit."

"Not now, Steiger. I'm traumatized."

"You probably think I'm going to say something about behaving yourself around the King but you're wrong. I know better. That'd be like me telling a lioness not to kill a gazelle. That lioness might look at me and seem to nod in agreement but you know that she is going to tear the gazelle to pieces no matter what."

"Please, Steiger, I don't care what you were going to say. I wasn't going to listen. I'm taking a meeting nap."

"What's that?"

"A stealth nap, a nap where no one knows you're napping."

"Nix, there are only two of us in the car and you've told me you're napping. It won't be very stealthy. Just listen with half an ear."

They hit the Tobin Bridge and traffic opened up. Steiger stepped on the gas and the tires made that fast low hum as they sped over the steel grating above the Mystic River. Nix settled in and closed her eyes, her breathing growing regular. She thought if she had to die she'd want it to be to this road chant.

Then Steiger started in, low and dozy, "Our office has an Employee Assistance Program. It's really a get out of jail free card. Before you got here I had a nasty porn collection on my computer. Some of it was so bad it was work for me to watch it. Well, someone said she saw something and before you know it I'm in the office with Buffum and the Union Rep. After all the accusations and denials, I get two weeks off, with pay, and they send me to a resort to correct my behavior. The food was good and I had lots of laughs. Met some nice people and learned some things, like how to hide my porn better and do you know what NSFW stands for?"

"Everyone knows what that stands for, Steiger."

"Okay, but that's not the point. The point is that I know you're going to do something terrible to the King."

"Like what?"

"I don't know. You threatened him. You locked him in a potty. You backed into the potty and knocked it over, don't deny it, covering him in shit, and then you left him there."

"He got out. You saw it on TV. And I deny everything you said ."

"The situation is escalating, Nix."

"You think?"

"Yeah, Nix, I do. Anyone but you would."

"So how is an Employee Assistance Program going to help me?"

"It came to me while I was dozing off last night. You have to go see a shrink and tell her how you feel about people and the crazy shit you say and do. This next part is crucial. Say whatever you have to so the shrink thinks you're just 'walking around crazy'. You don't want her to think you're 'jumping off buildings crazy'. It's not a thin line, Nix, but it's not a super-highway either. You should be able to pull this off. A word of advice though, don't embellish. That way, when the King is discovered hanging from the Zakim Bridge, missing, presumed dead, maybe in an emergency room, in a coma, or a mental hospital, bingo."

"Bingo?"

"Yeah, if whatever alibi you cook up fails, you have mental illness to fall back on. You're JFC."

"I'm what?"

"You're just fucking crazy. You can't be held responsible. It's the law. You might even keep your job, but no guarantee of that, not when there's a corpse."

"So, Steiger, did you go to a shrink before you got caught with porn?"

"Oh yeah, for years. I used to whack off in church and sometimes at the supper table. Drove my mother nuts. I don't know why, I just liked doing it. We had this guy working at the Agency back then. You know those nervous people, always in the bathroom, the ones that wash their hands until they bleed?"

"Yeah."

"I was in there more than he was."

"You're a sicko, Steiger."

"Oh yeah, but now I take medication. So, don't forget. Go to the shrink first so she can water the seed that nurtures the growth of a little green shoot that will become a forest of job saving cover. If it were me, I'd let the shrink know I have a particular loathing for monarchs, but that's me."

"I'm going to tell the shrink I have a big crush on your mother."

"Funny, Nix. You don't even know her."

"I'm going to tell the shrink that you talk about your mother and sister all the time and all I really want is to have a threesome."

"No, Nix."

"Yes, does your mother like girls?"

"Oh, Nix, stop it."

"How about your sister? Does she go down?"

"Please, Nix."

"If you want to join in you're going to have to dress like one of the girls."

"My mother is a good woman."

"They're the best kind. They're all wound up after years of frustration. Release them and watch. Mom will be eating pussy like it's chicken dinner. I'm getting excited just thinking about this."

"You have to stop, Nix. I'm your friend. I know your dirty secrets."

"I'm not worried about you, Steiger."

"Because you have a bigger dick?"

"That and you couldn't rat me out if you wanted. You know I'm right. It's not something you'd let yourself do. In fact, you'd protect me even though you're a natural, maybe a born coward."

"I am a born coward, Nix."

"That's perfect, Steiger. Now tell me about the girls"

"Please stop, Nix."

"I feel like you've been pimping them out to me for years and I was too innocent to catch on... until now."

"Begging you, Nix, please stop."

"You want me to be nice to them, don't you? You don't want me to turn them against you?"

"Ahh," Steiger's shoulders slumped and a sigh escaped, "here we are, Nix. Never wanted to get to Leo's office so badly."

XIII

My hands aren't healing like I'd hoped. They seem to have taken a turn for the worse. I called St. Tillo Hospital and spoke to someone. I told her my hands had gone weepy around the bullet holes and grey around the edges. I said they'd begun to ache and my right hand is starting to claw. I let her know it had me a little worried. She asked me for my PID number, which I didn't know so I hung up and caught the bus to Horseshoe Falls where there's a clinic at the pharmacy.

The nurse, who said she was a clinician, whatever that is, showed me to a small examination room where I took off the bandages. She backed away with a sharp intake of breathe. They didn't look as bad as I expected, but still greyish to the wrists. The smell was another thing. In the confines of that examination room even I had to admit that it smelled like the devil snuck out of Martin Luther's fanny and slipped under the door to join us.

Hanky to her mouth and nose, the clinician, or whatever she called herself, got out of there fast and returned with the pharmacist, a big fella, and both of them squeezed in and shut the door behind them. Now it was the four of us in there and way more embarrassing. There was the same stink but there was less free airspace for the stink to dissipate. The ratios were off.

The pharmacist, a man with obvious retail experience, was shallow breathing through his mouth behind a palm to chin filter, index finger and thumb closing off the nostrils. He muttered, "Hmmm, ahhhh, and eeeww," before elaborating, "young man, you really ought to be in a hospital. Your hands may be gangrenous which could end up costing you one or both of them. I don't want to be an alarmist but it could even kill you. Here at the pharmacy, we can't deal with that level of infection. Besides prescriptions, we mostly give flu shots and fill out forms for school and summer camp. We're worried about you, son. We'd like to call you an ambulance."

I thanked them both and told them I had to be going. At first we all waited for someone to make the first move and then we all made for the door at the same time. It was funny and I wanted to laugh, but neither of them was even smiling. I finally got outside and got lost in the tiny downtown while I waited for the bus. I thought about going back to the hospital to get my hands checked out, and I might have, but I remembered we had our first big weekend of the season coming up so it would have to wait.

This is a big weekend for a couple of reasons. First of all, next to Halloween, there's nothing bigger than Octoberfest for county, aggie, and olde tyme fairs, but nobody ever calls it Octoberfest. At King Henry's we call it Fartnight because it runs for two weeks, usually in September but sometimes it spills into October. No one knows what Fartnight has to do with Olde England but we sell a lot of beer and tee shirts with the words 'Pull My Finger; and 'Smells Like Fartnight', so who cares. Stan used to say, "If you want to make a buck you have to generously interpret the holidays."

For the kick-off of Fartnight we booked the Elvis impersonator again. He showed up early this afternoon, drunker, fatter, and more broke than last year. He tweaks the lyrics of Elvis' classics to fit our Olde English Faire, like Love Thee Tender and In Thy Ghetto. We also have a recurring attraction with the Best Wet Wench Rack Competition, which doesn't need describing except to say, of course we sell spray bottles with our logo and it's extra for water. We have the same event the following weekend except the competitors are amateurs who, honest to God, pay to be pawed, drooled on, and harassed.

Baffles me why anyone would pay to have herself treated this way, but then I remember I hit my head with a rubber hammer about twenty times a night, run around like a simpleton, trip, fall down, and get laughed at, so who am I to judge? For the Wenches, pros and amateurs, I suppose it is or once was the lure of fame. I never had even that. What I've got, all I've got is that I can play the Fool as well as or better than anyone.

Anyway, there's a five-dollar fine for touching the Wenches or amateur Wenches and a ten dollar fine for touching them inappropriately. All fines are payable immediately to King Henry's Faire. The Wenches never see a cent but they get all the aggro. We have other attractions too, like an ax throw, a karaoke competition, and a hot dog eating contest. It's a pretty good line up for this early in the season, when people will come anyway, just because we're open. We had a waterskiing demonstration with waterskiing rides scheduled for this season but the lake next door ran dry so we had to cancel. The Wave Ridin' Water Babes, that's their name, say they're going to sue but I don't know. Carny folk don't sue. On the other hand, by the time a Carny has exacted his fill of revenge, anyone would wish he'd been sued.

The other reason this is such an important and well-remembered weekend has to do with Stan. This is the tenth anniversary of his death. Poor Stan, and poor me too. I don't envy the King much, but sometimes I wish I had his memory 'cause it's for shit and there's too damn much in my library. Maybe I just want to remember things differently, or clearly or not as clearly. Sometimes I wish things were cut and dried but they never are. Instead, I run through possibilities, mostly while I'm in bed, thinking the way I imagine the Mastermind of the train tracks over at the Hobby Shop in Horseshoe Falls must think while he's laying out the tracks that will intersect down the line. 'What do I have for time?' the Mastermind must ask himself. Of course, he needs to know. What do I have for time? That's what I want to know. I need to know.

Stan didn't go peacefully. To this day, I can barely look at cotton candy, let alone eat it. Back then the Faire ran like a well-oiled machine and it was Stan who made it run that way. He was larger than life, a Carny god. He was always prepared and knew what was going to happen and roughly when. I only saw him surprised a couple of times. Once when there was a tornado and the other when, ah, that's personal, maybe later, once I get to know you.

And Stan never once ran out of beer, not even once. He never ran out of food, either, but it's a fact that a fair number of people got sick from it. I never said Stan wasn't a penny pincher. He sure was but what kind of food do people expect to get at a fairground? I'm just saying he never ran out and never ran out of prizes, cheap plastic trophies, flammable stuffed animals, swallowable trinkets or rolls of redeemable tickets for rides, events, and activities. He was always on the job.

The weekend Stan died was a hot one, like this. We were set up just about where we are now and what happened is someone messed with the cotton candy machine. This was Stan's pride and joy. He claimed it was the largest cotton candy machine in the free world and had some faked-up letter from a phony organization to prove it. Every week, usually on Sunday morning, Stan would put on a sterile paper suit with paper shoes and climb into the machine to clean, oil and test it. Stan took his time and wiped down the plexiglass walls with a soft sponge and squeegee until they gleamed. He'd check all the light bulbs, inside and out, and he'd run a test of the machine to make sure everything was working fine.

The day he died Stan got into a terrible argument with the King. The King wanted more money and a twenty percent interest in the Faire. He demanded that he be featured in all the promotional materials and posters for the Faire. The King also said he wanted to make personal appearances at store openings and car dealerships and things like that. The King said if he didn't get his way he was going to walk and take anyone who wanted a fair shake and more money with him.

Stan hadn't just fallen off the turnip truck. He'd been dealing with what he called 'prima donnas' since he opened the Faire. He told the King to go ahead and leave and take anyone foolish enough to go with him. He added that the King was a two-bit overpaid drunk who couldn't hold a thought, a woman or his dignity. Then he laughed in the King's face and told him to go screw. Stan was tough and didn't fuck around. I loved him for it, but the King didn't.

In fact, the King got pretty mad and started spitting and screaming at Stan, accusing him of this and that and then he asked when Stan was going to tell me who my father was. I don't remember much after that. I was so bowled over that everything was just a buzz in my ears. Momma ran a concession stand at the Faire. She never told me who my Daddy was before she died but I'd always looked up to Stan and walked in his shadow without knowing anything about any of this.

For some reason I stopped talking after this. I don't know why. It happened after I found out about Stan and Momma. No, it was after Stan died that I stopped talking. But the King had something to do with it too. Hold on just a minute, I've got to take a breath. Whooo, I get confused. The King whispered things to me back then, sly things that get in the way, dangerous things about me staying quiet. He pestered me like a mosquito on a hot summer night, night after day after night. He got me thinking, which I don't think is good for me.

I was robbed of my Momma and by my Momma. I was robbed of my father by Stan. I was robbed by the King but I wasn't looking when he did it so I don't know what he took. It happened after I found out about Stan and Momma. That I know, I'm sure. No, no, I'm not. It was after Stan died...I have to stop. I have to catch my wind. I have to slow my thoughts, slow them way down. I have to think of something else when I get confused like this.

Momma had a record player. She'd sip from a bottle at night and listen to it. After she was halfway through she'd get a little teary and play this one sad song over and over. I still hear it in my head. She played this song so many times there was a skip in the record where the song was. She put a quarter on the arm of the needle to make it play through.

Well, there's a skip in my head. It happened when I found out about Stan and Momma. Or was it when Stan died? When I realized what happened to Stan, I knew I'd never get the chance to talk to him again. I'd never hear his voice or his big laugh. Yeah, maybe it was what happened to Stan. It was so bad I can't think about it. Maybe it wasn't that. It was when Momma died, or when I found out about Stan and Momma. Then again, maybe it was when Stan died. Or maybe not. Anyway, for some reason there's a skip in my head. There's still a skip in my head, but no one can hear it. I've got a quarter on it so I can play through.

There is a price for everything. I have denied everything that happened that day, the day I lost Stan. I have fought so hard against the truth that I don't remember it. The truth is blurred and buried, bound in lies, deceit, and need. I made it so I couldn't know what was true and what wasn't. I had to fuck with the truth or I wasn't getting out of the worst place I'd ever been, the worst place anyone could ever be. When I was there I wondered if I existed or was I just the thought of someone else?

After Stan died I was declared a ward of the State and committed to a mental hospital. I was there a year in a big little room with metal walls with hooks for padding and a bed with no parts you can hurt yourself with and a tiny window with cross hatched wire safety glass. There were twenty-four diamond shaped cross hatches in every small window, ninety-six in the large ones. I was there a year and never spoke a word. I never even talked to myself. I just watched everything, like a security camera, and stored it away. Finally, they let me go. I was there a year but it was like a day because everything that happened was the same. But it was also like ten years for the same reason. I made my way back to the Faire. I had nowhere else to go.

I'm mooning around today, not really doing anything, but not relaxed about it either. I had a few drinks and half a spliff but that hasn't helped. I was walking through the park thinking of Stan when I heard the King.

"Hey, Fool?"

"Hmmm," I turned to see the King coming my way, waving an envelope.

"What's up, Your Majesty?

"A process serving Deputy Sheriff dropped this on me five minutes ago. Says it's a...it's a...you read it, Fool. I don't have my glasses."

"You don't have glasses, Majesty."

"That's what I'm saying, now what does it say?

"It says it's a subpoena duces tecum and let's see, that there's fifty-five dollars cash inside..."

"There wasn't a goddamn cent in there, Fool. Go ahead, take a look. You're a witness. Goddamn government."

"This envelope was open when you handed it to me, King."

"There wasn't no money in it, Fool."

"It also says you're supposed to be at a deposition next Wednesday at two o'clock in Boston. You're supposed to bring with you all kinds of records we probably don't have."

"That's crazy, in the middle of the day, two o'clock, in Boston? Boston? Have you ever heard of such a thing? Who the fuck goes to Boston?"

"You'd be surprised. It's not too hard to ..."

"I know where it is, sort of, but I ain't going. Doesn't that IRS po-po understand that I work? Scheduling something in the middle of the day, what's she thinking? I'm not going."

Shortly before he died, Stan said to me, "You got to watch out for the King. He's a stone-cold dummy and that's the nicest thing I can say about him. He don't listen to anyone, particularly me. You have to help him stay out of his own way. Keep him away from himself as much as you can."

With that in mind, I said, "Well, King, this ain't like a no show at the clinic or sleeping in instead of going to the food pantry. You have to call and tell somebody you won't be able to make it to wherever it is and be nice about it. There's a telephone number here."

The King held up his phone. He had a new phone case but the same shitty Port-A- Potty phone, "Why don't I just call it."

He dialed and someone must have picked up, but I only heard the King's side of the story.

"IRS? Yeah, my name is King, spelled the way you'd spell king. Tudor. Henry. If I had a social security number I wouldn't give it to you. I don't have that either. I do have a subp...a letter from Agent Nix and I can't make the meeting she mentioned. Her name is Nix, N-I-X, I think. Can you put her on the phone? Yes," there was a long wait. I could see the King getting steamed up, "Ah, Agent Nix, it's me, the King. I thought I was going to have to sit up and beg to get to talk to you. So, I wish I could say it is a pleasure, but...I know I called you... but before you get to that...No...Listen, I can't make this subpony, however you say it. No, I'm busy. Never mind, I'm just busy. But I don't want to tell you... I don't have to... If I wasn't a gentleman and a king, I'd call you a fucking cow bitch and tell you to go fuck yourself. Huh? I did call you that? Must have slipped out. Okay, but I won't be there and this is the only notice you're getting...So what? I don't care. Go fuck yourself, Nix. See ya in hell, bitch."

"I don't know if that was a good idea, King."

"What do you know?"

"I know that two o'clock in the afternoon is a good time for most people and it ain't unreasonable or bitchy to ask you why you can't make it. And you were a plain old jerk, Your Grace."

"She's trying to bust my balls."

"I don't think so, but she's going to if you keep this up."

"Then I better apologize," said the King as he hit redial, "IRS? This is King again. Yeah, I must have got disconnected. Put me through to Nix, please. Yes, sorry, Agent Nix." There was another long wait. "Nix, my associate tells me I was rude to you. He says I called you a fucking bitch and other bad names like dildo breath, pussy mouth, and...Glad you get the picture. Well, I called to say I'm sorry and I shouldn't have said those things right off the bat like that. Why don't you come down to the Faire tonight? It's on the house....... No, it's not improper... Sure, bring a friend, man, woman or child, whatever your pleasure. You won't spend a nickel...No, it's not a cheap bribe. It's a new start for you and me... Great... Yeah, great. Okay then."

"That idea wasn't any better, King."

"What do you know, Fool? You're the one who told me to call her back and apologize. That's what I did."

"Your Grace, do you think it's a good idea to keep calling her bad names and then invite her down here?"

"You don't know anything, Fool, especially about women."

"I know you should never meet her while you're drinking, shooting up, or taking amphetamines. I know she doesn't like you. I know she's not afraid of..."

"Zip it, Fool. She's never going to come. I was just having some fun."

XIV

Nix walked around the office, into the break room, made herself a coffee and walked to Steiger's squaricle. His face was about two inches from his computer screen, checking out the Vegas odds for Sunday's games.

"STEIGER," Nix whispered harshly behind his ear.

"Yaaaah!......Don't do that, Nix. I was working."

"Ha, you jumped in your chair! And only a complete jackass bets New York."

"I was taking a break from that application for a search warrant. Jets?"

"Either. You told Buffum you did that last week."

"I only said that because you put me on the spot. You knew I hadn't done it. We hadn't even talked about it."

"Listen, Steiger, do you want to go out tonight?"

"Out? With you? Tonight?"

"Yeah."

"Well, sure I...oh, I have a Deacon's meeting."

"It's Friday night."

"Yeah, it's tonight, Our Lady of a Thousand Sorrows."

"It's Friday night, Steiger. You're not going to church on a Friday night. I won't let you."

"Well, let me or not, I have this meeting and I have to go."

"Skip the meeting and come with me. You won't regret it. Ask for forgiveness on Sunday. The Lord is just and merciful."

"I can't, Nix."

"Don't make me go to Buffum's office and tell him that you never did the application for a search warrant for that Faire. He'll have you at your desk until you finish. So much for your meeting."

"You wouldn't do that, Nix."

"What would you bet on that, Steiger?"

"Well, now that you've made it a big issue you will. Fuck me, Nix, where are we going?"

"It's a surprise. I'll pick you up at six. Where do you live?"

"I don't want to tell you. I'll meet you downstairs, on the corner at six."

"I'll see you outside your house at six. I know where you live, Steiger. I was only being polite. Now, if I'm hot, wet hot, it's for Mom and Sis. Don't look disappointed. Girls dress for girls. Ready at six or knock, knock, I'm coming in."

"Yeah, Nix, at six."

Nix pulled up in her beat-up Toyota something at whatever o'clock and leaned on the horn. Steiger came running out in a suit with a doughnut in his mouth.

"Hey, Nix," he mumbled, "this is my neighborhood. Do you have to lean on the horn?"

"Yeah, and what are you wearing?"

"A suit."

"Go back and change into something, I don't know, rustic. And put sneakers on or something comfortable. And get a hat."

"Rustic? I'm comfortable in a suit and these shoes."

"Go change."

XV

I was keeping a weather eye on the King as he staggered through the Faire, knocking over stalls, leering at every girl he saw and pawing at those within reach. The Queen might have let this pass. She was used to his boozy, drug fueled antics. But when he grabbed Wench Clara, the Blacksmith's new girlfriend, and introduced himself to her breasts, she'd had enough. The Queen reached over and grabbed the King by his ear and pulled him into the Potter's shed. Then she stepped back outside, pointed at me, and said, "Inside."

"What are you up to now?" she had her hands on her hips, looking down at the King wobbling on a stool, "Just look at you. We talked about this. I told you, beer, smoke, and bourbon at night and that's it. No amphetamines, no needles, no blow, no fentanyl, no excuses. You said that you'd keep it down. You promised to behave. Now, look at you. You said no one would ever know if you had a little toot. Well, I'm here to tell you everyone knows and they know because you're staggering around like a bug-eyed pervert, grabbing every girl you see. What an embarrassment. If they only knew that you're all bark. That pecker of yours wouldn't reach for the sky if it had a gun to its head. Everyone's plain sick of you crashing into people and knocking over stalls. We've all had enough. This is going to stop and it's going to stop now. I'm putting you in the stocks until you sober up and learn to behave like a human being. Fool, don't you let him move or get more booze and drugs in him or I'll skin you alive."

I stood next to the King with my lip buttoned while he was slurring, "C'mon Diane, I ain't that bad."

"You're worse," shouted the Queen and then she turned on me, "It's your fault, Fool."

"Me, Majesty?"

"Why'd you let him get this way? Now put him in the stocks and don't let anyone give him any more booze or drugs. If I hear he's had any, your life ain't going to be worth a tin nickel. Understood?"

"Yes, Majesty, I do," I stood up straight and tall, "but I ain't going to be able to stop him."

"No buts, just do it."

"I hear Your Majesty, but if I don't free him or get him drugs, someone else will. I know he seems ignorant and sounds stupid but he has a way of twisting things. You get tired of trying to follow his reasoning. It wears you out and you just end up doing what he wants. If not me then someone else will get him what he wants. That's what happens when I try and shut him down. It's his ju-ju."

"Ju-Ju my left butt cheek," the Queen glared at the King, "we'll take care of that then. Clap him in the stocks like I said and then go to our trailer and get the gag that, well, that we, ah, just never mind why it's there. Get the red ball gag with the black straps. It's in my delicates' drawer. Strap it around his head so he can't talk. I'll have one of my ladies in waiting make a booth around the stocks and she'll put up a sign saying this is a pie throwing booth. Then you have the Baker make some whipped cream pies for throwing. It's going to be three pies for ten dollars. Tell him he better make a hundred. I want an endless line of people throwing pies at our jackass King. That ought to keep the horny dope addict quiet and save some poor helpless girls from getting groped any more than they have to. See how the Royal Swine likes being at the other end of the stick for a change."

It sure seemed like a good plan to me. When the Queen gets angry, watch out. She ain't flighty like the King. I clapped the sleepy King in the stocks, just like I was told, and made that gag nice and tight. Then I hustled over to the Baker to get him started on the pies. I told him to make a hundred and fifty of them for starters. I know a good plan when I hear one. There are going to be lots of people wanting pie tonight.

XVI

"So, Nix, when are you going to tell me where we're going?"

"You'll find out soon enough."

"Well, we're traveling South."

"You must have some hunting dog in you."

"There's a compass on your dashboard."

"Ahhh, that's your trick."

"C'mon, Nix, tell me where we're going."

"I'll give you a hint. We're dining al fresco."

"What does that mean?"

"Not exactly a linguist, are you?"

"I can say 'facial' in seven languages. I can say 'pussy' in twelve."

"I didn't know you were so well educated."

"I went to parochial school. I can say 'reach around' in Dutch: 'bereik rond'."

"That's why we should spend more time together. Out of the office, I mean, so we can learn to appreciate our individual strengths, weaknesses, and peculiarities. And you, Steiger, are peculiar from head to toe."

"Thanks, Nix, so where are we going?"

"Al fresco means outside."

"So, we're going on a picnic?"

"No, we're not picnicking. Let's see, another clue. There will be games of chance."

"Games of chance?"

"Yes, games of chance and entertainment, of a sort, low rent royal entertainment."

"No, Nix."

"Yes."

"Oh, Nix, I don't want anything to do with the Olde English Faire. It's the weekend. Can we please do something else? Anything else?"

"It's King Henry's Faire and what else would you rather do on our date? Go to a strip club?"

"I have the App on my phone. It tells me where the closest ones are and how they're rated."

"Like Michelin stars?"

"They go by cum shots, like two cum shots or five cum shots. Five cum shots is the best. A few years ago, there were some independent strip clubs that used a 'splooch' system but it didn't stick. "

"You need another hobby, Steiger, like stamp collecting, or coins, or baseball cards."

"I'm okay with what I've got. If anything, I've gone in the opposite direction. I've incorporated porn into other aspects of life, like porn on my computer at work, as you know. But lately, my favorite 'porn and' activity is going to confession."

Nix gave him a fresh look, "You mean 'confession' as in confessing your sins, begging forgiveness, and making heartfelt prayer in the hope of forgiveness?"

"Not so much the Sacrament of Reconciliation itself. It's more the stage and setting, if you will, of the confessional experience. What I like to do is,... do you have time for this?"

"Not another word from your mouth, Steiger, unless it has to do with forgiveness. I'm all ears."

"I liked the dark Confessional booth of my youth and the scary sliding screen because, well, just leave it at that. Perhaps it was nostalgia."

"Steiger! Focus!"

"Okay, okay but I never imagined how much better the sitting in chairs, face to face confessional experience could be. I'll go to confession three times a week, even more often, always different parishes. What I do is confess to auto-erotic experiences, lewd public acts, prosecutable voyeurism, gang bangs, circle jerks, threesomes, self-abuse, and one time, necrophilia. It's stuff off the beaten track. Anything that I might have done, read about, heard, or just made up, I weave into a story of seduction and disgrace, rise and inevitable fall. I try and mirror the Greek tragedians."

"Steiger!"

"Okay, I go into graphic, minute detail, identifying loathsome smells and describing the sex acts, all the while staring at the priest in the chair across from me, staring him right in the eyes until my vision lowers, dropping ever so slowly until I'm fixed on Father's holy mackerel which, when I'm good or just lucky, is fighting against the trouser net. If I'm able to mark a boner on a padre, and my standards are pretty high, I'll often pop one myself, in solidary. Semis mean nothing to me. That's walking around junk. As far as I'm concerned, it's a full-on trouser boner or it doesn't earn a hard spot in the win column."

"What's this fixation you have, Steiger. I can feel your damp thoughts worming their way into my head."

"Really, Nix? That's what I'm shooting for in confession. You can really feel them? Whoa! I'm good."

"What's the 'whoa' for?

"Oh, nothing," Steiger looked away.

"I know when you use that expression you're thinking filthy thoughts."

"It's just a word." Steiger looked Nix in the eye.

"If you're putting me in some kind of sex role in your head so you can get hard, Steiger, there's going to be trouble. And by trouble, I mean pain and disability."

"No trouble here, Nix. Just reliving how this priest in Brighton couldn't get out of his chair, he was so boned up. That was the 'whoa' and nothing else."

"That's good because we're here."

Nix parked her Toyota in the space closest to the exit. There must have been fifteen hundred cars and trucks in King Henry's Faire parking lot, but there wasn't one within a hundred yards of them. Nix was thinking ahead. While this promised a long walk to the Faire, it also guaranteed a quick, traffic free exit, should they be in a hurry. They could hear the tinny commotion of the Faire all the way from the gate.

"Have you got any money, Steiger?"

"I have a hundred bucks."

"Give me fifty."

"You asked me out."

"I never said I was paying. I just asked you to come."

"Ahh, it's implicit that you're paying when you ask."

"Says who?"

"Everyone."

"Name one."

"Every prostitute that ever street walked the earth."

"Give me fifty anyway."

Nix paid for their admission and they wandered around, stopping by the Elvis impersonator, and buying a couple corn dogs.

"Hey, Steiger, did fat Elvis just sing 'Thou Ain't Nothin' But A Hound Dog'?"

"Yeah, he really captured it, didn't he? This one's called 'Love Thee Tender'."

"Damn, Steiger, if this Elvis doesn't have type II diabetes I want to know his secret. He looks like he's made of cheese. Bet he has a cardiologist on speed dial."

"Hey Nix, what's that line forming over there?"

"Don't know. Let's find out."

Elvis broke into 'Thou Suspicious Mind' as they wandered over to where the line built.

"Hey Steiger, isn't that the King, clapped in the stocks?"

"I think so...... Christ, Nix, you're right. He's gagged and wild eyed. This is a pie throwing booth. Keep walking."

"No, no, no, Steiger, give me that other fifty."

"Don't do this.

"The other fifty, Steiger.

"This is a bad idea, Nix."

"That's your opinion."

"No, I think it's more than that. This is going to lead to trouble."

"Did I tell you I played softball in college, Steiger?"

"You went to college?"

"Well, junior college is what they called it then. Full boat scholarship and I still hold the school record for striking out twenty-two hairy dykes in one nine-inning, two hit shut-out."

"Wow, that's something. C'mon, let's keep walking."

"I was almost unhittable. It was my semi-sidearm delivery that had them fooled. It looked like a frisbee toss, but at eighty-five miles an hour. My slider dropped eight inches."

"Eighty-five, that's impressive. Look, Nix, they're making mead over there. I always wanted to learn how to make mead. It's a honey-based beverage, let's go see."

"You go. I've got some business here."

"Don't do it, Nix, please don't. You know the agency can make us pay for our own lawyers if we're criminally charged. You told me Buffum was thinking about that and they can refuse to defend or pay a judgment for intentional torts."

"Life isn't to be feared, Steiger. Go on, you're not involved in this."

"Of course, I am. I'm your partner. We're here at this goddamn Faire together. We're both assigned to this case. I'm as screwed as you're going to be."

"Run along, Steiger. Put that hat on that I told you to bring."

"I left it in the car. Can you just be quick about this?"

"No, I will not be quick about this."

"Let me tell you something, Nix. I think you're the cause of my colitis. And it's things like this, your stubbornness, your refusal to listen to reason, that exacerbate my symptoms. So, you fuck me in the ass every time you try and fuck that King in the ass. Even still, still, I'm not running away from you or anything. And I'm not leaving you in the lurch, either. What it is, though, is I've got to get to the can and pronto. If I don't I'll shit my pants. You're the cause of this condition, Nix, the direct cause. You make my ass bleed so badly my doctor says I'm anemic. I have to bring wet wipes everywhere I go because of you. How pathetic is that? So, I'll be back in ten or fifteen, maybe twenty. Can you be careful until then?"

While Steiger hurried off to a Port-A-Potty, Nix called after him, "I can....but I may not."

Nix got busy stretching and loosening up her neck, left arm and shoulder. She ran in place and did some squats before it was her turn at the pie booth.

"Give me fifteen pies."

"Lady, that's fifty dollars-worth of pies."

Nix slapped fifty dollars on the counter and said, "I'm not just buying pie. I'm having dessert."

"You got it," the Carny said, "fifteen pies for the southpaw, coming right up."

Nix stood in the line before the stocks, forty feet away, and stared at the King. While pies littered the ground around him and the stocks surrounding him were covered in cream and crust, very few seem to have reached the King. She gave the King a tight smile and a wink. The realization of who she was and what she was up to finally broke on the King's cerebral cortex as she stepped to the mound and scuffed her feet. His eyes widened and darted both ways. Then the King started stomping his feet and trying to shout something but the ball gag in his mouth wouldn't have it. All anyone heard was a garbled, primal, moan-scream.

Nix smiled more broadly, "Okay, Your Majesty, don't crowd the plate."

Before the King could do or say anything, an aluminum pie plate slammed into his upper lip at the junction of his nose. Much like the loose change, the half-eaten sandwich you were going to finish later, and all the other crap that accumulates in your car; when you slam on the brakes or rear end another car, all that crap flies forward, even after your car reaches a dead stop. The same thing is true with pie plates and the contents of pie plates. This is Newton's First Law of Motion, although I don't think Newton ever thought about pie, pie crust, or pie plates when he was trying to explain it. Nonetheless, when that pie plate came to a sudden stop at the King's nostril delta, a substantial amount of that whipped cream and pie crust kept traveling up the King's nose at the speed it had been traveling.

This was certainly uncomfortable, but not dangerous. Unfortunately for the King, though, Nix had reloaded and another pie was on its way, sidearm, traveling fast, and striking him in the same spot. Then another pie was let loose before the King recovered from the second assault. In quick succession, came pies four, five, and six. Nix was in the zone. The King looked dazed and disoriented, terrified, and unable to catch his breathe. Trying to breathe around the red ball gag wasn't working. Once again, Nix let loose, this time with pies seven, eight, and nine. The King's eyes rolled back in his head and his body shook convulsively.

The Carny at the booth held up his hands like a referee and walked over to the King. He opened one eye, found a weak pulse, and wiped the King's face with a towel. Then he pressed each nostril shut, in turn, allowing the King to focus a pressurized blow from each nostril to try and clear the passages. The King gave him a pleading look but the Carny just shook his head and shouted, "Play Ball!"

Nix let loose with pies ten, eleven, and twelve. The King was rattled and afraid, trying to get someone's attention, but then he was struck with pies thirteen, fourteen and fifteen. It was when the fifteenth pie was on its way that the King seemed to lose consciousness and a broad wet spot spread across his crotch and down his right leg.

The Carny said to Nix, "No more pies for you. You throw too hard. Can't you see the King can't breathe?"

"No," said Nix, "I can't. Sell me a few more pies so I can be certain."

Steiger was washing his hands at the little sink in the Port-A-Potty when he heard the wail of an ambulance siren getting closer. Whatever nascent bits of poo hadn't fled to the blue fecal pool chose this moment to rush the gates. Steiger sighed, turned around, and dropped back down on the horseshoe toilet seat awaiting the firehose exit of the excreta chaff from his otherwise clean and shiny rectal sleeve. The sound of the siren grew closer.

XVII

The King awoke as a substantial needle with a syringe attached was inserted into his chest cavity. He would have been unconscious but for an otherworldly tolerance to morphine derivative drugs. He watched the plunger on the syringe get depressed by a strong lined thumb in a blue surgical glove. He didn't feel anything but he did wonder where he was and how he got there? He stuck out his tongue and it cleared his lips.

He watched some hands snake a tube into his chest and wondered why they'd do such a thing. That tube doesn't belong in there, he thought. Did he swallow the gag? Are they fishing for the gag with that tube? Then he saw someone in scrubs with a defibrillator. He was running towards him, running towards him with the cardiac defibrillator. Not the cardiac defibrillator! The King was familiar with this apparatus. He'd been tased and he'd been resuscitated, both more than once. He much preferred a tasing.

"I'm awake," he wanted to say. "Don't turn that fucking thing on. Whenever they turn that thing on," he warned himself, "they use it."

BLAM, he was in the middle of a desert. His back arched as he gurgled nonsense. There was a white sun high in a pale desert sky. Heat warbled distant hills. A long flat road going nowhere shimmered above the desert floor.

The King's eyes fluttered but he wasn't breathing.

BLAM, he was screaming but not making a sound. A man floated down from the high pale sky. He was in the lotus position on a little blue motor scooter, right hand up near his face, palm outward. He was coming into focus. It was someone he knew from long ago, putt-putting his way over. It was Stan who motored over to the King. He was all business.

He said to the King, "Over and over, in your dark and desperate dreams, I told you that your debt to me can only be discharged if you take care of the boy. I told you this is your only way out, but instead of caring for him you made him your Fool. You took the business and all the money the Faire had, but you didn't do right by the boy. You should have been his guardian, but you made him your slave. You betrayed his promise. You broke his mind. You buried his opportunities. You hid him in a mental hospital to sully and question his recollection of what you did. I can forgive everything you've done to me, but never what you've done to him. This you may only get from the one you made into your Fool. You failed him and in doing so, failed to redeem yourself for killing me. You owe two souls. They weigh you down. There will be no lamentation and no one to mourn your passing."

Tears jumped to the King's eyes, "I'll mend my ways. I'm sorry. I'll be good, good to him. I can change!"

Stan wouldn't bend, "It's late for that, I'm sure you'll agree." His eyes glanced down to the gas gauge, "He's all grown now. And of what worth is your promise? The shifting sand below your feet is firmer and more resolute. Your life reflects your character, your character, your life. Look at yourself as though you were me. Why would I believe you? Why should anyone ever believe anything you ever say?"

"You should, Stan, because you're my ghost and I'm your King. You have to believe in me because without me there's no you, okay? You're nothing without me, Stan, nothing but nothingness. You don't exist. You're only alive in my head, where you torment me and replay the misdeeds of my life, but that's all you can do. And I have the remedy for that. It's a shot of this and a snort of that. It's a gun in my arm on the couch at night. Then I'm in the clouds, nearer you, but farther away. Fly away, Stan, fly away and goodnight."

When the King opened his eyes, he was in a room with two statues on beeping monitors in the beds to either side. His cell phone was on a nightstand. He'd scrubbed it and wiped it and left it in a container of rice but it still barely worked. He'd lost all photos and video and the phone wouldn't ring, but he could make calls. Whenever he did, though, he thought he smelled poo. He called the pay station at the Faire and asked for the Fool and told him to get a bottle of Comfort, some drugs, some money, and the new nickel-plated six shot revolver that he bought with the Fool's money and get over to St. Tillo's, on the pronto. He was busting out.

"And, oh yeah," he added as an afterthought, "I think they cut off my clothes. I'll need some clothes and my sneakers. Just a sec. Forget the sneakers. Roommate with the same shoe size. Bring me a sandwich and a Mountain Dew."

The Fool called Alfred who said he could get his friend Anquan's old K-car. It was a 1986, he said, but Anquan treated it like his baby. Only thing is, Alfred continued, he needs you to put down a twenty-dollar damage deposit. The Fool said he'd pay for the damn car and fill it with gas, but he wasn't gonna pay no damage deposit.

They went back and forth about this and finally the Fool said, "I'll call this Anquan myself and settle this once and for all."

"Go ahead," said Alfred.

"Fine, I will. What's the number?"

"Ah-ha," says Alfred.

So, the Fool had to pony up the damage deposit, half of which he knew was going into Alfred's pocket. He gathered some amphetamines, the Duragesic, a fingernail of blonde hash, a bump or two of coke, a bottle of Comfort and put them in the trunk. He got some clothes, including the King's robe, a box of ammunition and the nickel-plated six gun, which the Queen had been calling Cock Killer, and threw everything in the back seat. The Fool had just enough left to fill the tank, get a sandwich, and a two-liter bottle of Dew.

They headed north in the K car, which was not handicapped accessible. Alfred's stumps were standing on the seat at the wheel. The Fool was sitting on the same piece of seat, behind Alfred with his right foot poised above the pedals. Alfred's high low ass was just under the Fool's chin and the seatbelt held Alfred snugly in place.

"Touch the brakes, now. Now!" Alfred would order, like some double amputee Ahab on the foredeck.

"Watch your fucking stumps, Alfred, you're mashing my nuts."

"Then tuck 'em back to the watering hole and out of my way. Now give her some gas, c'mon now, you weakling, more, more gas... not so much."

"Listen, Alfred, your ass is in my face. Pull over and I'll steer too."

"Anquan said only I can drive. He trusts me."

"I know, but..."

"Anquan said."

"He'll never know."

"I'll know, won't I?"

"Fuck you, Alfred, why can't you put this on cruise control?"

"Oh yeah, how are we going to brake?"

"Use the cruise control control?"

"No wonder you're the Fool. Cruise control don't work that way."

It was a disputatious drive all the way to St. Tillo. As they pulled into the free parking area for food service employees, Alfred said, "I think she's burning oil. Yup, she's running hot. Look at that goddamn temperature gauge. Anquan set a trap for us. He's going blame us for overheating his engine and maybe cracking the block. Sakes alive, this is a 1986 K car. It's gonna run hot. It's gonna burn oil. We walked right into this one."

"We?"

"Yeah, us."

"Let's go get the King and let the car cool down. Come on, help me with the clothes."

"Unless I'm riding on your shoulders, I guess I'll be staying here."

"Oh yeah, be back."

The Fool took the elevator up to the floor with the room number the King gave him. There he found two guys doing a fine job pretending to be corpses but the King wasn't either of them. The Fool wandered the corridors, two nurses telling him that these were not visiting hours. He mumbled some inane reply about delivering a sandwich, finally finding the King in the solarium where he was sneaking a cigarette that he stole from the jacket of one of his living dead roomies. He waved a magazine at the smoke plume to keep the alarm from going off.

"Ready to go, Your Majesty?"

"Ah, Fool, I didn't think you'd make it. Help me pack up and then it's adios to this place. Where's the car? "

"Downstairs in the food service lot."

"Okay, did you bring..."

"I brought your clothes, Your Grace."

"But did you bring..."

"Everything else is in the car with Alfred. We got to get down to the car to get it."

"Alfred?"

"Long story, Majesty. We have to get down to the car."

"Let's go then, Fool, but did you know they have a drug locker on this floor and a pharmacy somewhere else in the hospital?"

"We have to go."

"If you brought the gun up here and forgot to tell me, I'd understand. And if you did, well, on the way out we could stop by the drug locker or the pharmacy and help ourselves."

"That's going to have to wait for another day. I left the gun in the car and you know we've both been on camera since we got here. Not only that, King, you were admitted so they know who you are and where we live. Think about that, Majesty."

"Yeah, it's just a drug locker, though."

"Maybe, but I think it's still a felony."

"Okey-dokey, let's go, ...still."

"Hey King, what's that tube coming out of your chest?"

"Oh, it was there when I woke up. I dreamed or maybe I saw them put it in. Can't be sure."

"What's it for?"

"I don't know but I heard I had a seizure and a collapsed lung."

"What was the tube attached to?"

"Air tank. I cut it so I could escape."

"I don't know about this, Majesty. Should we be leaving here with you in this condition? Seizures are serious things, so are collapsed lungs."

"Lung, Fool, lung. I have another."

"I don't think that's like having a spare. This sounds serious."

"I can't stay here, Fool. I'm in peril. We're at war with the United States. They're everywhere and they're after my kingdom. I'm a dead duck if I stay here. I've got to get mobile. Do you have a dollar fifty in quarters?"

"Yeah, but only just. It's for meters."

"Great, if I stop breathing or start to feel bad or pass out, just find a gas station with tire air and give me a blast through this tube at like, I don't know, say, twenty PSI. That sounds safe."

"Why don't we just get a can of Fix A Flat?" asked the Fool. "That way we won't lose time stopping at a station. We can jump start you on the fly."

The King, a literalist to whom sarcasm was a foreign language, nodded, "Even better, off to my castle, posthaste."

XVIII

Nix and Steiger sank into the long pleather couch in Leo's dingy office. What light there was fought its way through dirty grey windows before being cut to ribbons by heavy, yellowed curtains. The glass on the door read, Leo Ianetti, Private Investigator. Leo sat behind a big broad desk. He must have been sitting on a box on his chair because his slippered feet dangled high above the floor. Nix reminded herself that appearances can be deceiving. Then she reminded herself that they generally aren't, not unless one has a good lawyer.

Nix wanted to sound casual and friendly, "So, Leo, how do you know Steiger?"

"We run into each other at the clubs," Steiger answered for him.

"Well, yes and no," equivocated Leo, "I do run into him at the clubs, but I'm there in my professional capacity."

"I see," nodded Nix.

"No, really," insisted Leo, "eighty percent of my business is domestic. You know, cheating spouses. I got a little pen camera and catch the douche bags getting lap dances and, once in a while, a hand job in the sketchier clubs. My clients say it's for a divorce or whatever, but really, the principal reason is revenge, revenge by embarrassment. It's a holiday tradition with some of my clients, especially around Christmas, which is prime time for the kids, mothers-in-law, and my client's friends to see my videos. I've had forty-five of them posted to Facebook and I'm an Instagram sensation. By the time they get taken down the damage is done."

"Interesting job you have, Leo," Nix was still sizing him up.

"Yeah, the domestic stuff is my bread and butter."

"Tell her about the lap dance that got you in trouble," offered Steiger.

"Ahh, that's nobody's business and I'm still fighting it on appeal."

"It's a good story, Leo. Tell her," Steiger rolled his eyes.

"Well, okay, but I was framed, you know, and that girl lied."

"Yeah, yeah, Leo, just tell Nix what happened."

"So, I go to this club. It's called the Purple Pussy and it's kinda raunchy. It's in a strip mall and has a terrible reputation."

"It's gotten better, Leo. After their license got yanked they drywalled the glory holes, painted the whole inside, and added some lights. If anything, the girls look too old now."

"Anyway, I get hired to go in there and find this guy who's been fucking around on his wife and girlfriend. They told me that they found out about one another, got together, compared notes, and decided to fuck this guy over good. So, I'm there, discreetly, and in comes the guy and I got my pen camera going but for some reason he seems to be on to me. I look away and go to the bar and get a drink but he's still eyeballing me so to break the tension and change the narrative in this guy's head, I ask a girl to go to the Champagne Room for a lap dance. She could have been anyone. She could have been any age. It was just part of doing my job, trying to blend. I had no way of knowing she was sixteen. She didn't look sixteen. She was an easy eighteen, I figured.

Nix raised her head, "What are you, Leo, forty-five?"

"I'm forty-two. Why did you guess forty-five? Is it my receding hairline? Everyone else says I look young for my age. I have a lineless face. Geez, forty-five? Back to what I was telling you, I'm in the Champagne Room suffering that lap dance when in marches the asshole I've been surveilling and he pulls out a badge and tells me I'm under arrest. Then a squad of blues crashes the joint and there are more arrests and the club gets shut down for a month by the License Board and the ABCC. It's a total set up."

"A set up?"

"Total, entrapment, but I still had to register as a sex offender even though my conviction is on appeal. Can you believe that? I mean, where's due process, huh? I had to tell the neighbors and all the people in this building that I am a Registered Sex Offender. There's no good way to spin that."

Nix pursed her lips and nodded sagely, "You could say that you want to thank your Lord and Savior that you're no longer an unregistered sex offender. No?"

"Really, Nix, is that being helpful?" Leo scowled and Steiger smiled.

"I guess it's just an unjust world, Leo. Anyway, what about King Henry's Faire?"

At this Steiger got up from the sofa and wandered over to the window.

"Oh, that," Leo got down and walked over to Nix, "I got something for you. I did some research online and talked to some cops I know in Chelmsford. It seems this King has another name. He's Ronald Overbee, originally from Chelmsford. Let's see, thirty-eight, twice divorced, four kids, two of whom he denies. Real prince. Arrears on child and spousal support for, hmmm, let's see, wow, every Order issued. There's a capias out of probate. He has outstanding warrants from district courts for failure to appear, probation violations, blah, blah, blah. New Hampshire wants him too. He's got two felonies, washed out of the Navy, and has a record going back to juvie. Besides being a genuine piece of shit, there's this."

Leo tossed a handful of photocopied newspaper articles, an 8 x 10 color glossy of a younger, fleshier, less booze ravaged incarnation of the King, an autopsy report, the Medical Examiner's notes, and photocopied police reports concerning the death of a Stanley Zimochowski.

"Holy shit," Nix sat up in her chair, "this is the guy, Zimochowski, the last known taxpayer at King Henry's Faire. Take a look at this, Steiger."

"In a minute, Nix."

"It says here this guy Zimochowski...let's see, who died, whoa, the fuck you say. This poor bastard died in a cotton candy machine."

"World's largest cotton candy machine," Leo added.

"Dah-da, da-dah, da-dah, let's see," Nix's eyes sped down the page, "foul play suspected. Poor mother fucker, the cotton candy machine was latched from the outside. Good heavens, he couldn't get out. And Steiger, it says here our King was the prime suspect but....let's see, money missing too but, aaah, it says there wasn't enough evidence to prosecute. Didn't even present it to a grand Jury. Wow! You listening, Steiger?"

"Yeah, Nix, all ears."

"It says here another person, Charlie Aspirance, a/k/a Charlie Crow, a ten-year old who worked at the Faire and had for most of his life, learned that day that Zimochowski was his father. That's awful. It goes on to say that Aspirance was the only witness to an argument about money and a contract dispute that was said to have taken place between Zimochowski and Overbee an hour before Zimochowski's death. This says Aspirance ended up in a mental hospital two days after Zimochowski's death. He stopped speaking and, let's see the Supplemental Report, he didn't speak for a year. There's a picture. Hey, Steiger, we saw this guy. He's working at the Faire now. He dresses like a fool and has big hands. Remember him? He was at the parking lot when the King locked himself in the Port-A-Potty and tipped it over. Hey, Steiger, are you listening?"

"Hold on a minute, Nix. Hey Leo, who's that woman in the little tube top and short skirt hanging on the corner?"

"You like her, Steiger?"

"You eat the fish in the sea, Leo."

"Ahh, Steiger, you have a way with words. Poetic, really. Too bad I hate fish and I hate poetry even more. So, ah, what do you think of her?"

"Is she expensive?" Steiger hadn't turned around.

"She's not a blowfish, dummy. So, that must mean she's a ....come on, work this out. She must be a...?"

"I don't know, Leo. What is she?"

"A bluefish, of course. She's vice and been holding up that signpost for the past three weeks, Tuesday through Saturday, four to eleven."

"No shit. You're certain?"

"Look at her shoes," Leo continued. "Are those hooker shoes? Not smoking, is she? Look at her hair. It's her hair. This woman is in shape. No burn marks, no track marks, no black eyes. This ain't a corner scruff. You can't just look, Steiger, you have to see, like a private eye, like me."

Nix rocked herself up and out of the deep pleather sofa and headed for the door, "You guys are fucked up. You know that, doncha? You don't belong around normal people. You ought to be disappeared and the stains of your existence obliterated from the world. I'm taking this stuff with me, Leo. You got anything else?"

"Yeah, but you've got to have dinner with me to get it."

"No offense, Leo, but I'd rather choke on Steiger's vomit."

"None taken. All that stuff is yours. You want me to do anything else? I can interview the King and this other guy, Charlie."

"Hey Steiger, what's the budget you got approved for Leo?"

"Ten grand, another five if he gets demonstrable results."

"I think this shit is demonstrable. Where you at, Leo?"

"I'd be tripping over my lies if I put in for four grand."

"I think we can use you. We'll let you know when. And you can ride with us and make up meetings and phone calls we haven't had, and still bill for travel and phone consultations and all that. We don't care."

"Thanks, Nix. You're okay."

"Promise me you'll leave no money on the table. It's the only thanks I ask."

"Not even a nickel on the floor, Nix."

Nix stopped at the door, "I don't know if Steiger told you but you're going to have to hound Buffum to get paid. He's always holding cards he's not showing. The man is sly, but indecisive and a scaredy cat, so a threat to go over his head will generally work. We'll be in touch. Steiger is driving me back to work in his cum mobile We were going to go to the casino, but I don't think so now. I've gotten lucky enough today, even though Steiger is still my partner."

XIX

The K-car trailed a pall of noxious smoke down the highway. Alfred said, "Tap the brakes and slow down, Fool, I'm pulling over. This motherfucker's overheating again. Fuck you, Anquan, fuck you."

We couldn't hear the radio, let alone the directional tick as the car steamed, moaned, and sighed over the rumble strip before shuttering to a stop in the rest area.

Alfred asked if there was any water left for the radiator?

I wasn't feeling conversational, "Take the fucking seatbelt off, Alfred. My Adam's apple is buried in your ass crack. Come on now, this has to stop. I don't care what Anquan thinks. You ain't using me as brakes no more. I'm done."

"Yeah, we'll see, but is there any water left?"

"There was just over a pint and I used it to water down the Comfort 'cause otherwise the King wanted to stop and get more."

"Once the car cools down we're going to have to take the next exit and get more water and maybe another container."

"Well, you ain't using me as brakes and gas no more and that's that. I've had it."

"Who's going to do it?"

"I will, but I'll be steering too. I'm not letting you rest your ass in my face again."

"Anquan says only I drive."

"Then go ahead and drive but leave me out of it. Why don't you use the King as brakes? He's not doing anything."

The King had been passed out against a back window, mouth open. When the car stumbled to a stop he pitched forward and hit his nose on the back of a headrest. Suddenly awake and with tears in his eyes, his Majesty opened the door and fell out, blood streaming through his fingers, He staggered over to a tree against which he passed out, cradling the Comfort.

"The goddamn King is passed out under a tree," Alfred responded.

"Then hit the horn and wake him up. This is your problem now."

"It's your problem too."

"Not the way it's yours," I rubbed it in, "I can walk from here. It might take me all night or more, but I'll make it home. You, on the other hand, well, you've got a little bigger problem."

"You sonofabitch," Alfred started, but he didn't get any further because blue lights and a yelp siren were getting closer and louder in the rear view.

The State Police cruiser slowed to a stop about seventy-five feet behind the K-car and idled. This frozen moment is always tense and full of apprehension. It's at times like this that people get ideas. And these ideas cascade into worse ideas. Regrettable plans are hatched while a state cop waits in his cruiser. And these plans ferment into more dangerous and destructive plans. It's nothing the trooper is doing or done. It's the work of the wait on the person pulled over.

There are tens of reasons why a person gets stopped. It could be anything. Maybe a taillight or a low tire. But these possibilities don't come to mind because the take down lights are blinding, the epilepsy lights are winking wildly, and the person pulled over is going through her catalogue of wrongs and wondering what lies the dispatcher is whispering in the trooper's ear. But every once in a while, maybe only as often as a blue moon, the tables get turned and it's the trooper who ends up worried and scared.

After what seemed like half an hour the trooper got out of his cruiser and walked over to the driver's side of our car where Alfred was standing on the seat, belted against me with his ass in my nose.

The trooper's right hand rested on his hip above his gun as he said, "License and registration. Whoa, what have we here?"

Alfred tried first, "So, ah, officer, aaaah..."

"We overheated, trooper," I finished for him.

"I can smell that," said the trooper, "but who's driving? I've never seen such a thing. Let's see a license and registration."

"You see, officer," Alfred started again, "our friend Anquan, really my friend, let us use his car and it started running hot. It's a 1986 K-car. I told these guys it was sure to run hot. We were finishing up an errand of mercy and as you can see..."

"Who's driving?" the trooper interrupted.

"That's a funny story, sir," Alfred began tying his story in tighter knots.

I broke in, "The guy sleeping under the tree is driving. He's taking a snooze so we're playing around with the car trying to see if we can figure out what's wrong."

"Yeah," the trooper asked, "and what's wrong with him?"

"Who?"

"The guy under the tree."

"He's a sick man, trooper," I shook my head, "and we don't know what's wrong with him. They sent us out from the science lab to pick him up at the hospital. No one else would go. They were all afraid and we don't have those suits, you know, like space suits."

"Haz-Mat suits?"

"Something like that. They're on back order."

"Well, what's wrong with him?" the trooper pointed at the King.

"We don't know but at the hospital they told us not to bring him back. They said this was beyond them and they cried and pushed food and money on us to take him away, which we were going to do anyway. They were grateful and said, 'God bless', over and over, so much so that Alfred thought it was a church, not a hospital."

Alfred nodded solemnly.

"What hospital?"

"St. Tillo. Nice people, but they still slammed the door in our faces."

"What do you work on back at the lab?"

"I'm a custodian and 'Stumpy', here, works security. He runs the video surveillance of the cages. The scientists work on infectious diseases."

"Infectious diseases!"

"Yeah, for national security."

"I thought there was some treaty about that stuff."

"I don't know about that, Mister Trooper. I mostly use a broom at work. The floors under them cages is unholy."

"You're sure that skinny guy over there ain't drunk?"

"I don't know what he is, trooper, sir. I just know he's a sick man. Do you think we're going to get sick too? I think Alfred might be running a fever."

"What?" said the trooper backing up, backing up a bit further and even a little further, until he was shooting, not speaking distance. He shouted back, "How long are you going to be?"

"We'd like to leave now but we need water to fill the radiator."

The trooper looked relieved, "I have a four-gallon container of water in the trunk. I'm going to leave it over here on the pavement. It's heavy plastic. Fill your radiator and keep the container in your trunk for when you need more. Now get going. I mean get going on the car. Keep the container. It's yours. I'll be back in twenty minutes to make sure you're gone. You're done, I mean. Twenty minutes."

As the trooper sped away I said to Alfred, "Go get the water and pour it in the radiator."

Alfred said, "I can't do that. You know I can't."

"Who's driving, Alfred, or are you and the King staying the night?"

XX

Nix was reading a back issue of Soldier of Fortune when her phone buzzed.

"Yeah?"

"Agent Nix?"

"No, it's her secretary. Who do you think answers her phone?"

"This is Mr. Buffum, Nix."

"Oh, Mr. B, I didn't recognize your voice. Do you have a cold?"

"Can you come down to my office and bring Agent Steiger?"

"Righto," she punched the phone dead.

It rang again and Nix picked up, "Yell-ow?"

"Nix, it's me, Buffum. Don't hang up. Not for fifteen minutes, Nix, you and Steiger. In my office in fifteen, not before."

Nix walked the long way over to Steiger's squaricle, past the kitchen, having decided to startle him, "STEIGER!"

"Oh, fuck me, Nix, you're awful, you suck. My doctor thinks that maybe we need a safe word. She says I've developed a heart murmur and you're going to turn it into a full-blown cardiac event doing just what you did right now; her words, not mine."

"The good news is there's proof you got a heart, so I'm happy for you. Many of us don't bother with one. Truthfully, they aren't for everyone."

"Fuck off, Nix. You must think I'm here for your amusement. But the thing is, I really did see my doctor this morning and she heard a murmur loud and clear. With that and my colon behaving the way it has, she asked if there was anything out of the ordinary going on in my life. Granted, I could have answered the question five ways, but what I told her is what it's like having you as a partner. Can you imagine that? I'm seeing my doctor about things like blood in my stool, chronically loose bowels and sexual hysteria and I end up talking about you. And

I want you to know she was impressed with my self-diagnosis of proximal experiential colorectal anxiety particular to you. She thinks I'm spot on and suggests you're toxic."

"Does something I do rub you the wrong way?"

"Lots of things, but for one, you like to see me worried and uncomfortable."

Nix nodded thoughtfully, conceding, "That's true. Sometimes it's the highlight of my day."

"Tell me, Nix, what kind of person finds my discomfort to be the highlight of her day?"

"The kind of person, Steiger, whose days are so flat out shitty and her future so grim that your exaggerated discomfort is a welcome and harmless distraction from everything else. But speaking of your discomfort, am I to understand that you think you got the shits because of me? If so, I'm flattered. Something's working."

"It's not the shits, Nix. The shits are a symptom."

"Oh, the shits are nothing but a symptom now? I see. Is this some new age bullshit? Someone ought to tell dysentery about this, cholera too. Spread the word that the real villain is colorectal anxiety. Sounds more like an excuse for scuffing your undies. "

"Can't you leave me alone, Nix, just for today? Can't you go haunt someone else for a while? Give me the day off."

"Not today, that skid mark Buffum wants to see us, stat."

"He said stat? Like in TV hospital shows? Stat?"

"Stat."

"What's up?"

"I don't know. It's probably about King Henry's fucking Faire."

"Oh fuck, Nix, I started to tell you I went to the doctor this morning."

"Yeah."

"She gave me a pill to take. It's huge and it has a little camera inside and it activates, let's see, ahh, right about now. It's going to take pictures of my digestive tract and neighboring countryside, poke around here and there. I have to wear a shiny vest with blinking lights on it for the rest of the day. You know that yellow color you see on the vests of shopping cart wrestlers, construction workers and bicyclists?"

"Baby shit neon?

"That's it, there's some of that, plus reflective silver, black, and orange tape. For some fucking reason there's a rape whistle."

"That's nice. That outfit says outdoors the way a wet bus stop says shelter."

"Well, it's attention grabbing, I can tell you that. I'm not supposed to get excited while wearing it."

"Excited while wearing it? Excited how?"

"I'm not supposed to run and no jerky motions."

"Got it, keep the jerky motions down. Okay, put on your vest, Steiger, and light it up. We're going to see Buffum. Stat, remember?"

"Yeah, okay, we're late then. Hurry up. Why do you antagonize him like this, Nix? We could have been there on time."

"You do it too, Steiger."

"Yeah, but you take it to another level. You enjoy antagonizing him too much."

"It only seems that way. Honestly, Steiger, I daydream about bending Buffum over a thick plank table and slapping ham until he squeals like a taxpayer. I'd teach that boy to moan, maybe cry. Go ahead, knock on the door, Steiger, I'm right behind you."

"Who is it?" from behind the door.

"It's Steiger, Mr. Buffum."

"I said not for fifteen minutes. Don't you people talk? Don't you listen? Go see Nix. She'll tell you what's going on, when to come back."

"Okay Mr. Buffum, sorry," and under his breath, "You suck even worse than I told my doctor."

"He's right. He did say fifteen minutes. I guess I got that wrong. Sorry, Steiger."

On the way back to his squaricle, Steiger stopped in the hallway and asked Nix, "Does my vest go with these shoes?"

"Do you want the truth?"

"Not especially."

"No one is checking out your shoes, okay? You look too stupid from the ankles up to focus on the shoes. Now I understand why you go to strip clubs. You're as washed out as old wallpaper and common as concrete. But in a strip club the bar is lower, the teeth are fewer, and the lights are dimmer. No one sees you for the rusty nail you are. You're a solid tip and considered to have personality, or something. Do they call you Shakespeare or Professor?"

"No, Nix, I don't have a nom de club. And you know what else? Shit happens and good people go to strip clubs. I've met lots of nice people in strip clubs, even a couple of guys. You think all the nice people go to country clubs?"

"It's probably the same with church," Nix continued, "though I'm sure you don't tip as well. Strip clubs and church allow you to be someone, to stand out against the even greyer greyness of life and they both give you an identity. It's a pathetic and creepy identity, for sure. Kind of a Jekyll and Hyde identity, maybe even a Mr. Hyde and Mr. Hyde identity."

"What's that?"

"Bad to worse, but you know what?"

"No, Nix, what else?"

"You're not as grey as every shmuck. You've got that, Steiger. Sometimes I don't see any grey on you at all. Most people can't claim that. Most people are the walking dead. At least you've got something, Steiger. You've got something that separates you from the crowd."

"Thanks for seeing me as not grey, Nix."

"Sometimes you're not grey."

A few minutes later Nix knocked on Buffum's door, "It's Nix, Mr. Buffum. I'm sorry about Steiger. He don't ever listen. Can we come in?"

"Come on in."

"Thanks, Mr. Buffum. Hey, Doyle. Excuse Steiger's, errr, vest, I guess that's what he's calling it, a medical vest. He swallowed a camera pill before we came in here. He was supposed to swallow it. The vest somehow tracks and stores data as it makes its way through the twists and turns of Steiger's reproductive system. Did I get that right?"

"You are so clever, Nix. It's my digestive and excretory system that's under review, Mr. Buffum."

Nix looked over each shoulder and then back to Buffum, "It's a surveillance camera. Be careful what you say, Mr. Buffum, in case he's got the mic on."

"Funny Nix, very amusing, but Mr. Buff......" Steiger began but Buffum cut him off.

"Very well, very well." Buffum cleared his throat, "You and Steiger have a seat. I read your application for a search warrant, approved it and it's been issued by a Federal Magistrate. I had it sent to the Horseshoe Falls Police Department with instructions. You'll be coordinating with them about executing the warrant. I want that warrant returned by five today."

"But Mr. Buffum...," Steiger squirmed in his seat.

"Wait a minute, Steiger, I'm not finished. Legal said that what we want are books and ledgers, deposit slips, bank accounts, investment account statements, payroll services, third party vendors, anything they have from accountants' offices, lawyers' correspondence, stuff like that. Here's the Complaint that legal filed for us today. Remember, our cases are paper cases and computers are the new paper, so scoop up all the computers you can find. That means, folks, that we want the King's computer and if there's a Queen, her computer too. I don't care as much about the parking attendant's computer. Understand? Is everything copacetic?"

"Ah, Mr. Buffum," asked Nix, "what exactly does that word mean, 'copacetic'? I've heard it over the years, you know, and have a general idea. I always thought it was a security guard word."

"A security guard word?" Buffum was curious, "What does that mean?"

"You know, the way a security guard will find a word that sounds impressive and he'll use the shit out of it. Like the guys who string together words like 'surveilling the situation' and 'observing nightfall'. 'Copacetic' is one of the words they use. It's funny until you find yourself dating one of these brain surgeons, in which case it's not copacetic."

"You've got the gist, Nix. Doyle, fix."

"I know the gist, Mr. Buffum, but I'm looking for a more precise definition because I'm not sure you were using the word correctly."

"The gist is enough for present purposes, Nix. Back to cases. I don't want you getting in any fights, not even disagreements. That's what Horseshoe Falls PD is for. Let them be your buffer. You are there to supervise and gather evidence. You too, Steiger. And make sure you always have a witness. If things get out of hand, call and we'll send you some state police back up."

"Mr. Buffum," Steiger raised his hand, "I'm not supposed to be moving around very much while I wear this vest. I was wondering if I could sit this one out?"

"No, you're going, Steiger, and not another word about it."

"Okay, but..."

Not disguising his impatience, Buffum cut him off, "Say no more, Steiger, unless you want me to write you up. We've moved on. What do you want, Nix?"

"We're a federal agency, Mr. Buffum," Nix whined, "why are you sending state cops? We deserve federal marshals."

"I'm not sending anyone. This is a contingency plan. Mother goddamn, you two. Doyle!"

"That's a union violation, Mr. Buffum," Nix tsked, "swearing at us that way and on the record. Don't strike that, Doyle. That's spoliation of evidence, which is a crime. You're both on notice. I read about that in the manual, Mr. Buffum. Spoliation is not one of the IRS's favorite things. It says that somewhere, I'm sure. We fine the shit out of people for spoliation of evidence."

"Would you two please pay attention," Buffum wiped his face and neck, sweat spots darkening the sides and back of his shirt.

"I didn't say anything, Mr. Buffum," Steiger sulked, "even though you've been pointedly rude, I haven't said a word. Don't damn me because of her."

"Please," Buffum looked around hopelessly, perhaps for an object to throw.

"Something's wrong with Steiger today, Mr. B." Nix inserted, "He's crankier than usual. I don't know what it is, but as soon as there's work to do I'm certain I'll find out."

"You suck, Nix," Steiger mumbled.

"Ovulating much, Steiger? Nix smiled.

"Please, stop it you two," Buffum wiped down his face again and then held his temples, "For heaven's sake, please listen and don't speak. Go to the Faire. Execute the warrant. It's your job, okay, but if you do it and you do it well, and do it without any problems, without any complaints, without any newscasts, I'll give you both next Friday off."

"And the Friday after?" suggested Steiger.

"What?" asked Buffum, dumbstruck.

"Yeah, the Friday after that, too," Nix urged.

"I don't believe you two. No one else gets days off for doing her job. But okay, and the Friday after, but you have to produce and you have to be good while you do so."

"Deal," said Steiger.

"Going to do my best," agreed Nix.

XXI

It's eleven AM and the sun is reflecting off the broken glass strewn throughout the parking lot. It hurts my eyes. I squint into the distant purple clouds, rolling our way. A soft breeze ripples through the Faire, rustling the high dry grass and cooling off nothing. They call this murder weather, thick and heavy, hard to breathe.

I have a bad feeling and ain't sure if it's my hands or my head. Today's a big day. I have a ring of keys to all the different buildings and trailers at the Faire. You're probably wondering why anyone would give a ring of keys to the Fool. If I wasn't me I'd wonder too. I have these keys because the King kept losing them. Since I'm with him most of the time, I hold the keys.

I'm heading to the Dispensary, which is where the nurse worked when we had one. I have to take off my bandages and clean my wounds. Even though we haven't had a nurse in years, the King still orders drugs under her name and prescription number. If I don't get a Z-pak I could lose either of my hands or both, maybe even die. That's what an article I read said, same as that pharmacist in Horseshit told me. I find the Nurse's Office in the Dispensary but I don't have a key for that so I break in and take three Z-paks. I grab some cough syrup and some pain pills the King must have overlooked. I reach for the jar of valium but it's been cleaned out. Got to let the King know that someone is stealing drugs. It is at least a hundred and ten degrees in the shack and hard to breathe. If I stay here any longer I'm going to pass out so I sneak out the backdoor, which is across from the moat, which is nasty to the max.

Over a stretch of hot days, the still moat became a nursery for hundreds of billions of mosquitos and, therefore, mosquito borne diseases. Oxygen depleting algae blooms cover the bottom of the moat, where it is wet. Where dry, the algae crawls up the sides, seeming to have an eye on the Port-A-Pottys. Row after row of portable toilets baked in the sun. They were mostly full and a gaseous bacterial plume rose from the crap and chemical pools in the bottom of each toilet to press against the poured hard plastic walls and hard plastic joints, probing for weaknesses, trying to escape.

A huge campaign tent rose from the midway, royal pennants limp in the slender breeze. The Faire hadn't opened, but the King and Queen were in full regalia, as was most everyone else. With all the spectacle and finery, what may have passed unnoticed is that everyone was armed. Whether it was a sling shot, an apron of rocks, a wooden hammer, a pistol, or a crossbow, everyone carried something.

Those with outstanding warrants or otherwise preferring anonymity wore camouflage clothing and headscarves with thick black sunglasses and anti-glare sun block under their eyes and across their cheeks. Regardless of how they looked, these Carnies were not warriors. They wore nervous looks and were jumpy and not one of them could remember the signals or code words.

There were no firm plans and the King was loaded. He forgot to call the media so the Queen was busy doing that, mentioning to all the outlets that the invasion was expected any minute now and if they hurried they might be able to get the best parts. She closed every call by advising whoever was on the other end that the whole Faire prayed God for low casualties on both sides.

While she was taking care of business the booze addled King staggered into the campaign tent, which was hiding the trebuchet, an impressive siege engine made of steel, timber, and hemp. It was designed and built by four engineering students from the college down the road. It doubled as a semester project so they provided all the parts and equipment to build it. The Blacksmith, the Mason and a welder named Nikki from Horseshoe Falls helped too. And next to the trebuchet was a roughly ten by ten by two-foot-deep pit of sand, hot ash, and cinders nestling a harvest of glowing red tree stumps. This was the ammunition dump for the trebuchet. Two of these red-hot tree stumps were sitting in the bucket of the trebuchet at the moment.

The Fire Crew for the trebuchet was having lunch. Steady Eddie was named Chief. He's also the Armorer for the Faire, and a volunteer fireman with the Horseshoe Falls Auxiliary Fire Department. Eddie thinks he knows everything there is to know about fire. He knows a lot, for sure, but not everything.

Steady Eddie also suffers from an obsessive- compulsive disorder on the high side of moderate, so he's great with rules and routine and would have been an asset at the Alamo or in the Seventh Cavalry, but color outside the lines and he can get mulish.

Always safety conscious, Eddie stopped the Fire Crew from digging a hole in the ground to serve as a barbeque pit. Treating this as a teachable moment, Eddie asked if anyone on the Fire Crew had checked to see if there was a fire anywhere else they might utilize before starting this one? Eddie was staring at the trebuchet bucket as he said this. Then he asked whether anyone had considered the weather conditions before deciding to burn charcoal on the ground? He wanted to know who had inspected the grassy fields to determine whether they were too dry. Without waiting for any answers, Eddie began lecturing them on the characteristics of fire and how insidious it is. That's the word he used, insidious. He used the word just about every time he spoke of fire.

He had them gather up their pile of charcoal briquets and throw them in the bucket of the trebuchet, next to the tree stumps, telling them that no wind was going to whip in and spread fire from the deep steel bucket of the trebuchet and, as if trying to illustrate how safe it was, Steady Eddie doused the little pile of briquets and two giant tree stumps with a gallon of gasoline which skied flames to the tent roof and singed a few members of the Fire Crew, but the flames didn't set the tent roof on fire. It looked like a happy accident, but as things played out, maybe it wasn't.

Eddie got an old portable TV with a VHS slot out of his truck, plugged a two-hundred-foot extension cord into what I still call the cigarette lighter and dragged the TV and some lawn chairs back to the campaign tent. Eddie had every episode of Matlock on VHS. Slipping in a good one, he and the crew sat back and waited for the fire to die down and the tree stumps to go grey before dropping a cross-hatched storm drain as a grate over the mouth of the bucket for grilling their burgers and dogs.

Standing there and watching this, the King gave a drunken nod that looked like a benediction because he lost his balance and held out his hands to break his fall. Farmer 7, having just run in from the field, dropped the thick tree branch he'd been carrying so he was able to steady the King.

The King was about to say something not unkind when some wasps from the tree branch Farmer 7 had been carrying got a little too pissy, circling the King like harriers and stinging him on the back of his neck and on his right wrist.

"Damn you, doltish serf," the King brushed at himself and backed away from the tree branch, "right on the back of my royal neck. Did you bring these pests with you? Ouch, We hurt so."

Still smiling ear to ear, Farmer 7 said that indeed he'd brought a branch from the woods with a large grey nest of wasps on it. He said he wondered if it could be used as ammunition for the trebuchet?

Dampening Farmer 7's enthusiasm, the King replied, "You bumpkin, do you think me some kind of auxiliary Gunner's mate? Do you think that simply because We're standing near this infernal contraption I somehow know its requirements or how to load and fuel the thing?"

"Majesty, I found this angry wasp's nest and..."

"We're beyond that now, aren't we? I've been stung and I hold you responsible. Whatever you have to say is for lesser minds than mine. Ask those people over there, the Fire Team, We think they're called."

Farmer 7 was back within a minute, "The Armorer, Your Majesty, told me that the crew was on lunch break and I should fuck off before he cuts off my nuts with a farrow tool and feeds them to his chickens."

The King barked a high laugh, "Haha, what a cut up that Armorer is. Always with a wry comment. Eddie doesn't keep chickens."

"What I mean to say, Your Highness, is there's something wrong with the Armorer."

"Of course, there's something wrong with him. He's working here, ain't he? Don't bother him. He's got what doctors call 'Oh Sadie' which makes him some kind of an asshole about certain things and stubborn as fuck about others. Figure this out for yourself, groundling. Pretend you're not a farmer with a head full of dirt."

"Okay, Majesty, let's see, well, wasps have a terrible temper and they sting..."

"I don't mean for you to wrestle with this now. Do it later. Do it when I'm not around."

"But it's fresh in my head, Majesty, please?"

"What I do for you people, very well. Go ahead and tell me but don't make an ass of yourself. I warn you."

"As far as I can tell the only thing wasps do is sting and make these grey papery nests. Never seen them do anything else. And they're aggressive and always in a bad mood. So, what I'm thinking, Majesty, is why not put them to good use stinging our enemies? Make the wasps finally do something worthwhile."

"Now that is using your squash, Farmer 7. You're more than just a soil rat. Drop the nest in the trebuchet bucket, on the side, away from the fire, and we can forget about it until later. You are a loathsome and illiterate fool, it's true, but we all have our uses, don't we, from the mightiest to the smallest, most insignificant bit of dirt. I'm sure you appreciate it when I say it's a comfort knowing one's place. Now make thyself useful and bring me a libation. Something from the vodka family, or any clear spirits would be acceptable. Make it at least a double. Bring it in a mug. I'm famished."

"You mean parched, Your Majesty?"

"I mean stop being uppity and get me a fucking drink, okay, some spirits in a vessel. Now! And tell my subjects to gather 'round. Bang the angle iron and raise a hoot and holler. I have good reason to address them."

Farmer 7 wandered off and the King took a moment for himself, worrying a nail and mumbling, 'Almost half the day gone and not a cop in sight. Three-legged dog shitting on a hillside, I hope those stooges at the Horseshit Falls Po-Po got it right. I've got this one chance. I can't fuck it up without losing these fucking Carnies. They'll desert me. Well, today's supposed to be the day. Why don't I hear sirens? They should be here.' The King paced and grumbled, 'I could use a drink. Where's that villein? Oh dammit, here comes everyone.'

The King's subjects didn't look pleased. The King, all smiles, began, "Friends, loyal subjects, citizens of the realm, on this beautiful day...."

"Shut the fuck up," barked half of the crowd. "Yeah," barked the other half, "tell us what's going on. No more of your lies and bullshit. None of us want to go to jail for this place."

"Friends and subjects, we have spies in the Horseshit Falls Police Department," the King began, only lightly slurring his words, "Thanks to our lovely Wenches we know that sometime today the IRS goons and I don't know what federal law enforcement agencies and the Horseshit Falls Po-Po are going to try to search our premises, take our guns, and search our tents and trailers too. This is the chance we've been waiting for."

"What!" from everyone.

"Opportunity knocks," the King smiled and held out welcoming arms, "we simply have to see it for what it is."

The Blacksmith stepped forward, clad like a camo ninja, "Listen here, I don't see no opportunity for nothing but trouble. I gotta think it's time to make peace with the law. We gotta try peace. That or maybe just drift away. I'm too old for prison. I don't even know if I could do jail no more. Too many punks inside. We can't fight the government, no siree. They just keep coming."

"Listen everyone," the King tried calming his subjects down, "don't leave now! Everything is working as planned. The psychic, don't forget the psychic. She saw this coming. She knows what's going to happen. She told us what to do. Stand firm. The feds will be here today with the Horseshoe Falls Police, but we're ready for them. The bridge is up. They can't get in. The Queen called the media, which is the asshole radio station and the drunks over at the Horseshoe Falls Gazette and they'll be here sometime soon. What else? Ah, Diane, I mean Your Highness."

The Queen took out her gum and palmed it, "So, Boston Channel 5 asked us to delay any confrontation until later this afternoon. The 'Eye Spy Cam' is on its way from the Berkshires. How about that? The producer said we might be the lead story. We are going to be on TV! Whooo-hoo! I told 'em we'd do our best but we couldn't make no promises."

Now that he had his composure back, the King continued, "We got some college kids who want to help too. They have a radio station of their own and talked about an 'Occupy', whatever the fuck that is. And they're bringing that cannon. Ahhh, and two guys with a truck from the laundromat want to help. They'll be here so, you know, we won't be alone."

"Two guys with a truck from the laundromat," mocked the Blacksmith, shaking his head, "what are they gonna do, make sure we go to jail with clean undies? Listen, we don't mind dressing up, making a few threats, and rattling our sabers for the cameras, but that's about it. We ain't fighters. We're pretenders, like you. We're Carny rats and we know we're rats. We don't pretend to be anything better, so rat rules apply. And rat rules are that if something don't smell right we scatter. Those are rat rules. Why don't rat rules apply?"

The King jumped in, "Because the government won't do anything to us that the people can see on TV. That's a rule too. That rule trumps the rat rule, don't you see? We're safe."

"That didn't stop the IRS po-po from locking you in the shithouse until you almost went cuckoo. It didn't stop her from tipping the potty over either," said the Mason.

"And covering you in blue," added the Potter, supporting his friend.

"The TV crews weren't here that day, were they?" reasoned the King, swallowing his pride, "That's my point. And I'm not done with that IRS bitch, not even close to done."

"Let's just hope she's done with you," someone yelled.

"Listen to me, folks. The psychic laid out this plan. It's a certainty, it's in the bag, it's going to happen. What else do I have to say to convince you?"

"Do you swear that you had nothing to do with this plan," asked the Potter's assistant?

"I had nothing to do with any of it," said the King, raising his right hand with his left hand over his heart, "I swear and I promise. Ask the Queen."

"It's true," verified the Queen.

"What's this psychic's batting average," someone asked from the back?

"What the fuck? Batting average?" asked the King. "This ain't baseball, it's a different kind of game called war. Listen, who here hasn't called the Psychic Hotline at least once? C'mon, who? Not one of you, that's who. I've called the Hotline, all right, more than once and the Queen is always on the phone with them. She spends a fortune. Do you think the Psychic Hotline is going to screw us over? The Psychic Hotline is an organization of professionals who see the future and make decisions for people like us. You can trust them. They're dependable and they know what's going to...hey, shhhhh, listen. Quiet. Everybody listen. Do any of you all hear a siren?"

"Sirens," someone said.

XXII

The Horseshoe Falls Police cruisers, wagons, and SWAT Team could be heard turning into the park and accelerating across the rock and pebble parking lots. They screeched to a halt at the edge of the moat where the drawbridge was up. Nix and Leo stepped out of the Five Hundred. Steiger stayed in the back, adjusting his camera vest and taking it easy. Nix and Leo walked over to the Chief's car, IDs out, and introduced themselves. Then the three of them walked over to the space where the drawbridge was over the moat and the Chief took out a megaphone.

"Hello y'all, this is Chief Cynthia Beauchamp of the Horseshoe Falls Police Department," began the Chief, unfolding the search warrant and scanning it. "Some of you know me and hello, but I'm here on business. I'm here to serve a warrant to search certain premises within the curtilage of King Henry's Faire, bound and described herein, including the open space, visitor space, parking lots for King Henry's Faire, King Henry's Faire offices, including the video room, two storerooms on either side of the video room, the business office, the kitchens and attached storage space and the trailers, tents and cabins...'

It went on like that and when she was done the Chief heaved a sigh and asked for the registered agent for King Henry's Faire to step forward.

The King had a megaphone of his own and yelled back that the Chief was trespassing and could suck Hep-C water. He warned of dire consequences should any police try and breech the moat and alluded to booby traps and a secret weapon that he was ready to activate. He finished his comments by adding, "We will accept nothing less than unconditional surrender. Tora! Tora! Tora!"

Whether the King said exactly this, the news media said he did. What we know for certain is that after the King got done threatening law enforcement with this and that, Cindy Beauchamp, Chief of the Horseshoe Falls Police Department, accidentally depressed the talk button on her megaphone with her Sam Browne belt as she leaned in to hear Agent Nix whisper, "That clown King is shit-faced and it ain't even noon. Why don't we just drag his fucking ass in and serve the warrant on him while he's in Protective Custody? He has outstanding warrants as far away as New Hampshire. Let's get the drunken dopehead and PC him."

Nix said this in a whisper, but the Chief's megaphone made certain that everyone heard her. What Nix was suggesting is that they use the pretext of Protective Custody to detain the King because they arguably did not have probable cause to arrest, at least not yet. Nix and Chief Beauchamp shared a look. The look said: 'That was a sneaky thing we were just talking about doing. Now the King and everyone else knows we were thinking about screwing with His Majesty's rights'.

The newspapers printed Nix's words in quotes, with asterisks as needed to keep their readership safe and the content wholesome. The headline over the story read, 'FIGHTIN' WORDS' and in this case they were correct.

The King drew his sword, struck a pose and sputtered into his megaphone, "Battle stations! Shield's up! Repel the non-believers! Fire the trebuchet!"

The people on his side of the moat scrambled about, dropping things, running into one another, and causing a general panic in the Faire grounds. Someone fell in a tiger trap, followed by his friend. Only the Trebuchet Fire Team seemed unconcerned. While Matlock was trapping the perpetrator with his own words, the Fire Team was finishing a hot dog and hamburger extravaganza with homemade potato salad, grilled corn on the cob, chips, and cold beer. They had watermelon and supermarket chocolate cake for dessert and hadn't even started on it.

The King looked their way and swore at them through his megaphone, "You lazy bastards, put down those hot dogs and fire the trebuchet!"

"We're at lunch," announced Steady Eddie, Chief of the Fire Crew. "This is a scheduled break at a scheduled time. We are on duty for eight hours and then on call for sixteen. That's twenty-four hours a day. You can't deny us lunch. Are you looking for a job action? You better be careful if you try and fuck with us. We fuck back. We ain't afraid of you and not afraid to talk Union. We got the law on our side."

Another member of the fire team added, in a more conciliatory tone, through a mouthful of bun, "There's nothing we can do. The tent's still up, Highness. Nobody's firing nothing until the roustabouts take down the tent. Also..."

"Fire the fucking trebuchet," screamed the King through his megaphone.

"We can't until, like he said," reasoned Steady Eddie, "the tent comes down."

"Then I'll fire it," the King screamed through his megaphone as he marched behind the trebuchet and began hacking and sawing with his dull blade at the twisted hemp lines restraining the weight and the bucket.

Steady Eddie stood tall and threw his head back, right arm and index finger pointing at the King, "Sir, you will desist immediately from sawing that rope. In matters regarding the trebuchet I speak for the Fire Marshal and, therefore, as the Chief Safety Officer. You will desist from this nonsense immediately. This is an unsafe activity by an untrained operator."

A chubby Fire Team member translated, "It's a bad idea, Majesty."

"I wouldn't do it," chewed another one of the Fire Team, laying on the grass, "unless it's your aim to fire through the tent. We put hot tree stumps in the bucket so they're going to take down the tent. Going to take down the tent and keep going. You haven't thought this through, King. It's more complicated than you want to know. Damn, these are good fuckin' hot dogs, Eddie."

BOING, the trebuchet bounced. The whole machine, all two tons of it, jumped a couple feet in the air when the twisted hemp ropes loosened, the weight fell, and the bucket arm flew forward. When the bucket arm stopped it released the storm grate, flaming tree stumps, grey wasps' nest, and a couple of hundred red hot charcoal briquets, along with forgotten burgers and dogs as well as the assorted trash.

The whole mess crashed into and ripped through the tent ceiling, scattering hot ash everywhere, inside the tent and out, igniting the dry grass and sending strips of burning tent roof to the concession stands, where the propane tanks exploded minutes later, spreading the fire further, all the way to the business office trailer, which was consumed in a flash.

The Faire was storing a skid of full propane tanks along with some diesel and gas cans and landscaping equipment in two of the food trucks. One of them took a direct hit from a flaming tree stump, holing the side of Tacos Tonite. The explosion was so loud no one could hear anything, not even their own voices, for minutes. The truck was vaporized. The only parts left were four red-hot wheels still on their axles, resting in puddles of melted rubber. Gardening tools rained from the sky like a horror movie.

Fire was beginning to land and light the trees in the surrounding woods. The red hot grated manhole cover, flying through the sky like a comet, found Ciao Chow, the pizza truck, cleaving it before it went BOOM. The explosion was deafening, so powerful it was difficult to breathe just after. Fires were everywhere, distant sirens wailed.

Nix stood next to the Chief and confided, "This is better than I expected."

"So, ah, why do you think they fired that ah, what did you call it?"

"Trebuchet," Nix finished for Chief Beauchamp, "it's like a catapult.

"A catapult? Why'd he do that? Fires are breaking out all over. That jackass King did it this time. Well, here come the firetrucks." Cindy let out sharp two finger whistles, rotating the index finger of her left hand high above her head, "Let's move 'em back so the firefighters can get in, close anyway."

"Why don't we just follow them in when they get here?" suggested Nix.

"Yeah, why not follow them in," added Leo.

Steiger walked over in his illuminated, flashing neon vest, "Nix, do you have a minute?"

"Hey Steiger," Nix clapped him on the back, "did you see what that cocked King did? He set the trailer park ablaze. He's a tax scofflaw, a suspect in a murder, and now a drunken arsonist."

The Chief offered that arson is a specific intent crime and difficult to prove. She went on to say that the fact that he's a drunk, unstable asshole is actually going to work in his favor with this charge. Consolingly, she assured Nix that he was a scofflaw beyond reasonable doubt and a drunk for certain.

About following the firefighters in, Chief Beauchamp said, "That's not something we ought to do. It'll look like a pretextual search without service of the warrant."

"But we have a warrant, Chief, and you read it and then the King set off the trebuchet and started all the fires," Nix pushed back.

"We have to play by the rules and wait until the firefighters finish fighting the fires. What I could do is spot some officers in the woods behind the Faire so if anyone is trying to get away or conceal evidence, we can stop them."

"That's cool with us, right Leo, right Steiger?"

"Nix, can I talk to you for a minute?" Steiger seemed uncomfortable.

"Go ahead."

"Yeah, but it's not about this," Steiger looked at the Chief and Leo. "It's private."

Chief Beauchamp interrupted, "Take a minute if you like. It's Nix, isn't it? I like the cut of your jib. There's no hurry. We have to let the fire department get control of the situation."

"Yeah, it's Nix. Thanks, Chief, I won't be long."

Steiger took Nix aside and said, "I have to talk to you. I've been thinking myself silly. This camera I swallowed is taking pictures, movies really, of my insides."

"That's what you said it was supposed to do."

"It does that but I think it does more. You see if there's one thing I know cold dead certain it's pornography. There's every kind of porn. There's more sick porn out there than you can imagine. So, I've been wondering where inside the body porn comes from? Know what I'm saying?"

"I can usually piece these things together but, no, I haven't a clue."

"It's not computer graphics," Steiger continued as though Nix said nothing, " It's not animation. Where do they get the footage?"

"I'm a step behind, Steiger. Catch me up about the kind of porn we're talking about and why I should care."

"I think the camera pill I swallowed and the vest I'm wearing are taking inside the body porn videos of my balls, penis, large intestine generally and, moving upriver, the prostate, all the way to Bowman's capsule."

"The scenic route, eh?"

"It's not funny, Nix. It's freaking me out, as a matter of fact. Why are they filming the whole of my excretory system from the rim of my touch hole to Shangri La?"

"Hold the reins, Steiger. I'm trying to catch up but I'm not even close to understanding what you're driving at."

"They're in there with their camera, Nix. I'm going to end up seeing my own asshole, dick and balls in some inside the body porn video with a superimposed Matchbox car, or a Hess truck, or Happy Meal figure meandering through the boulevards and backroads of my digestive tract. I know how these things work. I won't have it. My private parts are just that."

"Walk with me, Steiger," Nix took him by the arm and they walked along the safe side of the moat while the fire built and spread on the other, "And slow yourself down, will you. C'mon, take a deep breath. Control those thoughts. There you go. Deep breathing. Now exhale and relax, Steiger, relax and take another long, deep breath. Now, listen to me. Just because there's a camera in you doesn't mean it's taking porn pictures. Exhale. You only think that because you spend more time with porn than anyone. Of course, you're going to think that any video of you is going to have something to do with porn. Take another deep breath now, Steiger. You're connecting the porn dots in your head. Porn is your primary frame of reference. Porn is the only thing you really comprehend. It's your bedrock so, ironically, it seems that you're being undone by the very corruption that motivates you to keep on living and enjoying life. Best part is it's all in your head."

"What the fuck, Nix. The corruption that motivates me to continue living?"

"And enjoying life, I added. I'm trying to say that all of this is in your head. Forget this camera stuff, Steiger. It's a distraction."

"I can't. I'm more certain of this than anything I've ever been certain."

"That statement is almost meaningless, Steiger."

"I should have known. I should have seen this coming, Nix. I feel like such a loser, such a chump."

"Do you know how shit-house crazy you sound, Steiger? Stop talking for a minute and listen. Because you engage life on a strictly sexual level, that's your perspective, understand?"

"I think so, yes."

"Then why are you surprised that when you swallow a camera pill you assume it's for pornographic purposes? Everything else in your life is geared that way so this must also be, right? What do you think you're going to think about? What conclusions do you expect you'll draw, considering what's on your mind all the time? You're going to think about pussy, dicks, and associated shit. You're actually bougie in this regard, Steiger, bougie and one dimensional. To a man with a hammer, everything's a nail."

"What the fuck does a hammer have to with this? And do you mean an actual nail, a fingernail or an ovarian teratoma with nails?"

Nix was nonchalant, "The fact that you never got pussy until you were twenty-eight hasn't helped."

"Keep that to yourself. Why do I tell you anything, Nix?"

"I don't know, but I do know you're a sexual hysteric. You venerate the jade gate. You've created a mystique about pussy and the whole sexual experience. You have to get over that."

"Come on, Nix. I feel bad enough without you putting cigarettes out in my mind. They hurt, you know."

"Watch your step, Steiger. You don't want to fall in the moat. C'mon, get a grip. You got one foot in Pussy Town and the other one kicking your ass about it. Choose a side."

"Okay, Nix, I know you're right, but I've got to get out of this vest and shut down that camera pill I swallowed. I'll feel better if I do."

"Well, Steiger, I think you're goofy, but if you feel this strongly about it why not take off the vest and see if the cops or the firefighters have syrup of ipecac, I think that's what it's called. Throw up the camera pill or poop it out if it's gone too far. You might need to go to a pharmacy and get some Mirilax and Colace to help with that. Better still, some of the King's blow. It was in his trailer but good luck with that. Anyway, once you squeeze out the pill, step on it to break any transmission. I saw it done that way in a movie, but that movie had nothing to do with porn or even taxes. It was a spy movie. Are you okay now?"

"I feel a little better, Nix. Just talking about it helps. Whew, I don't feel as violated now that I've vented. Fucking pornographers. Filthy scum. I'm going back to the car and call my lawyer. See if she'll take my call. Then I'm going to think this through again. I'm going to have to destroy the vest too. It could also be a transmitter."

"Okay, Steiger, you do that, go back to the car. You can always burn the vest. Say you got caught in the fire that this douche King started. You could even file for worker's compensation if you think you need a soft landing. Don't forget, you warned Buffum that the doctor put you on restrictions. He insisted on sending you. I'm a witness and I'll beat that eunuch Doyle half to death if he's scrubbed those notes."

"You're right, Nix. I have to clear my head of this stuff."

"Whatever you decide to do, just let me know, okay? I've got Leo stepping in for you so I'm going to have to let him know what's expected."

"Thanks, Nix, you're okay."

"Fuck you, Steiger. I have to go."

"Hey Nix, I don't understand. Sometimes you're awful to me. Other times you're my best friend. Sometimes, like now, a little of both."

"Who knows how things work, Steiger, trial and error, rats in a maze."

"Really? So why..."

"That's it, Steiger. I'm talked out. Find another ear."

XXIII

The firetrucks pulled up to the moat and blasted their horns as their sirens continued to wail. Finally, the King, the Queen and some of the Maidens in Waiting walked over to the drawbridge and asked what the firefighters wanted.

"Lower the damn bridge so we can put out the fires."

"If we do," asked the King, "are the police going to stay on their side of the moat?"

"Lower the bridge!"

"Not until I hear that the cops and their tax goons are going to stay on their side!"

The Chief pulled out her megaphone so the King could hear her over the sirens, "We'll wait until the fire department puts out the fires."

"Okay," shouted the King as he, the Queen, Farmer 7, and the Fool began lowering the drawbridge.

As soon as the bridge was down the first vehicle, Tanker Truck 2, Forest Fire Division, began slowly crossing the bridge when the boards snapped, the frame bent and the two front wheels sank into the moat.

"Oops," said the King, as the driver climbed out, holding his mouth with the hand that wasn't broken, while blood coursed through his fingers.

The firefighter in the passenger seat stayed in the truck, complaining about his neck. The four firefighters who had been holding onto the sides of the truck with one arm, holding fire axes in the other, were all laying on the bed of the moat, one of them motionless, spread eagled on a wet spot. The rest were moaning and holding their necks, backs, heads, or legs, some with multiple complaints. Other firefighters sprang forward to rescue their fellows and some of them slipped and fell in the moat as well. Finally, some ladders were lowered to facilitate the removal of those stuck down there. Other ladders were laid across the moat and boards were laid over the rungs so the firefighters could cross the moat on foot.

The Faire was now fully involved. Portable water tanks with pump hoses were taken from the disabled fire truck and placed on the backs of firefighters so they could attend to the grass fires, which were spreading out of control. Other firefighters started on the structures with fire axes. The bucket truck on the far side of the moat hoisted two firefighters with hoses to douse the roofs of the buildings, food trucks and trailers. Three teams of firefighters armed with fire axes, pikes and shovels tried to contain the fires popping up all over.

Firefighters like certainty. They're black and white people this way. There are no grey areas for them, at least not in firefighting. For a firefighter, a fire is only out when it's dead, usually by drowning. Firefighters will continue to pour water on a fire long after ordinary people would have figured it was time to go inside for a snack. It's because they know more than we do, I suppose, that's why fire fighters keep pouring on the water and that's what happened at King Henry's Faire that day.

The offices, storerooms, kitchens, and trailers were soaked through. They were all old particle board construction so everything just sandwiched. Eight-foot-high trailers full of records, account books, ledgers and documentation were soaked through and collapsed into four-foot-high impermeable lumps of glue, paper, and metal. All the records that Nix and Steiger came to get were destroyed. All of the computers had been baked to death and then drowned for good measure.

The Fairgrounds were burned to the sandy soil. The rides and stages, stage seating, booths, and attractions were gone, incinerated. The Faire and the fields around it were a hellish blackened landscape under a still smoky sky. All this wreckage took only twenty minutes.

The King, his hair having started to grow back after the car crash and explosion, was now bald as a baby's knee, steam still rising from his head. More unsettling, his eyebrows were just white shadows on his soot darkened face and he was naked, the ceremonial robe, true to its Dacron-polyester roots, having shriveled into nothing around his neck.

Steiger watched these developments with growing horror. Firefighters were getting injured and fires raged throughout the Faire. Endless hours of report writing loomed. Explanations would be expected and lawsuits filed. Someone had to be blamed. His stomach hurt. He was going to have to scrub his computer again.

And how was he going to explain the appearance of his innards on inside the body porn videos? What was he going to do about that?

He couldn't keep his thoughts from racing. Shakily, Steiger got out of the back seat of the Five Hundred and put on his camera vest. He took a lighter from the car and held the flame to the vest until he was sure it had it caught. Then he ran towards the moat and threw himself in. The flames were extinguished when he landed in a wet spot. He checked for broken bones, got up, looked around and used the lighter to get the vest going again. Then he dove to his left, where he immediately started screaming like he was being paid by the decibel.

The wasp nest had to land somewhere and fate chose the moat. The wasps, Hymenoptera Apocrita, were in a foul mood, having had their nest cut out of their tree, then having been transported half a mile, dropped in a hot bucket, scorched, and finally sent flying into a wet and nasty moat. Their patience, not a wasp strong suit, had worn thin. It had all been too much.

If wasps ever adopt a religion and some kind of recording of their faith is made, today would have to be one of the books. And in this book the part of the wasps' bete-noir would be played by Steiger. Most modern religions at least pretend to advance good fellowship and cooperative discourse among its adherents and the world at large. It's unlikely that a wasp religion would bother. Which is why the wasps set on Steiger so viciously when he jumped in the moat and then dived on them. Steiger was stung everywhere that wasn't covered up.

Nix held a handkerchief to her mouth and nose as she walked across the jury-rigged bridge over the moat. Below she saw Steiger squirming and thrashing about. She had a good idea what that was about so she left him alone. Making it across, Nix hunted for the King, finding him huddled together with the Fool and Farmer 7, the Queen having walked away in disgust. There were tears in the King's eyes.

Nix walked up to him, held out the search warrant and said, "Sign right here. Don't matter if you don't. I actually want to put down that you refused, but I have to ask. What'll it be?"

"Go 'way. Leave me alone. Look what you've done. You've ruined everything."

"I didn't do this. This is something you did, Your Goddamn Majesty. You got that, Majesty? What'll it be?"

"I said go away."

"The way I see it, you torched this place to prevent us from being able to search your records. It's the only explanation for what you did. That's arson. You were also interfering with a federal investigation and engaged in the willful destruction of evidence. So, it's fine with me that you refuse to sign for the search warrant. Your behavior is consistent. And you still owe ten years taxes, plus interest, compounded annually. So, I got to tell you that anything you say may be used against you in a court of law. You have the right to an attorney and if you can't afford one, an attorney will be provided for you by the court at no cost to you. Blah, blah, blah. Do you understand the rights I have explained to you? If so, sign here. Or, I'm guessing, just like with the search warrant, you probably won't. And finally, you piece of shit, I know you murdered Stanley Zimochowski ten years ago and fucked with his kid's mind so he couldn't testify about what he saw and heard you say to Zimochowski before you killed him. I know about you. I know what you're about."

"You can't prove anything. You don't know what you're talking about."

"Oh, I can't?" asked Nix as Chief Beauchamp and Leo joined her, "That's funny. Hey Chief, Leo, I was just telling the King about his rights and that this stunt he pulled is arson, willful destruction of evidence and interference with a federal investigation. They're all multi-year felonies. He refused to sign the search warrant and refused to acknowledge that I read him his rights. I also let him know that I'm wise to him murdering the last known taxpayer of King Henry's Faire, Stanley Zimochowski, ten years ago."

"You can't prove nothing."

"What he just said, that's what he said when I accused him of it a minute ago. See, he doesn't deny it. He only says I can't prove it. Interesting, isn't it?"

"That case is over seven years old," argued the King. "It doesn't matter what you think or think you can prove. That whole thing was ten years ago. It's over. There's nothing you can do about it now. I answered a million questions and nobody ever charged me with nothing. I could stand here and say I did it. I could swear on the bible and say I killed him. I could admit it in front of the heavenly host and there ain't a damn thing you or anyone else can do about it."

Nix was nodding her head, "Is that right, King, or is it Ronald Overbee. Is that right, Mr. Overbee?"

"It's called the statue of limitations, Nix."

"Statute, you Royal Numbskull."

"Whatever, it means it's too goddamn long ago to charge me with anything."

"I'm afraid you're wrong about that, King, I mean, Mr. Overbee. There is no statute of limitations for murder."

"It's a closed case."

"I'm reopening it."

"You can't. You're not that kind of cop."

"Watch me."

"I never said I killed him. I said if I killed him. I never admitted to a thing. You have to admit that. I never admitted to a thing."

"Good thing I read you your rights before you told me that you killed Stanley Zimochowski."

"I never said I killed him. They say he died of a peanut allergy. How was I to know anything about that? You're blinded by your hatred for me, Agent Nix. And you caused me permanent nerve damage in my neck, locking me in that portable shitter and knocking it over. I got a lawyer looking into it."

"Good for you," Nix smiled.

"You're not going to get me, but I'm going to get you, Nix, yes I am. I don't care how long it takes. I'm going to take your job and all your things and leave you with nothing. You can't fight me. You can't win. I've covered my tracks."

"Why would you do that, Majesty?"

"Do what?"

"Cover your tracks."

"I didn't say that."

"You sure did. We all heard you. Those are the words of a guilty man at ease."

"I must have said, 'It's in the sack'. I might have said, 'I checked my tracks'. That's what I said."

"I don't see why you'd say that, Your Majesty? It's no better."

"Don't call me that anymore."

"Everyone does. You're the King. It's who you are. You rule over this fire purged wasteland."

"When I'm done with you, Nix, no one is ever going to know you were here. You'll just be another spectator at the show."

"When I'm done with you, Mr. Overbee, you'll be doing thirty-five to life. That's a thirty-five year minimum. Hope you get lots of visitors."

"You can't scare me, Nix."

"Yes, I can. You don't know me. I can terrify you. But I don't want you terrified. I want you at ease, like this. I want you chatty."

"Well, I'm glad you told me because you're not going to hear anything more from me. I'm done talking. You can talk to my lawyer."

"Chief," Nix asked, "can you take in the King and put him in a holding cell for the night, maybe a couple or few?"

"Sure, anything else?"

"Let me know if the issue of bail comes up. I've got some paperwork to finish. I'm afraid that most of the charges I want to bring won't be under state law. Feds think their shit is special. But can you hold him on something, if necessary?"

"Sure," the Chief told her, "I can hold him on a Detainer or how about assault, arson under state law, and disorderly? I'll put in the report that we expect jurisdictional issues and we'll have to consider dismissal or nolle prosequi if there's Supremacy Clause bullshit. That way the DA won't get his nose out of joint."

"That'd be great, Chief. You may not even need to bring anything because I remember there are arrest warrants out for him from Middlesex Probate and a Capias from Charlestown District Court, another one out of Worcester, I think, and New Hampshire wants him too. He's not going anywhere. When should I come to interrogate him?"

"Any time, day or night, I'm there."

"Thanks, Chief. I'll come by when his Royal Highness starts to jones without the booze."

"It's Cindy."

"Thanks, Cindy, see you soon."

XXIV

The Fool wandered among the burning tents and trailers, helping people pack up what they could and make it to the parking lots. He didn't care for fire. It was too unpredictable for him. Even bonfires made him edgy. He didn't care for smoke either, but he stuck around to lend a hand for those in worse shape than he. Relocation buses were drifting into the parking lot to take them to shelter.

Shelter turned out to be some motels on the outskirts of Horseshoe Falls and a nearby field with FEMA tents around a one-story common building they called the Welcome Center. It had a large kitchen, bathrooms and showers, and a lounge area with vending machines, comfy chairs and sofas facing a big screen TV. The motels were for the families and couples who worked at the Faire. The tents were for single people, like the Fool. He thought he got the better deal, having heard that the guests at these motels included scabies, bed bugs and crabs.

In his tent the Fool could watch nightfall and listen for the whoosh of the bats as they gorge on mosquitoes and introduce the nightly cricket and bullfrog serenade. He chose a campsite away from the others with a little stone ringed fire pit and a view of the lake a quarter mile away. He had two half-filled bottles of Knockabout gin and an unopened bottle of Folly Cove rum, clean sheets, a warm blanket and fluffy dry white towels, courtesy of FEMA. He figured he was set for the next four days, even if he had company. He also had canned goods that the FEMA people gave everyone and flour, butter, eggs, milk, coffee, juice, chicken, bacon, and beef, all in refrigerated containers in individual refrigerated lockers at the Welcome Center. All in all, the Fool was doing okay.

Stepping out of his tent after his first night's sleep, the Fool sniffed cool fresh air. It didn't smell like unwashed people, booze or fried food. It smelled like gin. He took off the bandages from his hands and smiled because they weren't grey anymore and didn't smell like death. They were getting easier to use, too.

At a far corner of the field, he saw a mother fox and her kits crossing from one patch of woods to another. A big eared spotted fawn, munching acorns and early fallen apples, started at the sight of them, crashing into the woods. The Fool smiled at this, pulled on a sweatshirt and a pair of cheap canvas shoes the FEMA people gave him and walked down to the lake. It wasn't so big he couldn't see all the way around, but big enough. The Fool walked the circumference, seeing standing trees gnawed by beavers and others felled by them. He saw muskrats and rabbits and halfway around he found a feeder stream and thought he would like to follow that, but for today he contented himself with a walk around.

Flushed and perspiring, he walked the path back to his tent, stopping when he saw Nix sitting on an upturned box at his campsite.

"Hello Agent Nix, what do you want?"

Nix smiled. It was the first time the Fool had seen her smile. Her face didn't crack. He couldn't help but smile back. She said, "Your name is Charles Aspirance, I believe, or maybe you go by Charlie Crow."

"My name is Charles Aspirance. My mother gave me that name, but I used to go by Charlie Crow because I thought it sounded cool. Now they call me Fool because that's who I am."

"I like Charlie Aspirance more than the other two. Do you mind if I just call you Charlie?"

"No, I don't mind. It's better than Fool."

"Yeah, it's better than that, Charlie."

"What's your name, Agent Nix?"

"Ha, turnabout is fair play. This is between us, right?"

"Sure."

"My family name is Nix, but my given name is Gwen."

"Gwen, huh?"

"Gwendolyn, to be precise."

"You have a warm smile, Gwendolyn. This is the first time I've seen it. When you smile you look like you could be a Gwen or a Gwendolyn."

"Thank you, Charlie. That's sweet."

"But you're here to ask me about the King, aren't you?"

"Yes, I am."

"Well, see, I'm not sure I want to talk about that."

"Why not?"

"Not to protect him, if that's what you mean. I got problems of my own. I don't think I should be talking to the law."

"I pulled your record, Charlie."

The Fool tensed up, "Are you going to arrest me?"

"No, Charlie, I don't do that sort of thing. You have some stupid things on your record and there are two or three things you have to get cleared up, but not paying your excise tax and skipping out on a couple of speeding tickets isn't going to get you arrested. You do have to take care of that old disorderly conduct charge, but that's the worst of it. You're not going to jail for any of that and I'm not saying that just to get you to help me. They're just not jail worthy."

"That's good to know. So, if not the King, what do you want to talk about?"

"How about your father, Stan, and what happened to him ten years ago."

"That's clever, Agent Nix. Asking about Stan is the same as asking about the King, but I don't like talking about that."

"Why?"

"All my troubles started then. I became lost and afraid. I was only a boy when that happened."

"What happened?"

"When Stan and the King were, ah, they were, ah. See, I'm having trouble now. My mind doesn't want to go in that direction. There's a scratch in the record, if you have to know. I mean, there's a skip in my head. There was a time when I couldn't stop thinking about that day and what happened. But that, well, that, ahh, landed me in a mah, a mentahh, a mental hospital. I was a ghost back then, a piece of dust on the edge of a ray of light, nothing but a germ. I'm bigger than that now, but I don't want to end up like that again. I don't think about that stuff."

"How bad was it, Charlie?"

"I sat in a room until it got dark. I did that every day. Didn't see a knife or fork for a year."

"It must have been bad, especially right after you found out who your father was and then he died."

"I hid in my head the whole time. I still hide there. Sometimes I do."

"I think I know what happened to you, Charlie. I think the King got in your head. I think he whispered things about why Stan didn't tell you he was your father and how he didn't love you and didn't love your mother and how you weren't good enough. Is that about right?"

"You don't know. Nobody knows. I don't even know. I did know, once upon a time. I knew who did what and when. I knew it all and that's what landed me in the looney bin. Ever been to the looney bin?"

"No, Charlie, I haven't."

"That's good. I don't know nothing now, not a thing. You wouldn't want to remember anything either."

"But I've been in my head, Charlie. I know what it's like in there. I don't understand people half the time. I turn their words over in my head. I mix them up and scatter them. I rearrange them to find the clues to who means what and what she wants, sometimes what she did and why."

"I'm sorry, Agent..."

"Just call me Nix. No, call me Gwen, Charlie."

"I'm sorry, Gwen," Charlie sighed, sadly, "but what you just said is the kind of thing people say when they're on the way to the looney bin. I know things like this. I don't want you to have to go there."

"Charlie, that's the nicest thing anyone ever said to me. Want to know why?"

"Yeah, really?"

"Because I can be scary and I put people off. Importantly, you know that. Still, you went and told me I was thinking crazy thoughts and maybe I shouldn't. I know me and that took balls, Charlie. That took big balls."

He smiled, "Yeah, it did, didn't it."

"Straight up."

"To be honest, Gwen, I never thought you'd hurt me. I thought maybe you'd insult me and treat me like an asshole, but I never thought you'd raise your hand to me. Know why?"

"Don't try and figure me out, Charlie."

"Because you're fair, Gwen. You're a little nuts, if you want to know the truth, but so am I. But I can tell you're fair."

"I've never been accused of that before."

"You know I've been trying to help the King but you don't hold that against me. You understand how things are. But most of all, the fairest thing you do is listen. Most people don't, not unless they want something from you. And then they're not listening, they're waiting. You'd be surprised. I notice when someone listens. It means they are willing to hear. No one can ask anyone for more than that."

"You're a lot smarter than you let on."

"A little."

"And you ain't gonna tell me what the King said to Stan just before he died."

"I can't pull it up. Well, I won't. That's more like it. I'm afraid if I do I'll end up back in the mental hospital and this time I'll never get out."

"Okay, Charlie, I understand. It's cool. Sometimes the price is too high. I'll figure something out. Anyway, it's a nice lake you got here."

"It is, isn't it?"

"That's where you were coming from when I got here. What's it like?"

"Hmm, well, when I was little Momma and I and this fella she was with went camping in North Carolina. I think it was the Blue Ridge Mountains. This fella knew all about the wild plants you can eat, like poke and mushrooms, dandelions and berries and he found wild garlic, greens and herbs and he'd gather them fresh. Then he'd set out with a rod and go down to the lake and before you knew it he had a big catfish. Then he'd reel in the trot line he set in the morning and bring in some perch, walleye and maybe a smaller catfish. Mama would make biscuits in a fry pan and a salad. He'd cook our catfish up in lard with garlic and juniper berries and then he'd cook the trot line fish and put them in the dogs' bowls. We'd all eat real quiet until our spoons were scraping tin. Then I'd lay back, smelling the campfire, and watching the sun go down and the magic of the stars. It's like that."

"Sounds nice. Listen, Charlie, I'm going to take off but I've got something for you in my car. It might help you pass the time and help your hands get stronger. I'll be right back."

Nix returned with a fly rod and reel and a fishing basket with a good set of flies. "It's yours," she said. "It once belonged to my ex-husband, Larry. His health isn't what it once was. He'll never miss it."

"That's awful nice of you, Gwen."

"It seems right that you have it. It's not a bribe or anything. It's just to help you get the strength and flexibility back in your hands. I'll be back in a couple of days. Maybe we can talk. Maybe we can fry up some fish, have a drink and watch the sun set. You know, Charlie, I came here to get information. I didn't expect to like being here. I didn't expect to like you, but I do. You're not yapping all the time."

XXV

Nix was on page six of a Form 62P, Appeal from a Denial of Reimbursement. This was about an ill-advised four-day stay in Las Vegas at a Tony Robbins seminar. By the time Nix figured out that no amount of positive thinking was going to end her losing streak or pay her tab, it was too late to claim her stay as professional development. But that hadn't stopped her from hounding the Agency about it for the past year. Nor had it stopped the Agency from continuing to deny her claim. Form 62P would be her last shot before having to request an Adjudicatory Hearing, and that would be another long year away. Ugh, and she'd have to testify under oath before some bitter government Hearings Officer. She was wondering how she'd ever be able to get through that without at least mouthing the words, 'Fuck off'.

"Nix," Doyle stood behind her, "Mr. Buffum wants to see you and Steiger in his office."

"You're blocking my light, Doyle. You need to go on a diet."

"He'd like to see you... now."

"Why doesn't he tell me himself? Why didn't he just pick up the phone?"

"I don't know, Nix. He mumbled something about the lawyers saying he couldn't record calls anymore so he sent me. Just get Steiger and both of you get to Buffum's office."

Nix turned to face Doyle, "Tell Buffum that Steiger was injured on duty and he's out of work right now on workers' compensation. Tell him I thought he knew, everybody else does. Ask him if he'd like to see me alone. Pause here for a long moment, but don't say that. Then tell him that my preference is to wait until Steiger gets back before we have this meeting because I don't want to have to do it twice and I doubt he does either. Do I tip you or will Buffum take care of that?"

"Come on, Nix. Go see Buffum."

"I'll wait here."

Doyle was back in less than a minute, "Mr. Buffum says the message was clear and unambiguous."

"Unambiguous, huh? If he said unequivocal, I might have to give it to him, but unambiguous, hmmm. I won't cave on that. I mean, there is a degree of ambiguity in just about every human action. I smile when I fart. Really. Are they connected in some way? I don't know. It's ambiguous. So, tell Buffum that we have a difference of opinion regarding the clarity of his..."

"No, no, no you don't, Nix. We're not doing that. I'm not your messenger boy."

"You delivered his message to me. You delivered my message back to him and his message back to me. I think maybe you are."

"Nix, I'm taking Prilosec for GERD. I have a bowel stricture and a hip surgery scheduled in a month. All I want to do is make it to retirement and die. I'm not playing your game."

"That's bleak, Doyle. How often do you think about buying some rope or are you one of those run into traffic problem solvers?"

"You're a brutal, cold-hearted bitch, Nix."

"It's nice to know I'm appreciated."

Doyle stuttered, "I have integrity and friends and three wonderful grown children, Nix, three of them. Hardly smooth down there."

"Glad to hear it. I'm a big proponent of adoption. There are too many people in the world without adding to the problem."

"Hahaha, my wife gave birth to our children. It's unfortunate she didn't live to see them grow into the people they've become."

"And?"

"And what?"

"And did you find out who the fathers were? You know, HLA blood screenings are ninety-nine-point nine percent accurate."

"What's wrong with you, Nix?"

"I don't know, but I don't use my dead wife to get sympathy or make headway in a conversation. So, as far as I'm concerned, there's nothing much wrong with me. But that, Doyle, doesn't mean there's nothing wrong."

And just as Doyle was about to ask Nix what the heck she meant by that the phone rang. Doyle and Nix stopped talking and shared a moment of apprehension. Nix picked up the phone and started to say hello but Mr. Buffum talked over her.

"Put this call on speaker, Nix."

"Roger, Mr. B."

"Are you there, Doyle?

"Yes, Mr. Buffum."

"Where should you be?"

"In your office, Mr. Buffum."

"With whom?"

"Agent Nix."

"Can Agent Nix hear me?"

"Yes, Mr. Buffum."

After the 'click', Doyle said, "Why is he mad at me?"

"C'mon, Doyle, let's go. You're hopelessly stupid and smooth as a spoon, but I've developed a soft spot for you."

"Those are my children, Nix. I'm not smooth."

"Of course, you're not and I'm sure you love them as much as their real dads but we'll have to finish this later. Oh shit, Buffum's got that constipated look."

"Oh, I hate that look, Nix. It's not good for anyone."

Buffum walked back and sat behind his desk, "Sit down you two. Doyle, didn't I tell you to go get Nix?"

"Yes, Mr. Buffum, but she wouldn't come."

"Didn't I tell you a second time to bring her to my office?"

"There was some confusion about that."

"There was no confusion on this end, Doyle."

"Well, ah, you see, it was like this..."

Buffum looked to Nix, saying, "Forget it Doyle. Sit down, pick up that file and say nothing. I printed out the minutes of the meeting we're about to have. All you have to do is sign and time stamp the bottom."

"Okay Mr. Buffum."

Nix got her back up, "Woah, woah, woah, Doyle, you can't do that. And you, Mr. Buffum, can't make him."

Ignoring the interruption, Buffum said, "Agent Nix, all you had to do was serve a search warrant. I engineered things so the local police would do all the dirty work. I approved an outside contractor to reduce the opportunities for conflict between the Agency and this King. How could you screw this up so terribly?"

"You mean about the fire?"

"We'll deal with that first."

"We didn't start anything. That King torched the Faire to keep us from serving the warrant. That's arson. And this King had a moat dug around the property, behind which he had a trebuchet."

"He had what?"

"A trebuchet, a siege engine. It's all in my report. Who has one of those and why?"

"That's your story, Nix,"

"That's not my story, Buffum, those are the facts."

"That's not what the papers say, or the radio or TV. Social media is exploding. That's what someone said and it's bad for us."

"Yeah, well, I was there and the media was not. And you know that we're never going to get a fair shake from the TV news or even the papers. They'll never admit that the IRS ever did anything right. People hate us more than the cable company."

"Have you seen the paper?"

"Which one?"

"Any paper."

"The Globe ran this?"

"The Globe, The Herald, the Worcester Telegram, The Patriot Ledger and the Providence Journal. It hit local cable and wire services. It hit the wire services, Nix. I got a call from the Washington Post and the FBI called. They're sending investigators up. Investigators, Nix, and you know what they're all asking me?"

"Not a clue."

"Why I let someone like you go to a place like that. How do I answer that?"

"Mr. Buffum, that drunken jackass King did this. He fired a trebuchet full of burning stumps and hot coals into a campaign tent. The local cops and fire department will verify that. The burning stumps and coals started fires throughout the Faire. We never crossed the moat until there was nothing left."

"What about your plan to violate this King's civil rights? It's all right here in the newspapers, in quotes. They call it 'incendiary and provocative goading with a megaphone'.

"Oh, that, that was the Chief's megaphone. As a matter of fact, the button got..."

"I don't care about excuses. I have to go to Washington because of you, Nix. They told me to bring some clothes. It's all your fault, you and that pervert Steiger."

"You've got to go on the offensive, Mr. B. I suggest we bring charges against this King immediately."

"Is that right, Nix, bring charges?"

"Right away."

"No one is bringing charges against anyone except maybe you and Steiger. Do you understand?"

"Why?"

"There's a public outcry. People want your heads and, as your Supervisor, mine."

"We can't roll over, Mr. B., not because of that. I'm confident..."

"You're off this case, Nix, officially off the case. That goes for Steiger too. If I find that either of you has any more to do with this, I don't care what it is, you'll be fired. Steiger too. You're going to sign a letter to this effect. The lawyers want me to tell you that you do not speak for this office or the Department. We can't stop you from talking, I'm told, but if you do we will make it clear that we do not share your thoughts and opinions, nor do we support your actions, nor will we provide you with defense counsel, nor indemnify you against any losses or judgments. Is that clear?"

"If you're saying you are going to turn your back on us and support that lying, drunken, brain damaged King, yes, you've made yourself clear. But before you say any more about what you know nothing about, make sure you tell these Washington investigators that Steiger was a hero. He was almost burned to death by the thugs at this Faire. Still, he somehow charged forward until he ended up in the moat. Who knows how many lives he saved? Watch your step if you denigrate him. He'll sue you and I'll testify for him. If you're looking to make a villain out of anyone, Buffum, have some balls and go after me."

"You don't have to worry about that, Nix. I'm way ahead of you on that score."

Nix turned her head, "Doyle, are you getting this? Doyle?"

"Ah," Buffum smirked, "Doyle is having a medical procedure, aren't you, Doyle? He's requested a medical leave. Of course, his numbers are down and the rules are fairly clear about that sort of thing, once one's behind. We're going to see what we can do and then, assuming he's eligible, face the rate of wage continuation battle. That's a wholly different consideration."

"Doyle?" Nix asked hopefully.

Doyle squirmed, "Why do you think I'm taking his notes and fetching you? I wasn't always smooth."

"While I'm away, Nix, you'll stay away from that King," continued Buffum, "the Faire and anything to do with the last taxpayer at King Henry's Faire. You'll let Doyle know where you are during working hours."

"You can't do that, Buffum. I'm a union employee."

"I can when I work it out with your Union Steward."

Nix stood up, shaking her head, "Don't tell me..."

"The new Union Steward...,"

"Is Doyle," Nix finished the sentence for Buffum, "isn't it? You must think you've got this all figured out, Buffum, but you ought think again. Anyone who would leverage a man's health into a tool to control him is wounded in his soul."

"I don't care what you think, Nix."

"You should because it's not just karma that's out to get you. I'm out to get you."

"Doyle, get out your pen and take down that threat on the back of a page. Date it and add a time stamp."

"Don't do it, Doyle."

"All I got, Mr. Buffum, is that line about leveraging a man's health problem into a tool. If there was anything before or after that, I missed it."

"Ha," Nix laughed, "I'm sure Doyle would like to take you down, though he likely won't be able. There are others who quietly seethe. I know them. You call them friends. The only difference between them and me is I see the fear is in your eyes. I may be done here, Buffum, but I'm not done."

"Please leave, Nix, right now. But don't go far."

XXVI

Nix downshifted into second, killed the engine and let the clutch out so fast it jerked to a stop in the middle of the road. Stepping to the curb in a nice tight skirt she tossed her keys to the valet, who chased after her with a ticket.

Smiling and holding out her purse, Nix continued to the elevators, walking between two guys in scrubs who stopped their conversation as the elevator sighed open and she stepped on, asking, "Where do I find 341 St. Tillo East?"

The taller of the two, a rumpled fellow with an early stoop and a hairline crying for a Kangol said, "That's my floor, that is, I'm the intern, one of them, an intern on that floor. Can I help you?"

"Yes," Nix smiled broadly, "I'm here to see Agent Steiger."

"Oh, Steiger, yes, I checked on Mr. Steiger earlier today. He was playing canasta when I came back on my afternoon rounds. It seems he was admitted as a precaution, maybe even at his request, something about bee stings."

"Wasp stings," Nix corrected.

"But he's doing fine now," the intern put on his soothing doctor voice, "We think he was just shaken up. We're working on his discharge."

"Just shaken up? Discharge? I can't say that's wise. Did you know that man was lit up?"

"Mr. Steiger, the guy in 341, lit up?"

"It's Agent Steiger, doctor, and yes, certain murderous cretins tried to roast him alive." Nix looked the intern in his eyes and said, "Do you understand what I'm saying? Can you appreciate the existential insult he's facing?"

"He seemed like a happy guy to me."

"You're a doctor, aren't you?"

"Yes, that is, well, I'm a graduate, a recent medical school graduate. Honors, I should add. I'm an intern at the moment, which is to say that I am a doctor."

"So, you well-understand that the patient's demeanor is not dispositive of a serious psychiatric insult, nor that the risk of post-traumatic decompensation is high, if not staggeringly so, when the survived threat is of an elemental nature, a primal fear. This goes without saying, doctor."

"I didn't know anything about fire."

"Was this patient triaged? Have you read the notes, the history? Do you understand that your failure to explore and address the underlying psychiatric aspects of a physical injury is malpractice per se? Do you deny that failure to ascertain the psychiatric dimensions of an injury may well lead to long term fucked-up behavior, to resort to the vernacular. Doctor, this poor man should be observed for a couple more days, maybe three. I also think you should know that while Agent Steiger was ablaze, while his clothes were burning to his skin, this man saved a small child from a perilous situation of some kind. Then, fully engulfed, poor Steiger fell ten feet, landing face first in a giant wasps' nest at the bottom of a dry moat."

"A moat?"

"A dry moat, doctor. This man is a hero. Who knows how many lives he saved from the fire at King Henry's Faire?"

The bell dinged and the doors opened. The tall, rumpled intern hurried to catch up with Nix, "I read about that fire. I didn't know that was where Steiger was, honestly. He never said a thing."

"Of course, he didn't. The man is a quiet hero."

"But we didn't know he was there. There was something about the IRS, too. I think they started the fire. I remember reading that the whole place went up."

Nix found room 341, adding over her shoulder, "Well, maybe not, but what's important is there was a fire," she pushed the door open. "but there were no deaths because of Steiger. He sacrificed himself. I'd do anything for that man. Anything. Please take care of him. Out of an abundance of caution, if nothing else, keep him a few more days. We owe him so much."

"We will," assured the taller intern.

"Just for you, Miss," added the shorter guy, probably thinking he had to say something and regretting that it was this.

Nix smiled as she pushed Steiger's door closed and turned around.

"Wow, Nix, look at you."

"Look at me? Look at you? Have you looked at your face."

"It's the wasp stings. You should have seen what I looked like when they brought me in. I was 'Bighead Bumble Bee', according to the nurses. But look at you, Nix, you're put together. You've never dressed like this before, not while I've been around."

"Stop thinking about me, Steiger, right now. Just listen."

"I can think and listen at the same time."

"I know you can but I don't want you to. Buffum has it in for us, especially me, but he won't do you any favors."

"What's he mad about?"

"He's more than mad, he's scared. Have you seen any newspapers or been watching the news."

"No. I'm taking a break from that. I made friends with a couple of nurses. We have similar interests. One of them is teaching me filthy needle point. The other is devout but she loves porn."

"Listen, Steiger, Buffum is going to have us criminally charged."

"For what?"

"He's going to say that we're responsible for the fire, me particularly, and violations of that asshole King's civil rights, again, particularly me."

"We have to get to that Horseshoe Falls Police Chief before Buffum does," added Steiger.

"Yeah, but here's the thing, Steiger. We've been kicked off the case and Buffum says if we have anything to do with anything he's going to make sure we have to get our own lawyers and pay any damages out of our pockets and we'll get fired too."

"But Nix, we can't sit around waiting for a knife in the back. We have to save ourselves. No one else will."

"I agree, Steiger, but I can do this part alone. You never wanted any part of this. I butted heads with that King, not you."

"Like the King said, Nix, 'Tora, Tora, Tora'!"

"Let's not start quoting that touch hole. You lay low for the next day or two. There are some things only I can do."

"Like what?"

"Like talk to Chief Beauchamp, who likes the cut of my jib and maybe interview the King. Then I have to go back and talk to Charlie Aspirance again, the Fool with the big hands."

"Again?"

"I don't waste time, partner. I'll be back late tomorrow night or early the next morning, unless they kick you out. I'm writing down the number to your room phone. Answer if it rings, but don't say a word until you hear my voice. And don't call me unless it's an emergency. Why leave a trace? Try and find a way to stay here. I told the big, goofy intern with the receding hairline that you're a hero and got burned at the Faire. Play it up."

"I know that guy, flirts with all the nurses more than anything else."

"I told him you were traumatized but still managed to save a kid's life. Can you work with that?"

"You want me to stay here?"

"Yeah, if you can. I just got through saying that."

"Well, thank you, Nix. I love it here. Of course, I can. I can pretend I have cancer if you'd like."

"No, too ambitious. Keep it simple. I told the intern you were turned into a S'more. Make it psychiatric. All we need is some time and a place where we won't get arrested by Buffum or tormented by the press. We can't go home. I'm sure there have been reporters staking out your house and that dickhead Buffum knows where you live so this is better than home."

"Poor Mum. I hope she's got some valium left. She must be stressed out with hives. Too bad. But this place is wonderful. It's full of nurses. I get examined morning and night. I get a rectal on request."

"Well, in between can you get Leo on the phone and have him run down Buffum for anything and everything: sex, money, drugs, associates, friends, and family. We need to throw something in his way to slow him down."

"Yeah, I got something better than that. Do you know Sava Prochuk, the night custodian at the office?"

"Creepy guy with the long hair?"

"Yeah, they call him 'Porkchop'. Well, Porkchop doesn't understand America. He says that back in Whathefuckistan it's perfectly normal to get engaged to your fourteen-year-old cousin."

"Oh Steiger, don't tell me this."

"Yeah, his little cousin wrote an essay for school about Porkchop and it was enough to get him arrested, tried and convicted of something and deemed to be a sexually dangerous person. He wears an ankle bracelet and lives in a rooming house now. I think the marriage is off."

"Fascinating tale, Steiger, but I think we can do without Porkchop."

"Except Porky is a huge fan of American pornography. He told me he uses Buffum's computer during breaks. He says Buffum is a huge pervert. Between the two of them, I can't imagine what kind of sheep shagging Turkish bath porn is on that hard drive, maybe on the IRS server. I'm going to let Leo know we need a hacker and we got one right there in the office if we can show him what to do."

"That's brilliant, Steiger."

"Thanks, Nix, and you know what else?"

"No, what?"

"He's got his own ID and pass key so we don't leave any prints, no ghosts, and no surveillance tape images. We're home free."

"That's great, Steiger, but we don't have any money. How do we pay for this?"

"There's still Leo money on the table that Buffum approved. Can't we do something with that? There's enough there and more if we have demonstrable results. We just have to be successful."

"You take care of that, okay Steiger? It's a good plan. I have to get going, but I brought these for you because I know you must feel cooped up." Nix reached into a big bag and pulled out four filthy magazines, "These are the nastiest ones I could find. I asked for jack fuel for sickos."

"That's where you're wrong, Nix. This one here, for example, is a pictorial essay. It's a classic, more a commentary on the plight of women in capitalist society than anything else. I see a woman chained...."

"There is a woman chained, Steiger, and three guys circling her with unsmiling dicks. I flipped through."

"Well, it was very thoughtful, Nix. I wish I could have watched you shop for them. My new friends and I will be going over these tonight and I'll be certain to credit you as procurer. I don't know what else to say."

"You don't have to say anything, Steiger. I like to see you happy. Well, actually, I don't, but I want you to be happy."

XXVII

It was late afternoon as the Fool made his way from the lake to the path that ran to his campsite. The sun was full in his eyes when he thought he saw Nix walking from the Welcome Center to his campsite and he couldn't wait to show her all the trout he caught. But as he got closer he raised a hand to block the sun and saw it was the Queen trudging through the grass, slapping at the bugs and losing her footing.

The grin left his face. He hefted his pack, adjusted his basket, and made straight for his tent and campsite.

"Hello, Majesty."

"Hello, Fool. What's in the wicker basket?"

"Fish I caught this morning. What do you want with me?"

"I came by to see you and, first of all, let you know the King says 'Hello'."

"Hello to him, how's he doing?"

"He's still in the can and no bail set. They said he was acting up so they got a psychiatrist down to examine him and the King turned him his way. He got the shrink to say he is an alcoholic and a drug addict."

"He is an alcoholic and a drug addict, Majesty."

"What matters is he got the shrink to believe it and the shrink is making the police give him a beer in the morning and another at night and Valium and Ambien too."

"I guess that's good."

"It's not cutting it for the King. He says it's just a tease. Anyway, he'd like to see you."

"Why does he want to see me?"

The Queen couldn't meet his eyes, "He wants you to do him a favor. He wants you to wear a condom catheter when you go there, with the tube full of pills and a cuff full of booze. Take it off and pass it to him through the bars."

"I could get in big trouble for doing that, Your Worship. I could end up behind bars myself. It sounds dangerous to me."

"You have to do it or we all lose our jobs. Winter comes early this year and no one has enough weeks for unemployment.

"But I don't want to end up in jail."

"Do it right and you won't."

"But even if I do everything right, you know the King could fuck up a royal flush."

"Don't ever say 'royal flush' in my presence again, do you understand?"

"Yes, Majesty, never, Majesty, but you know it's true. Our King could fuck up anything."

"I'll pretend I didn't hear that because you have to do this and you're venting. But make no mistake, I'm not asking. You don't do this and I'll have you removed from this cushy campsite and your smelly fish too, got it?

"Yes, Majesty."

"Come to my car so I can give you the condom catheter, the drugs and the booze. Do you know how to put it on?"

"No."

"Well, I ain't gonna do it for you. Just get it a little chubby and slide it over the head. That's all there is to it."

"Chubby?"

"Firm."

"Firm?"

"Get a little, you know... that is, have you ever, I mean, can you think of something exciting?"

"I don't know exactly what you want me to do."

"Want me to show you some titty? Want me to rub it a little?"

"I don't know."

"You don't know! Lots of guys, and I mean lots, would slide me a hundred bucks just to see a little titty of mine and have me pat jack."

"Pat jack?"

"Do you know what a condom is?"

"No."

"It's a rubber, you goddamn Fool."

"You want me to put on a rubber full of booze and pills and take it off in jail and give it to the King? Are you crazy?"

"Get in the backseat of my car, Fool. Unbuckle your belt and... Thor's hammer, I thought the Blacksmith had a friend. Where have you been hiding this crocodile? Seems to be doing a river roll right in my hands. Tell me, Fool, does this thing breathe on its own?"

"I'm sorry, Majesty. I've been fighting this thing since I was a boy."

"Pretty clear who's winning."

The Fool's penis began to arch, grow, and reach, "I'm sorry, Your Worship, forgive me," he reddened, "It has a mind of its own."

"Sorry? Don't I wish the King was a little sorry. Okay, now spread the opening of the rubber and stretch it over the lump at the end. Let me show you Fool, like this."

"What next?"

"Whatever you do, don't pee. Now take that off and you put it on by yourself."

"I know how to put on a rubber, Queen."

"Good, let me see you do it. Okay, that's the way. Now give it back. I'm pouring the booze in the cuff, like this, and now the pills in the tube, like that. Now, just before you get to the jail, pull over, put on the condom like you just did, run the sleeve down your leg and attach it to the cuff around your ankle. It's simple."

"How I'm going to get to the jail?"

"Alfred will come get you......"

"I'd rather take the bus."

"The bus don't go to the jail."

"Then I'd rather walk."

"Alfred got a lawyer who got him in a class action suit against the manufacturer of his car."

"Alfred thinks the car company shoulda known the King was gonna shoot the gas line?"

"Something like that, but some Order in the class action says they got to give Alfred a rental. So, he's riding around in a 2017 Hyundai four door sedan with heated seats."

"It ain't cold."

"Moon roof, back up camera and tinted windows, Bose speakers and Bluetooth."

"It ain't that. It's Alfred's ass."

"Oh, yeah, he told me. He says he's got that all figured out and not to worry."

"Ask me how I'll know what he had for lunch?"

"It's going to be different this time."

"I'll tell you, Queen, I don't like any of this, not one bit. It's too scary."

"I know, right?"

XXVIII

Leo stood at a high top at Dunks, looking out on Cambridge St. in a light rain. It was late afternoon with a grey chill. He nursed a weak coffee until Sava Prochuk pushed his wet way through the door and shook himself off.

"You're shorter than Steiger said you'd be. What you want with me? I'm going to be late at work."

"Nice to meet you, Sava," Leo smiled, "Want a coffee?"

"What I want is no trouble."

"Well, you're not going to get any. Steiger tells me you know your way around office computers."

"Computer systems."

"Okay, right, systems, but what I want you to do is access the hard drive of a computer on the seventh floor of that building, over there, where you work. Copy any bad things, anything criminal or embarrassing and give it to me."

"Like the porn on the computer?"

"Yes, like the porn or anything else. It's half an hour's work and I'll pay you three hundred green."

"You know I work at cleaning IRS?"

"Yes, Sava, that's why I'm talking to you, because you work there."

"What is wrong with you? You know is federal time if I am caught, yes? Are you some kind of cop? You wearing wire? For three hundred green, you say? Are you nuts?"

"It's personal, nothing to do with the IRS. There's a guy up there and he's a bad man and I have to take him down."

"Yeah, I'll bet it's worth more than three hundred. I'll bet it's worth a grand."

"Wait a minute, Sava," Leo looked disappointed, "You shouldn't ever do that, never."

"Do what?"

"What you just did, ask me for a grand. Get me off three before you drop a number. It's important, Sava. It's practically a rule."

"There are rules?"

"Yes, and now I know your reach is a grand, but more importantly, I know you'll do the job. And not just that, I didn't have to use anything but my ears to find out. It's your own fault that you reap shitty terms. From now on, Sava, think before you speak. Your number is five. Let's cut the bullshit and get this done."

"That's not my number."

"Yes, it is. Don't be mulish."

"But five is not my number."

"It is now. You fucked up."

"I don't know about this, mister. I'm on parole and I get caught doing this, I'm not going to state prison. I'm going to federal penitentiary with all sorts of other trouble on top of my head. That's not like the difference between coffee and cashew ice cream."

"What kind of ice cream?"

"Give me a grand, seven fifty, at least, and tell me who you want me to hack?"

"You don't need to know."

"Give me seven fifty."

"Don't beg, Sava. Beggars get scraps."

Sava took a deep breath, "You're gonna pay me seven fifty! It's what it's going to cost."

"Better," Leo nodded, "but say it in a normal voice, not like you're in a movie. Say it like you say it every day. Pretend you're talking to me."

"I am talking to you. This job going to cost you seven fifty, up front."

"You're getting there, Sava, but nothing is up front except, sometimes, expenses. You're almost believable. Take a look at this sketch, 7th floor East, at the end of the middle corridor, here. When you get there open the door that says 'Supervisor'."

"Mr. Buffum's door?"

"Yeah, that one. The computer is on his desk."

"I know where it is. What you want with him?"

"He did something...."

"To Steiger and his partner, Nix?"

"You don't need to know. You're talking to me."

"But I am right?"

"It doesn't matter what he did. He's a bad motherfucker and needs a dope slap."

"Dope slap? You want to slap him? Okay. You do what you have to. I look in computer and send it where you want. Pay what is fair."

"What's that, Sava?"

"Pay what is fair."

"Why?"

"Am late for work and must go. Pay what is fair."

"But tell me, Sava, why you'll take what I think is fair?"

"Okay, fiancé from old country come here. She and sister get names and papers mixed together at Immigration. Dushka is sixteen and Anna is fourteen, but they get here and is other way around. So, Dushka writes story about me for nosy teacher and they think she is turning fifteen and I get in trouble as sex criminal. How about that?"

Alone on a barren and unfamiliar stretch of moral high ground, Leo was perplexed, "Yeah, I see what you're trying to say, okay, but here in America, Sava, that's what they call a distinction without a difference."

"What is that?"

"The mix up with the papers makes no difference, Sava. You have to get over it."

"But she is now seventeen, soon to be eighteen, and our parents fix us up. Was decided for us in old country that way. We, me and Dushka, even sleep in parent's bedroom, on mattress on floor with heavy board between us and mother's dead eyes on me all night. I wouldn't touch myself, let alone Dushka."

"That sucks, Sava, but so what?"

"The little guy Buffum, my Supervisor, finds out I am criminal and tells me to pay him a hundred and fifty a week, cash, or he tells my boss at agency to fire me."

"That's extortion. I told you he was a motherfucker."

"He knows my job is required for to be on parole. No job and I am back to prison, so I pay him every week. I hate myself and want to kill him, but I'm no killer. I pray to Saint Gemma, patron saint of back pain, that she lay him low. I pray to Saint Ignatius, Saint Bastard and Saint Elmo for his early and painful demise. I light candles and pray to St. Rocco, patron saint of the wrongly accused. Then I remember the instruction of Our Heavenly Protector, through the teaching of Saint Barbara, who reminds us that we must help ourselves before looking for favors from above."

"That's good advice, Sava."

"Yes, so I have not been idle and angry. I am a cleaner because I am convicted sex criminal and don't speak good English, but I have degree in computer science from Russia."

"Really?" Leo was impressed.

"Yes, I know enough about computers to find the porn on them and there is very sick, very nasty porn on Buffum's computer and there is some porn on his computer that I put there, to be honest, but who's to know that? I'm just cleaning guy. Am not like kind of guy that would change the date and time on a computer to watch porn and other things and then change it back when I'm done. I don't look smart enough to always date the porn for when Buffum is in office. How would someone like me know about all the viruses that are on his computer and the bad places, very bad places they came from? How would I know there's a, what you call interest, no, uptick in bestiality URLs and links to snuff films and that kind of filth on Buffum's computer? It almost is like I am creating a profile for this sonofabitch that will draw attention of wrong people."

"Who are the wrong people?" Leo wanted to know.

"Many are the wrong people but I have searched the websites for the worst of them. National Security Agency wrong people are the worst of the worst."

"So, you were going after him anyway?"

"In a slow, you say deli, delib,..."

"Deliberate?"

"Yes, methodical way I am planting the seeds, but now we are working together, right?

"That's right, Sava."

"So, we go faster and you pay me what is fair. What I like to do for my vengeance is file Whistleblower Complaint. There's a hotline. I know all the hotlines. I will file a complaint with the IRS and forward a copy of the hard drive with it. I'll send to FBI, too."

"The FBI, Sava, what the fuck?" Leo went pale.

"I want him punished. I must ruin him."

"But Sava, we don't want to get ourselves punished and ruined too."

"Da, I know this but I almost don't care."

"But we do, Sava. We don't want any part of that. Nothing to do with the FBI or any initials except IRS, okay? This has to be anonymous, so no Whistleblower Complaint. You have to give your name when you file that, so we want none of it. Rat him out, but anonymously."

"Da, okay, okay, I do that later, on my own. But there's more on his computer. He's skimming and shorting IRS through blind discounts scheme."

"What's that?" Leo was puzzled.

"Russian child knows for how to do this. Is really just two sets of books, no? One that lives only on the internal server, the other on his desktop. Buffum keeps the difference between the two and no one is wise except for me."

"He's stealing?"

"He make so much money is silent partner in cleaning company where I work. That is ethical violation. They told me so on Ethics Helpline. He also shorts the Union on the first hour after forty, calling it flex adjustment something but it goes in his pocket under the name M & T Training LLC. He's President, Treasurer and eighty-five percent stockholder. This is for every union worker in Northeast Region, not just Boston office. That's millions of dollars just rolling in for nothing. With all this money this son of bitch make me pay a hundred fifty a week cash."

"Can you do whatever you just said and how soon can you do it?"

"I can do tonight after every people leave and I have surprise for him and you're going to like it. This guy has a camera in ladies' room. He can go to jail for that, no?"

"Huh, a what?"

"A camera, smile, click, click, in ladies' room."

"Why?"

"Why you think? That patches direct to his computer. He not just sell pictures, no, he sells streaming bathroom video to people and kinky porn sites. I have seen this and the records on his computer. Big money roll in from streaming video he calls 'The Girls' Room'."

"No kidding?" Leo was intrigued. He took out his phone, "Jupiter, you're goddamn right. Holy crap! 'The Girls' Room' is a narrated streaming service of a ladies' room. This has over two million subscribers. Get those records, Sava, but don't mention this to anyone else, no one except Steiger or me, do you understand?"

"Of course, I am quiet as buried stone, if that's what you want."

"Wonderful, Sava, and I'll get that grand for you somewhere."

"Where do I meet you when I am have finished?"

"We'll call you. What's the best number?"

"The one I have."

XXIX

Nix parked in the shadows, pulled a ball cap over her eyes, took out her cell phone and made a call.

"Horseshoe Falls Police Department, nonemergency line. This call is being recorded. How may I direct your call?"

"Put me through to the Chief, please."

"Who's calling?"

"Tell her it's Cuttof Herjib."

"How do you spell that?"

"The way it sounds. I'll hold."

"This is Chief Beauchamp. Is this...?"

"It's Agent Nix, Chief."

"Cindy."

"I mean Cindy. Can we get a coffee, Cindy?"

"Come down any time before seven AM. I'm covering the night shift. I've got coffee on."

"I'd like to speak to you outside of the station if you don't mind. I'm parked right here in the lot."

"You are?"

"Yeah, can you come out? I'll explain myself."

Cindy came out and Nix explained everything she could, "...and near as I can tell Buffum had his finger to the wind and decided Steiger and I had to take the hit. That's the story, Cindy, and I haven't left anything out, nothing important, I mean."

"Why is this guy Buffum trying to finger you?" Cindy asked like the cop that she is.

"Because he feels threatened. He's always afraid and he knows the best way to deflect blame is to accuse someone else, but he also doesn't like me. I don't care for him either."

"I can't keep calling you Nix, Nix. What's your given name?"

"Gwen."

"Well, Gwen," Cindy rolled Nix's name around in her mouth, trying it out before beginning in her reasonable voice, "have you given this fellow any reason not to like you?"

"We've clashed over the last seven, eight years about what he calls my 'high T attitude'. That's what he called it until I grieved him on every time he said it, which was a hundred and fifty-seven."

"Don't tell me you..."

"Yeah, that went into his record as one hundred and fifty-seven individual complaints of gender-based harassment. Oh, and I slapped him in the face at a party once. I'm big enough to admit that it might have been a misunderstanding. I've also called him a pussy, but never gratuitously. Otherwise, we're cool."

"Otherwise, huh? Well, Gwen, what do you think is going to happen when you call a man a pussy?"

"I call my partner a pussy, even though he isn't. He just ignores me or laughs it off. Buffum, on the other hand, looks like he's either going to cry or bake me in a pie. And for the record, he is such a ..."

"Okay, okay, I get the picture, but I shouldn't really extend myself, Gwen. I might end up as a witness, testifying in your criminal trial. On the other hand, I was at the Faire, saw what happened and know those news reports are false, mostly. What is it you want me to do?"

"Push back for us if you can. Don't let them bury us. And if I can, I want to talk to the King, but I don't want it to be on the record. Can you let me in on the hush-hush?"

"That's asking a lot, Gwen."

"I know, Cindy, and I understand that you have..."

Cindy interrupted, "It would look bad because it would be bad. They'd call it a conspiracy, Agent Nix, and they'd be right. I'd get sued. I'd lose my job and maybe worse. So, I can't help you. We're understaffed as it is. We can't afford to have anyone posted to the lock up. There's just the desk sergeant out front and me in the back. It's quiet here, like a little outpost and the only other person I expect to see tonight is the pizza delivery guy. It's someone new every night. It's how we feed the prisoners."

Nix smiled, "Are you saying...."

The Chief held up her hand, "What happens is the driver pulls up and gets out with a pizza and a bottle of Dr. Pepper. The sergeant, two years from retirement and a wizard at the New York Times Crossword Puzzle, will buzz him through. The sergeant believes, maybe correctly, that the less he does, the greater the likelihood he'll make it to retirement. I've heard this man say that he, 'almost saw something out there'. Don't you either see something or not? I could not understand what he meant until I tried to look at it from his perspective. From there I realized that if my objective was to avoid seeing anything, almost seeing something would be a near miss and, therefore, noteworthy."

Nix smiled and said, "Cindy, I understand and want to thank you."

"Well, like I said, I'm sorry I can't help. I did want to mention that if the pizza delivery guy was wearing a longish raincoat, sunglasses, and a hat, even gloves, this desk sergeant wouldn't care. He'd wave him through. And finally, there's only one camera and it's on the wall facing the cell door. That camera is fixed on the prisoner. But there's an inset plexiglass mirror on the cell's back wall. If the pizza delivery guy didn't want to appear on video, poor quality that it is, he'd want to keep the King between himself and that mirror. Every pizza delivery guy wants to talk to the prisoner. Don't ask me why. They'll waste a minute, sometime two, just talking to him. They never spend more than two minutes. I hope none of them ever make me come down to chase them away. Two minutes, tops."

XXX

Alfred came to get me and he hadn't done a thing to fix the driving situation. It was a good-looking Hyundai, for sure, I'll give him that, but his friend Anquan was being the brakes and the gas. They pulled up next to me and Alfred stuck his head out the driver's side window. Before he could say anything, I told him all bets were off and I was done getting my nuts mashed by his stumps.

"Why don't you just hold on there, Fool, and take a good look at the modifications I made. You see the way Anquan is sitting and I'm standing?"

"How are your nuts, Anquan," I asked, trying to be a smart ass.

Anquan didn't say a word, didn't even look at me. I looked inside and the only thing different from the last time we did this is that Alfred's stumps were straddling Anquan's left thigh and so Alfred's ass was resting on Anquan's left shoulder, not in Anquan's face.

"Is that it, Alfred?" I said, still looking in the car, "You're stepping on Anquan's nuts with one stump instead of two?"

"Anquan's nuts are fine, aren't they, Anquan?"

"I'm going to my girlfriend's house," Anquan lifted and slid under Alfred's right stump and opened the passenger side door. "Your rental needs to be made handicapped accessible, Alfred. It ain't street legal driving this way."

"You're welcome for the ride, Anquan," Alfred called snarkily.

"Welcome for the ride? You killed my K-car."

Alfred waved him away, "Make sure you meet me in three hours, Anquan."

"Or what, you're going to drive home without me? See you when I see you."

"Okay, Fool, I'm ready when you are. I got navigation on this Hyundai. Let's go to jail."

I told Alfred to take it easy and I was in no rush to get to the jail in daylight. Alfred wanted to know what we were going to do while we waited and I told him he ought to come over to my camp and have a drink by the fire. So, I got in the driver's side and he only put one stump between my legs and when we got near the campsite I told him that the drive wasn't so bad. I picked up Alfred and carried him over to the best seat at the fire and laid a little blanket on his lap. I went into my tent and got the bottle of Folly Cove rum, threw a few sticks of wood and some small logs on the fire.

"Just a sip for friendship," I passed him the bottle. Alfred liked rum so much it wasn't ever one sip. I ain't certain how many we had, but by the time we were done that bottle was only half full. As the sun was going down I asked Alfred one more time how the navigation works. When I was pretty certain I knew, I passed him the bottle and told him I was leaving for the lock up and he was staying here. I said I'd bring him back a cheeseburger and fries because that was his favorite and asked him not to bother getting mad, but he did anyway. He threw awful names and curses my way as I finished programming the navigation. Then I tooted and sped off.

XXXI

Nix found a black raincoat on the floor of her closet and a pair of overlarge sunglasses in a beach bag. She changed into sweats and sneakers, wiped off her make-up and stood in front of the mirror. She could tell it was still her. Once it got dark, she thought, it would be better, but the police station itself would be bright, so a solution eluded her. Before she knew it she was in the bathroom with an erasable marker, putting black dots along her jawline, chin, and upper lip, as though she was a seventeen-year-old boy that hadn't shaved in a few weeks.

Stepping back and peering in the mirror, she realized it didn't look at all like she had a beginning beard. It only looked like her face was dirty. Oh well, she thought, as she went to wash it off, but it didn't wash off. Looking more closely at the marker she saw the warning about putting marker on skin. The warning said it wouldn't wash off easily. She tried again, irritating her chin with a facecloth and some alcohol. Still, it wouldn't come off.

Shrugging her shoulders, Nix balled her hair up under a skully, put on the raincoat, put the sunglasses in her pocket and started the Toyota. She only got a few strange looks but that might have been because she was on a highway at night doing eighty. Exiting the highway, she traveled the dark backroads until she got to the sleepy town of Horseshoe Falls.

Downtown Horseshoe Falls was a hundred-yard strip and one building deep, but on both sides, they liked to brag. Everything was closed except, at one end, a convenience store gas station and across from that an uncool old man bar called The Taproom, and at the other end sat a pharmacy with Athena Pizza, Subs & Salads across from it. Nix parked in front of Athena and got out.

The bell dinged and a once handsome man raised his head above the counter. He had a look, a sad look, like he led a life of rolling disappointments. Standing up, he 'paused' the Greek movie he was watching on his iPhone and said, "Can I help you, sir."

Nix looked behind her, "Who?"

"I mean, ma'am. I mean miss, that is, young man. Young man, may I help you."

"Young man?"

"Or young lady, rather. May I help you, please, young lady."

"Give me a large cheese and a two-liter Dr. Pepper to go."

"Let me wash my hands."

"Don't bother."

"Excuse me?"

"The person I'm getting this for doesn't mind."

"Maybe so, but the Health Department does."

"A rinse will do."

"That'll be $14.75."

Nix put down fifteen, "Put the quarter towards some glasses."

Driving to the police station, Nix salivated at the smell of pizza in her car. She killed her lights as she turned in, put it in neutral, and coasted through visitors' parking. There was only one other car in the lot and it might have just gotten there because someone was stepping out of the driver's side. Nix turned on her headlights and froze the Fool where he stood, one hand up against her high beams, the other one deep in his pants.

Head out the window, Nix yelled, "What are you doing here, Charlie?"

"Who's that?"

"It's me, Charlie, get over here."

Charlie shuffled over to Nix's car, throwing one leg forward, then the other.

"Why are you crab walking, Charlie?"

"Hello Gwendolyn, did you forget to shave?"

"Don't ever ask a woman that, Charlie."

"Okay."

"What are you doing here and where did you get that car?

"Oh, I'm here to see the King and that's Alfred's rental."

"I don't like the smell of this, Charlie."

"I don't either, Gwen, not a goddamn bit."

"So, what's he having you do?"

"The King needs his pills and booze. I'm carrying a contraption to deliver them. It's on my wiener, down my leg and around my ankle."

"Why would you do a thing like that, Charlie?"

"Because I'm easy to boss around. The Queen told me I had to do it or I'd lose my campsite and everyone would go hungry. Also, I can't say no. I know it's stupid and I'm going to get in trouble."

"But you're doing it anyway."

"Yeah."

"Well, no one's forcing you. No one has a gun to your head. This is your choice and if you get caught, don't blame anyone because you were too weak willed to stand up for yourself. "

"I'm a weak old drunk."

"You're not old, Charlie."

"That's funny, Gwen."

"Not really, now take that fucking thing off."

"The condom catheter, pill sleeve and booze cuff?"

"Get rid of the works. Put it back in the car and we'll throw it away later. We're going in there to see the King together."

"We are?"

"Yes, and you don't have to say a thing. Let me do the talking. There's only one thing I want you to do. There's a camera on the wall that's focused on the King's cell and there's a mirror on the wall behind the King. The camera picks up the reflection in the mirror. Got me so far?"

"Sure."

"You have to stand between me and the King, so I don't get picked up on camera in the mirror. If you see my reflection in the mirror, block me. Got it?"

"Yeah, I guess so."

"It's important, Charlie. And one more thing, no matter what I say, don't react to me. Act like I'm not there, no matter what anyone says, you don't say a thing. I'll explain it to you later."

"I'm in trouble, aren't I, Gwen?"

"No, you're not and won't be while I'm around."

"Okay. And don't worry, I won't react. I don't react. I can't react. That's how I get by. I take it. I take everything. I'm a punching bag, not a fighter."

The Fool and Nix walked into the police station at the same time. Nix held the pizza box up but never looked at the desk sergeant as she and the Fool got buzzed in. They walked across the station, detectives' empty desks on one side, beat cops' workstations on the other until they reached the desk right before the lock up. Nix flipped the fat grey switch on the wall and the bars slid open. She walked in the Fool's shadow and stopped behind him as they stood at another heavy barred steel door, waiting for the first one to close again.

The King was laying on a thin mattress on a bed bolted to the wall and floor. Still as he was, Nix saw the flash of his eye.

"What have we here? Is that Agent Nix with the Fool?" the King didn't look their way. He was looking straight up, "What a pair, what a fine pair you make. Did you know, Nix, that I made this fool the Fool?" The King turned his head their way, but didn't smile, "I broke you, Fool. There was something wrong. I reassembled you, like a good father would, like a caring father, like a real father would. You are who you are because of me, Fool, and me alone. Always remember that.

The King clasped his hands behind his neck, "But what I wonder, Fool, what I'm most curious about is whether you've been listening to this IRS bitch. It's puzzling to me why you would. You've been listening to this IRS cop-bitch, haven't you? You're a stupid Fool, so stupid to be listening to someone like her and I don't doubt you are.

"Well, Fool, I'll tell you this. You better keep your goddamn mouth shut, do you hear? Telling tales can work both ways. Who had more reason to kill Stan than you? No one, that's who. You killed Stan sure as I'm standing here, following him around everywhere, like a puppy dog. Then you find out, after all that time, after all the jokes and stories, that he was your real Pa. Stan was your real Pa and he didn't think enough of you to let you know. What a low man. What a rotten, selfish man. I don't hold it against you that you took his life. Stan was asking for it. You had to kill him, Fool. You had to do it. I'll testify that you had good reason. Maybe that way you won't get the death penalty."

The King sat up and got out of bed and walked over to the bars, "Works both ways, Fool, don't it. I can say you killed Stan just as easy as you can say that about me. See how it works? But one last thing. If we don't agree on how Stan died, who do you think everyone is going to believe, me or some looney bin mental patient?"

XXXII

The phone rang at seven AM.

"Zdravstvujtye," Sava answered.

"Yeah, ahh," Leo was nervous, "you speaking American today?"

"Okay."

"Did, ahhh, is everything okay?"

"Is okay."

"Can we see you in a little while so you can tell us more?"

"Of course, I am getting up."

"Can you get to the Boston Garden?"

"Whose garden?"

"North Station. It's where they play basketball, you know? The TD Bank Garden."

"Hmmmm, no know."

"It's where they play ice hockey."

"Why don't you say? Big Bad Bruins. Of course, I see you there. I am good hockey player, best in my village."

"We'll see you at the statue of Bobby Orr, outside North Station, in thirty minutes."

"Flying hockey player, do svidaniya, see you there."

"Thirty minutes."

"Da, da da."

As soon as Leo hung up the phone, Steiger peppered him with questions, "Did he do what he said he'd do? Did he hack Buffum's computer and send the porn to the IRS? Did he send it to the Boston cops? What'd he do? What'd he say?"

"I wasn't going to ask him over the phone. We'll see him in a few minutes. Ask him yourself, Steiger."

"Think we can trust him?"

"Don't you think it's kind of late for that? The time to worry about that would have been yesterday."

"I know, Leo. It's just that I'm nervous. I have a terrible feeling. I oughta be with Nix right now. She's got a screw loose, you know, or worse, and a wicked temper when it comes to Buffum."

"You do what you're supposed to do. She'll do what she's going to do. Now get in the car. I got a parking spot in the North End, behind my cousin's funeral parlor. It's a two-minute walk to the Garden."

Crossing Causeway, they saw Sava posing like airborne Bobby Orr only Sava wasn't made of bronze, had one foot on the ground, and was in street clothes. Indistinguishable. They talked for a few seconds and made their way across the street to a coffee shop.

Steiger complained, "This coffee sucks. Why didn't we go to the neighborhood? This place is for gibrones."

"We're not here for the coffee," Leo explained, "We're here to talk to Sava."

"Of course, that's why we're here, but since we're here and we're having coffee, don't you think it ought to be good coffee, not this shit. That's all I'm saying."

"So, Sava," Leo turned away, "what happened, how'd it go?"

"Okay, so I open computer and copy all the files into attachments, but I put the receivable and payable files first and never say a thing about them or the phony discount prices, banking records or nothing. Same with the ledgers for the phony companies Buffum owns. They are there to be opened and discovered, like a gift from Father Christmas. A puzzle easy to finish. Next I put the porn files, which are bigger even than I thought, and nasty too, many illegal, of course, and I add the live stream he has of the ladies' room and all the URLs for that sick 'The Girls' Room', pee and poo porn...."

"Back up a second, Sava," Steiger asked, intrigued, "what was that about live stream porn?"

Leo started laughing, "I forgot to tell you this, Steiger. Tell him, Sava."

"Mr. Buffum has a chat room subscription live feed of the ladies' room for the IRS offices I clean. He makes big money. Sometimes he narrates. I know his voice."

"Narrates?" asked Leo.

"Is high quality live feed," explained Sava. "Is full audio too, so you not just hear conversation, you hear every fart and flush. That's what he likes to narrate. There's one lady Buffum makes the most money from. They call her Ramrod."

Steiger and Leo locked eyes but neither said a word.

"Buffum hates Ramrod," Sava continued, "but he sells more Ramrod tee shirts and coffee mugs than any other stuff."

"Back up again," said Steiger. "What was that about merchandise?"

"One tee shirt says she pees standing up. Another says she's very bad girl, but the biggest seller is a silkscreen of her from back, head cocked, one leg up against a bathroom wall as she pees standing up. This one just says RAMROD."

"So, what did you do with this stuff, the attachments?" asked Leo.

"I take everything, even worst kind of snuff porn and very bad things, and all of that goes to the anonymous IRS Hotline site and the Boston Police and Detective Bureau tipster site and copies of everything to the IRS Homepage Suggestion Box, they call it. It is really a revenge box. Many people have access to the suggestion box so nobody is going to try to bury anything after it goes there. You have to think ahead. This will spread through IRS like forest fire of cancer. All it took me is seven minutes. Seven minutes! How about that?"

"That's great, Sava, just great. Anything else?" Leo asked.

"Not that I can think of. Do you have my money?"

Leo reached into Steiger's jacket pocket and pulled out a roll of bills, "This is seven fifty, Sava. We're going to pay the full thousand but we're short two fifty. I'll have it Monday. I know this looks unprofessional. I'm sorry. Thanks so much."

"Khorosho. I trust you. I'm not even going to count it until I get out the door. Just one more thing. I put terrorist sites on that govnyuk's computer and I send it, with everything else, to FBI and State Department and Homeland Security, who are motherfuckers about that."

Steiger's eyes widened. He stood up and said he had to go to the bathroom. Leo's jaw dropped, "You did what! We talked about this, Sava. I told you we don't want to mess with the FBI. I said that to you, Sava."

"Proschat, I know. I could not help myself. Now that ublyudok has FBI folder, a big FBI folder and Homeland Security too. State Department will cancel his passport. Of course, his job is over but he doesn't know. Police are sniffing his trail and soon he'll be in jail. I could not stop myself when I see that skinny smiling motherfucker in my head and before I know it, whoosh, he's got an FBI file. Is not even my fault. He is so bad my hands did it against my will."

"Forget the extra two-fifty, Sava," Leo shook his head.

"I thought maybe you might. So what? Was worth two-fifty to get that ublyudok my way, Russian way, long and slow. Forgive Sava, but long may this one suffer. Praise be to you, St. Bastard."

"We have to go, Sava. Not a word to anyone."

"Soblyudayte tish? I am Russian. I don't tell myself the truth. Of course, I be quiet. You be quiet. Come have drink."

"You just sent Steiger to the shitter with all that FBI talk. He practically lives there anyway. Are you proud of yourself?" Leo checked his watch and looked towards the bathrooms.

"I didn't know he had weak stomach. You should have told me."

"Do you always drink this early in the morning, Sava? I'm not being judgmental. I know you work nights. I'd just like to know."

"This is holy day of revenge. Is not ordinary day. Things are now, how you say, in balance. I would sacrifice pig or chicken but I need one to kill."

"We have to go, Sava. I'm going to call you tomorrow at seven and then at eight if you don't answer. We live or die together, Sava. We are in the same pot of soup. None of us want the pot to boil, right?"

"Is not what I want, Leo. I have what I want. I don't want anyone to boil except Mr. fucking Buffum."

"Good, and we'll talk every morning or maybe meet if we should."

"Yes, Leo, if you want."

"And if anyone talks to you about this say nothing. Tell them you want your lawyer." Leo pushed a business card into Sava's hand, "This is who you call if someone comes to talk to you. Got it?"

"He is good lawyer?"

"He's not an idiot."

"Okay, lawyer on card will take care of me."

"Lawyer on card will help, Sava, if he can."

"Hey, Leo, I want to live good long life. I want to marry American girl and have family. I am not crazy and if I was little crazy, I have taken care of that by sending it away on a bad wind to darken my enemy's shore. Now is time to thank God and ask forgiveness for being mean and not turning other cheek. Heavenly Father, I swear and so do Leo and Steiger that we are done fucking with Buffum so don't punish us and don't let FBI know we stir pot. I put money in the church. Amen. Make the sign, Leo. Does Steiger know how to make the sign?"

XXXIII

I leaned into the bars, Gwen behind me, the King just inches from my face. I said, and this time I really said, "You shouldn't have said those things about Stan and me, Majesty. I loved Stan more than anyone in the world. What you said was wrong."

I was watching for Gwen in the mirror when I started talking, so I kept on talking and blocking the camera from seeing her in the mirror. For some reason, having Gwen behind me and watching for her in that mirror made it easier for me to talk. It kept me from thinking about what I was saying. I said, "But you know, King, in a way you're right about Stan's death. I am responsible. Even though I loved him more than anyone, I let him down. He expected better of me and so did I. He deserved better."

"That's right, Fool, he deserved better," the King nodded.

"It was the smell of Stan I remembered first. I could tell him from his smell. I could tell who he was the first day I knew that I was me. Does that make sense? Stan had that rolling walk too, remember King? He walked like a cowboy or a roofer. You could hear him coming."

"Keep talking, Fool."

"You could always hear the roll of him. When I was a little boy I waited for that sound to get to my door. I used to try and walk like him. Sometimes Stan would ask me to walk like him and I'd try and everyone would laugh and I'd laugh too and Stan would laugh but mostly his eyes would crinkle and he'd smile at me. That's the difference between then and now. I still make people laugh, but you won't catch me laughing. I don't even smile. What's to laugh at? Who to laugh with? Nothing and nobody, that's what and who."

"Poor Fool," said the King without meaning it, "full of regret now, aren't you?"

"When Mama took to her bed she'd be lost to me and the world. I would pray to be taken away from the loneliness of being with her in that little trailer. Back then I didn't know how to pray. I didn't even know who to pray to, so I prayed to Stan. After a while he would come by, pick me up, and take me to his trailer. I never would want to go home. I was afraid of the loneliness, even when Mama was better. I'd feel bad about it, for sure, but not bad enough to go. I still feel bad, bad about everything."

"And you should, Fool, you should," the King all but cooed.

"And Stan had a way of explaining things so I understood. And he was calm and had a smile most of the time and that's what I remember. I took it for granted that he was the one who made everything work, even me. And I can't forgive myself for his death."

"Well, Fool," the King put his hands on the bars next to mine and smiled, "what's important is you admit it now. That's the important thing. Just make sure you tell all the po-po what you told us here tonight, that you killed Stan and you're sorry. Tell agent Nix that you killed Stan and tell the fuckin' warden of this fuckin' dog pound that you're the goddamnn cotton candy killer. Tell them now and get me the fuck out of here!"

"I didn't kill Stan, Majesty. You killed him, you and you alone. I saw you do it. I just feel responsible. I could have saved him. I should have saved him. He saved me many times. But I didn't kill him. You know you did that."

"The hell you say. You're full of lies," the King sneered.

"I watched you go up to that cotton candy machine, King. Clear as day, I saw you stick your hand in the Skippy jar and wipe it on the centrifuge. I saw you do that and I saw you run away and hide next to the generator at the Ferris wheel. I knew what you were up to. I knew better than anyone that Stan would be along any minute and he'd climb in that machine and at some point he'd turn it on. You knew it too. That's why you did what you did."

"Shut your lying mouth, you damn, crazy fool. You're a fuckin' mental case."

"I didn't do anything. That's my crime. I just crouched there like a coward, hiding between two food trucks. I didn't call out to save Stan. He would have saved me. I was too afraid. Too afraid of you, King. I don't deserve to be Stan's son."

"You better watch what you say, Fool. Watch what you say about me unless you want the same thing that happened to that asshole Stan to happen to you. I didn't kill no one but that don't mean I can't. I'll be out of here soon enough and

I'll get you. You know it. These bars won't be between us much longer. I'm going to kill you hard. I'll piss on your dying body, Fool. Then I'll throw it in the garbage where the rats will get you"

Not listening to the King's threats, I kept talking and watching out for Gwen in the mirror, "Two days before Stan died it was my birthday. Stan got me a steak and cheese, my favorite, and stuck a candle in it and wished me happy birthday. He told me I was now a man. Some man I turned out to be. I whimpered and ran. I hid. In that way, King, I am responsible for Stan's death, just as sure as you are. But it was you, Highness, who did the killing. It was you who wiped peanut butter on the centrifuge and, once Stan got in, you threw the latch on the cotton candy machine doors so he couldn't get out. So, you sealed Stan's fate, King, and sealed mine too and you know what, you sealed your own as well. Yours too, King, yours too."

"That's a crazy story, Fool. You got a hell of an imagination. You must have made that up in the mental hospital to make yourself feel better about killing Stan. I saw you kill Stan but I never said a word. I protected you even though I saw you do it. This is how you repay me?"

"When you saw me, King, I was hiding between the food trucks and you set off after me. We ran through the cars and trucks and the tents and trailers. I was trying to circle around to get back to Stan but you were too smart, driving me farther and farther afield. I couldn't get back in time. You knew I wouldn't. When I did get back I saw his hand lying against the glass and I knew I failed him. Stan was dead and the stink of death was on me and on you too, King, stronger on you. You still smell like it. You smell like a murderer."

"You shut your goddamn mouth, you goddamn mental case. You shut it right now."

"I got to let this out, King. The time has come. Ever since Stan died, I've spent my whole life holding it in, like that story about the boy and the dike. Just like him, I can't hold it no more. It's coming out, like it or don't. It's bigger than me and bigger than you, too, King. You shouldn't have started talking about it. You should have let it be. Only good it's going to do is get you locked up in prison for the rest of your life. I don't like it no more than you."

"Don't worry about me, asshole," the King sneered. "I see Nix behind you. She put these thoughts in your head. You got nothing. You're a killer and a crazy boy and you killed Stan. They never should have let you out of that nuthouse. No one will ever believe you. No one should. And Nix is a violent psycho, as everyone knows. She's had it in for me because she thinks I cheated the IRS. And since she can't get me on that she's trying to frame me for murder. I'm going to walk away from this, but you ain't and neither is she."

Agent Nix put the pizza box on the floor and had the Fool kick it over to the bars where the King stood. She had the Fool roll the soda over too, but the King got upset.

"I tell those guys every fucking time, no two-liter bottles. I can't squeeze them through the bars."

XXXIV

When traveling, Buffum wore slip on shoes and casual clothes. Today he was Tommy from the ankles up but below he wore a pair of lustrous, hand tooled, soft leather Italian loafers that he picked up from a little shop in Georgetown. He didn't spend money like this back home, he consoled himself, and checked the thirty-six thousand-dollar Rolex that he bought somewhere in DC. Twenty more minutes, Buffum told himself, before I'm home and I don't know how I feel about that. He liked being himself when he wasn't.

He'd been thinking of retirement. He had more than enough money, enough for any of the disasters he saw coming and wondered why he put up with the aggravation of people? Agent Nix came to mind and he thought better about returning home. There were still things that had to be done, and grinding Nix down was at the top of the list. He wanted her broken. If her suffering has a flavor, he indulged himself, what will it taste like? He smiled a satisfied smile, assuring himself that she will pay ten-fold, as promised somewhere in the Bible. Yes, Buffum smiled, she'll pay for everything, every smart remark, all the laughter and the jokes, Steiger too.

***

Like it or not, no matter how he may have felt about it, Buffum was landing in Boston. And waiting for him in the concourse beyond the gate were four Massachusetts State Troopers, two Federal Marshals, an Investigator from Treasury and another from the U.S. Attorney's Office in Boston. Front and center were a couple of FBI agents. You could tell they were FBI because they were FBI. They all stood in a rough circle, arms crossed, not saying much, but looking imposing.

At the gate, leaning against the plasti-ceramic airport wall, were two East Boston police officers. They were there because whoever gets scooped at the airport gets locked up in the East Boston slammer and arraigned in the East Boston District Court the earliest weekday thereafter. Unlike the gaggle of suits and sunglasses on the concourse, this wasn't their first airport scoop. Everyone at the East Boston station gets a shot. Some of the calls were suspected terrorists. The husbands, wives and partners of these cops grew apprehensive whenever it was their loved one's turn. The cops liked it even less.

"Hey Sally," asked Officer d'Orsay Juarez, "what are we here for and tell me this ain't no terrorist?"

"I don't know, d'Orsay," answered Custanzu 'Sally' Salvatore, her partner, "it could be but, then again, you know, it might not."

"What have we got over there," Juarez nodded toward the important looking cluster of law enforcement. "Let's see, there are the Staties, of course, and FBI and those other suits are feds of some kind, but I don't see Homeland so maybe not terrorists. If not terrorists, then who?"

Sally turned to look at Juarez, "Or what."

"Yeah, or what, I mean look at all those feds over there. Except for the FBI, who do they really belong to?"

"The fuck would I know, d'Orsay? No one tells us shit. 'Course, we're the first ones to take down these pirate travel motherfuckers, every time, but no one tells us shit."

"True, Sally, true. But hey, do you think those guys are standing kind of far back. I mean, they're on the concourse. Why would that be?"

"Yeah, they are kinda far back. Could be a reason but, you know, maybe there ain't. What do you think?"

"What I think, Sally, is maybe some of those suits are from the CDC down in Atlanta."

"What would the CDC be doing here?"

"What do you think, Sally? Go ahead and say it or do you want me to?"

"You mean Ebola? That's what you mean, isn't it?"

"I didn't say that, Sally, but I'm saying something like that. I think there's something new, something worse."

"No, Mama, no, worse than Ebola? Fuck me, they say you bleed through your eyes from Ebola. Imagine that Juarez, bleeding from the eyes? What could be worse?"

"I don't know but maybe that's why they're standing back there and we couldn't be any closer."

"Fuckin' feds, I got a bad feeling about this, d'Orsay."

***

The landing was as seamless as Buffum could remember. He checked his Rolex, twenty minutes on the nose. He thought he'd have a veal chop tonight with a strawberry, cashew, and kale salad and a nice rosé. Maybe make time for the gym. But before he could consider this any further he felt a hand on his shoulder.

"Would you come with me, Mr. Buffum, so we might deplane ahead of the others," the flight attendant smiled.

"Well, thank you very much," Buffum was flattered.

As he tried to remove his carry on from the storage space above his seat an arm reached out from behind the flight attendant and shut it.

"You can get that later, sir," said a faceless voice from the planisphere, but it really seemed to promise nothing of the sort.

It seemed to promise trouble, and not just going without toiletries trouble. 'What could this be about?' wondered Buffum, 'What's going on? Am I in trouble? Has something happened at work? Has someone died? Got to call Mama.'

Buffum walked ahead of his shadows, out the passenger door and up the skyway. He wondered whether it was too late to call Mama and just as he was about to enter the airport he shook his right arm to encourage the bracelet of his Rolex to fall towards the back of his hand. He liked the look and the feel.

Officers Juarez and Salvatore saw something else. Juarez dropped to one knee and aimed a boxy pistol-like thing at Mr. Buffum's chest and two little arrows trailing wires headed his way. Salvatore stood behind her with his service revolver drawn, both hands on his weapon. Buffum had time to think, 'Oh no', but not much thereafter. He left his feet and pinwheeled backwards, back arching before finally striking his head on the metal skyway.

"Is he breathing?" asked Officer Salvatore.

Not getting too close, Juarez leaned forward, "Yeah, he's breathing but you better call an ambulance anyway." Now a little closer, but still a safe distance, she added, "Hmmm, he's spasming and there's froth on his lips. Hey Sally, is that normal with a tasing?"

"I think so. I think that's fine, expected even. 'Course, I could be wrong. Don't get too close, d'Orsay. Let's let the EMTs handle this."

"Look at those useless assholes, Sally, still standing on the concourse. This guy must be infected with something awful. Hey, that was a watch we saw on his right wrist."

"Watch, gun, it was dark, d'Orsay. How were we supposed to know? No one tells us shit."

She got a little closer, "Don't people usually wear them on the left? Wow, nice watch. Fifty bucks it don't make it to the station."

"A hundred says the shoes don't either."

XXXV

Nix and the Fool left the Horseshoe Falls Police Station and stopped in the visitors' parking lot to talk.

"Hey Gwen?"

"What is it, Charlie?"

"Thanks."

"Don't thank me. I didn't do anything. You, on the other hand, grew a pair. How do you even walk with those giant things?"

"You know what you did, Gwen. I'd have gotten caught smuggling booze and pills into that jail if you hadn't stopped me. I'm sure that's a felony everywhere. And I never would have been able to talk back to the King like I did if you hadn't stood behind me. I ain't had anyone in my corner since Stan died."

"Where are you off to now, Charlie?"

"Got to get the Hyundai back to Alfred but first I have to pick up a cheeseburger for him."

"I know just the place, right down the street."

"Sure, if it ain't far. Alfred's got an eye for the gas gauge."

"Follow me."

One thing Horseshoe Falls had was ample parking. Nix and the Fool parked right outside the Athena and as they walked in Nix said to the downcast pizza chef, "I'm sorry about the twenty-five-cent tip. That was rotten and I was unnecessarily an asshole. This is what I should have left," Nix passed him a five, "and my friend, Charlie, wants to order a cheeseburger to go. Anything with that Charlie?"

"Fries and a two-liter Diet Coke."

"For a dollar more," said the weary Greek pizza chef, putting down his phone, " I can make those cheesy fries. Makes all the difference in the world." He shambled over to the grille.

"Alfred's worth cheesy fries," answered the Fool, "go ahead. How about a cup of coffee, Nix, I mean, Gwen? Or a cold drink?"

"I could use a real drink."

"Me too," agreed the Fool, "Want to come back to my camp? I have liquor."

"Why you rascal, Charles, the way you talk. But I could use a drink right now. Hey, excuse me, Mr. Athena. I never asked for your name. I seem to have no manners at all."

"Lesous Gostanias is my name, and yours?"

"Call me Nix."

"Strange name for a lovely woman."

"That's not exactly the song you were singing an hour ago."

"It was the light, the night, and the shadows. And in my country, the birthplace of Western thought and the home of Aphrodite, a whisker on a woman is not an unappealing thing."

"You have a way with words, Gostanias."

"I am Greek, from Thessaloniki."

"May I call you Lesous?"

"I would be pleased if you would. And you?"

"Just Nix, but Lesous, if you have a bottle of something with a little kick somewhere behind that counter I'd be interested. You must or you'd go mad."

"I have nothing but a bottle of grappa, which I sometimes enjoy under the stars, if it's quiet."

"Three fingers for each of us, on me," Nix slapped down a twenty.

"I don't have license for this. I would need Common Victualer's license for to serve booze and I don't have one, not even beer and wine."

"Then here's five more bucks," Nix peeled off more bills, "and forty-seven cents, if I can find them.

"Just forget the money," said Gostanias as he filled three cups, "Yasou!"

"Life in prison," said Nix touching Styrofoam cups with Lesous and the Fool.

"To Stan," said the Fool, who started coughing even before the grappa hit the back of his throat.

"Edo," Lesous joined in, "and here is your cheeseburger, cheesy fries and Diet Coke. That's...."

The Fool reached for his wallet, but Nix restrained him, "Lesous, here's a fifty," interrupted Nix. "I wrote my number on it. Take out for the food and keep the rest. I'd like you to call me sometime, like next week. We'll go out and, if I'm broke, we'll use what's left from this. There's something sad about your eyes, Lesous, sad but not pathetic. Maybe you can tell me how they got that way?"

Nix followed Charlie all the way back to his camp. Waiting for them was a legless angry drunk sitting at a dying campfire, one hand holding a blanket to his chest and the other wielding an empty bottle of rum.

"You motherfucking Fool, I could have died of exposure out here. My nerves are shot with worry. I can't walk on these stumps and I crawl for no man. You're a sonofabitch."

"Easy, Alfred, ..."

"Don't come no closer, Fool," Alfred cracked the belly of the bottle against a rock, the jagged neck flashing in his hand.

"Cut that out, Alfred. What's wrong with you? I'm ashamed of you, and in front of company. Drop that bottle right now. It wasn't me paying you to take me to the hoosegow to smuggle drugs and booze to his Majesty, was it? It was the Queen and you were supposed to drive me so you could report back if I got caught, maybe when I got caught, so cut the bullshit. And I went to the trouble of getting you a cheeseburger. I must be crazy."

"A cheeseburger?"

"And cheesy fries and Diet Coke."

"Ahh, Fool, cheesy fries! I'm sorry. I must ha' been hangry. I was worried I'd never get back to my motel."

"My friend came with me in case Anquan didn't show up. She has a car and can help us get you where you got to go."

"Ahh, Fool, I'm in the Roach Motel all the way out by the reservoir."

"That'd be the Town Crier, right? We'll get you there, Alfred, don't worry. Have your cheeseburger."

"Thanks, Fool. Matter of fact, Anquan is spending the night with his girl so he ain't coming back tonight. Fuck Anquan."

"Yeah, but maybe you ought to get this car tricked out for the disabled, like he said, so you won't need anyone onboard for brakes and gas. Maybe you can keep a few friends that way."

"It's a fuckin' rental. I'd have to wait two weeks for one of them handicapped cars, probably a van. I can't wait that long and I ain't driving no van. They're for cripples."

After Alfred finished his cheeseburger and licked the queso off his fingers, they drove down the highway, Alfred resting his ass on the Fool's left shoulder, burping, pointing, and barking commands all the way. After they got to the motel the Fool got in Nix's Toyota and they drove back to the campsite, where he stirred the ashes and got the fire going.

Then he asked, "Gin or gin? I got both. That is, unless Alfred got into more than the rum. Wait a minute, happy days, there's a bottle of rum that escaped my notice."

"Rum sounds good, Charlie, what a night."

"Yeah, and it ain't over. Boy, oh boy, shit won't stay buried, no matter how deep you dig. Best you can do is try and cover the smell. Don't the past catch up to everyone."

"Ain't that the truth," Nix agreed. "Looks like it caught up with that King of yours."

"I have to wonder what it would have been like if Stan told everyone I was his son. Maybe we wouldn't have had this King problem. Maybe Stan would still be here."

The fire was healthy but Nix threw on more brush and some wet split pine so the smoke would keep the bugs away, "You're wondering if Stan loved you, or loved you enough. I get that. You want it so bad, but he's dead, so you're never going to know this thing straight up. But that doesn't mean you can't work it out. Did this man hurt you? I mean, how did he treat you?"

"Wonderful, and we were best of friends, inseparable. He taught me everything I know. He was patient, kind and there when I needed him."

"Did he use you or take advantage of you? Was he a good man?"

"He was the best. I wouldn't be here without him. I wouldn't be anything without him."

"Then there's your answer. You just never got it from him in words. He must have had his reasons. Maybe your Mom wouldn't let him tell you or maybe he was waiting for the right time. Who knows? Whether he loved you or not has been right in front of you, Charlie, all along. You just have to take the risk and open your heart to let his love in. Unanswered questions aren't the worst thing in the world," Nix laid down, hands behind her head and eyes on the sky, "Far from it, so stop wondering, Charlie, and start thinking about the good things that happened, all the good you got from Stan. Think about the little things."

"That's easy for you to say, Nix."

"No, Charlie, it isn't. Just because you've been hurt doesn't mean others haven't. I had a father. I always knew he was my father and he lived with us. He answered all the questions I ever had. In one answer he had my mother by the hair while he drove her face into the linoleum floor, over and over, while he was watching reruns on TV. When he was done I couldn't tell who she was except by her clothes. He raped me the first time when I was eight. He spit on me when he was done and called me a whore. He sold me to some men in a bar one night but my poor Mom grabbed me and ran before they could pick me up. He broke my arm four times, spiral fractures. We never went to the same hospital twice."

"Oh, Gwen,.."

"Don't say anything, Charlie. I'm not done, but even when I am, don't waste your pity on me. It's not appreciated. Pity doesn't work for me. I'm telling you this for another reason. Everything I said is true, every word and more, much more. My father answered every question I ever had."

Nix's eyes were open, hands locked behind her head. She was looking up at the stars through the grey pall of smoke and let out a long sigh, "And still......," Nix took a moment, "And still I miss him. Imagine that? Everything else and that too. What in the fuckin' world, Charlie? When does anything ever come to an end? When in the goddamn fucking world does it come to an end. That's what I'm waiting for. Maybe we should be grown in bottles. I don't know, Charlie, pass the rum."

XXXVI

Steiger flushed one last time and stood on shaky legs, "Whoa!"

Leo called, "You okay in there, Steiger?

"Legs went a little numb. That's a robust flush you have in this crapper, a fast fill too. That's a dependable toilet, overall."

"Glad you approve but you're not paying the water bill. C'mon, get out of there. I don't like you in my bathroom so long."

"You'll thank me for those flushes. Listen, Leo, my bowels are in an uproar."

"Don't fucking do this, Steiger."

"Do what?"

"Do what you do. Don't impose your life in the crapper or your sore ass as a justification for anything. Don't sympatha-bully me. That's passive bullying, Steiger, the most insidious form of bullying."

"What are you talking about? I was just going to tell you that my excretory function is excited. This is a sign. My waste disposal system is like radar for trouble. It's like my ass can smell the future."

Leo nodded distractedly, "No kidding."

"Yeah, Leo, and right now my ass is acting as badly as it ever has, like it's trying to get my attention, trying to tell me to be careful or something."

"Your ass is talking to you now? Oh boy," Leo shook his head, "what's it trying to tell you, use thicker ply?"

Steiger became thoughtful, "I'm not sure, Leo. But I think it's trying to tell me something bad is going to happen if we don't do something fast."

"What does your ass know that you don't?"

"My ass knows very little, but what it knows, it knows."

"Get out of the bathroom, Steiger, if you want to keep talking to me."

Steiger opened and shut the door fast, "It's not an intellectual thing, Leo. It's more primitive than that, maybe something as simple as my digestive and excretory functions reacting to stressors of which I'm otherwise unaware. Who knows? Who cares? I just know my ass in turmoil is an oracle. It's never wrong. It never makes mistakes. It knows when trouble's coming."

"What kind of trouble is coming?"

"I'm not certain, but I was in paroxysms of agony when I was thinking about Sava."

"Yeah, what about Sava?"

"As my knotted bowels were wrenching and twisting I had a vision, a vision born in agony. It was a dark night. You were there. We were in a train yard. Freezing rain was pelting us. Sava was running naked down a train track and a train was closing on him fast. He was hollering our names, crying for help. I lost sight of him as the whistle blew, steam rose and clouds rolled in. The train screamed as it disappeared into a tunnel. That's it. My ass won't get more specific."

"What does it mean, Steiger?"

"Hell, if I know, but when my ass acts this way, I listen. Sava's up to something is all I can tell you. I think it has to do with the file dump on Buffum. My ass is belching as I tell you this."

"We don't talk to Sava until tomorrow." Leo equivocated. "Think we ought to go find him?"

"He's up to something, Leo. Do you have his address?"

"It's somewhere here, Steiger."

"I don't know why we bother. Nix will probably execute the King; on his royal knees, BLAM, right between the eyes. That's a scary thing because if she murders him I'm equally responsible. It's called the Felony Murder Rule. I read all about it. Why bother with anything? Stopping Sava isn't going to stop her from killing the King and sending me to prison, maybe you, too."

"Get it together, Steiger. We aren't going to prison."

"What are we going to do, Leo?"

"We're going to Chelsea and see if Sava is home, okay? If he isn't we go to a couple of the Russian bars. If he's not there, I don't know. Maybe we wait."

"Okay."

"Good. Change your undies and get a jacket. We have to leave."

***

Sava walked to the Harvard Square T station. He'd been auditing courses at local colleges and universities through the Chelsea Neighborhood Center. He 'd taken an electrical engineering course at Northeastern, courses on coding and some on data systems at Boston University. Today he was returning from MIT, where he was auditing a class on the politi-cultural weaknesses of electronic security systems in progressive political democracies. He had a smile on his face as he hopped on the Red Line, considering the uses to which he could put this knowledge. Sava got off near North Station and took the commuter line to Chelsea, where he disappeared, popping up in a rooftop Russian cafe a little later.

A dumpy old man named Otto with a cascade of chins sat silently at the bar, watching Sava have a coffee and two splashes of warm bad vodka. He waited until Sava's face screwed up and he slammed the second glass down before signaling him over.

"So, Sava, how is probation?"

"Parole, Uncle Vanya, is called parole and is wonderful. I so wish you could enjoy too. In ideal world, Uncle, one day I'd like to graduate to probation. Happy days ahead!"

"Don't call me that."

"Call you what?"

"Uncle Vanya, it is disrespectful and only a fool wears an anchor on one leg."

"It is a monitoring ankle bracelet I wear all the time, even in the shower, so I don't go back to prison."

"There were two men looking for you today. What are you up to?"

"What kind of men?"

"Americans, not police."

"I'm not up to anything. What did they say?"

"They said you were up to something."

"What did you say?"

"I told them I didn't know you, of course. They said it was important. Two Americans, one short, the other squeamish."

"Did the squeamish one need the toilet?"

"Not the short one, yes."

"I know those guys. They are nothing and nobody."

"We don't want American trouble here, Sava."

"These guys are not trouble. These guys are friends. I don't know for how long, but they are now. Where are they?"

"They're in the Thai joint."

"I'll go down and take care of them, Uncle..."

"Otto, you clown, call me Otto."

Leo had a long thin drink in his fat little hand, occasionally finding the straw with his lips and sipping. Steiger was playing Keno and holding his own. He had a cordial of crème de menthe in front of him with a Metamucil chaser. There were no windows in this place. Leo was wondering if they made acoustic ceiling tiles that could suppress gun shots and the screams of the tortured. Smiling, Steiger looked up, holding a winning ticket as Sava walked through the door and over to their table.

"You guys looking for me?"

"Yes, Sava, thank you for coming over." Leo couldn't be nicer, "Have a seat. Want some Pad Thai?"

"You embarrass me in my neighborhood and act like all is fine. Is hard enough here without you, friend. What do you want from me?"

"I'm sorry, Sava, but Steiger has an ass that knows a thing or two and it thinks that you maybe didn't tell us the whole truth about everything you did the other day."

"Ahh, you mean back when you were my partners? Back then? We worked well but that is over now."

"I hope not, Sava. Steiger and I are playing the long game. We live here. He has a job and I have a business. We couldn't leave here easily and don't want to. What we have to know is whether you told us everything you did or if you've gone and done something else to a certain guy."

"I told you everything I did that night."

"Yeah, but did you do anything after that?" Leo persisted.

"When we were not partners?"

"At any time did you?"

"Like what?"

Steiger joined in, "Did you file anything else against Buffum?"

"Why do you ask me that? Because I am Russian? Because I speak bad English? Why?"

"So, you did! I knew it, Sava," Steiger gloated, "I knew it, I knew it. What did you file?"

"Was nothing. Was Whistleblower Complaint, deemed credible in hours. I figure we did what we did for good reasons, we are happy and that is over. Done. But if there is a pay-out for turning in this crook, I am all for it." Sava looked around before saying, "What is harm if I get to squeeze a certain comrade's yaichk dry and get paid for it."

"So," started Steiger, "there will be money coming your way from filing this Whistleblower Complaint?"

"Is possible, yes, but that I never thought of. At first I only thought one last kick to the nut sack would feel so good."

"You're going to find yourself in the middle of a shitstorm if you did this," added Leo.

"Is done. The sow is in the beet field, but I'll never mention you. Never. That is promise on my Russian soul."

"You can say that Sava," nodded Leo, "and you might even mean it, but in the end you'll give us up."

"Not me, Leo. I did this by myself, that's what I'll say."

"You'll give us up, Sava, because you'll have to. Because that's how it works."

"Call it off, Sava," Steiger leaned over the table in a more awkward than aggressive way. "If they find out you laced Buffum's computer with porn and then turned him in you'll be looking at fifteen to twenty. Takes big balls to gamble with twenty years of your life, Sava. And you'll need luck for things to work out for you. How's your luck been lately? Is there anyone you know that can depend on luck? No, that's why they call it luck."

"Listen, Sava," Leo picked up the narrative, "Steiger's saying it nice. I'm saying it real. You spill your guts about us and I let the government know you seeded Buffum's computer, which means you do your time and then get deported to Russia, Sava, back to Russia. I'll do it."

"Easy, Leo, easy" Steiger looked back at Sava, "What we want to say is..."

"We have pistols at heads of each other."

"Yes, Sava, exactly, pistols at heads of each other."

"You and Steiger have your worries but they are not the same as mine. Me, I am convicted felon, sex criminal, no less, on parole. I wear ankle bracelet and stay in a shit rooming house unless I am working or at school. Where do I get job? How I live?"

Steiger said, "I don't know, Sava, but there are programs...and workshops."

"There are no jobs for Russian speaking felon on parole, okay? That's it. That's fact. Only job is cleaning offices and giving someone my money. I have to be, ahh, ...is word for this....ahh, enterprising, yes? So, I file Whistleblower Complaint. What does Russian felon on parole have to lose?"

"That's asking for trouble, Sava, saying you got nothing to lose." Leo was shaking his head, "There's always something to lose, Sava. Don't fool yourself. We got to go now. If you have to get in touch with us call this number and leave a message. Okay? Bye, Sava."

"Yeah, bye, Sava," Steiger got up and followed Leo to the door. Once outside he said, "What did you think of that, Leo?"

"We're screwed, totally fucked," whined Leo angrily. "Sava's going to feed us to the feds. There are going to be interrogations and search warrants. The legal fees are going to choke us. Then we're going to get killed by the smut mob before the feds can send us to prison."

"About my ass, Leo, I mean what do you think of that? I told you my ass is never wrong," Steiger held a tight smile, "Admit it, Leo, never wrong."

XXXVII

Nix walked in the front door of the Horseshoe Falls Police Department, past the snoozing Desk Sergeant and into Chief Cindy Beauchamp's office.

"Hey Chief, are we still going to the range?"

"Oh, Gwen, how are you? Geez, I'm sorry. I've had my nose in this paperwork. It'll be great to get over there and blast the shit out of something."

"Maybe you ought to cut down on the coffee."

"Maybe I ought to get a new job. C'mon, let's go."

As they were bouncing down a rutted dirt road in the chief's 4X4, Nix asked, "Why would you mention changing jobs? I'd think that in the world of local law enforcement, you've arrived. You're the chief law enforcement officer in this town, which means this area. There's no higher place to go except to a bigger town or city and both will have their own problems. What's so rough about Horseshoe Falls?"

"Things aren't what they seem, Gwen. This Department of mine has been staffed generationally. Know what that means, generationally?" the Chief's head was swiveling from the road to Nix and back again.

"Easy, Cindy."

"Sorry, it makes me upset."

"I suppose," Nix replied, "it means people are born to a job. The father dies and the son or daughter takes his place. It's feudal that way."

"It's reverse feudalism, Nix. I'm the one that's powerless. This department is full of fuck ups and bad cops. What few good officers I have find a way to leave. For example, there were six firefighters injured at King Henry's Faire the day we went to serve that warrant. Only days later four of the firefighters filed for accidental disability retirement and four of my officers, all the good ones, put in for their jobs. Not one of them said a word to me first. They simply want out."

"I'm sure that sucks, Cindy, but this is America; land of the free to change jobs and home of the inconsiderate."

"I know and I'm sorry to be poor mouthing. I don't like it in others. And I know firefighting pays better, has a better union, so better benefits. And being a firefighter is more respectable than being a cop, especially in this town. But these are my four best. The only ones worth their salt. Did I mention that one of my sergeants has Alzheimer's disease? He told me himself. He says it's in the early stages. A touch, he actually said, and he'll let me know if it begins to affect the job."

"He could forget, Cindy. You're going to have to jump on that."

"There's more, there's worse, two of my patrolmen and the high school resource officer have gotten teenage girls pregnant, all in a year and a half. These are married men with families, carelessly ruining the lives of the citizens of the town they are sworn to protect. They are doing this behind a badge and all this has happened since I've been here."

"That's fucked up, Cindy."

"There's worse, my Captain, who I like and thought I knew, is under investigation by the Attorney General for misappropriation of the assets of the estate of a ninety-two-year-old woman, a recluse. I thought she was his great aunt. I get sick to my stomach thinking about it. He wrote her notes in which he calls her pussy, 'mumsy'."

"However bad this story gets, Chief, that is the politest term I've ever heard for gash, stuffy and whimsical at once."

"Demoralizing is what it is, Gwen. He's my most dependable officer and someone I called a friend. Full body targets okay? Let's see, I got head shots too, and bulls eyes, or what?"

"Head shots are fine for me. Nice range, Cindy. What are you shooting?"

"Desert Eagle Fifty."

"Nice weapon."

"What did you bring?"

"Just my gun, a Glock Twenty," Nix chatted as she chambered a round, "What you need are some police to protect people from the cops."

"I was thinking about just that, Gwen. The foxes are in the henhouse. That's what makes it hard. Watch me blast the fuck out of this target. We caught the Mayor's son stealing drugs from the Evidence Room. We caught him three times. He had a key and probably still has one. None of my cops ever showed for trial. Have you ever gone through the Massachusetts Police Academy, Gwen?"

"Excuse me?"

"If you were to work here you'd have to have graduated from the Academy."

"Are you offering me a job?"

"I'm trying to find out if you'd be interested."

"I graduated from the Academy and then trained with the Secret Service because the IRS is Treasury. I'm qualified, if that's what you're asking. Where I am on any list, I don't know. But why are you asking this? I mean, you know how I operate. At least you have an idea. Being honest, I don't know if I'd hire me. At least I wonder sometimes."

"Don't sell yourself short, Nix. I can't get the tree stumps that draw paychecks around here to do anything. You're not like them. You're the opposite of them. I'm not naive. I know being around you won't be easy. You're hard-headed, single minded even, but I'm desperate. I need a gunslinger."

"Let's hear more about how I'm the opposite of them."

"There'll be a price to pay in headaches with you but that will be worth it if you do what you do and be a straight shooter. And don't lie to me. So, what do you say?"

"Two things first, Cindy. I have a partner. You met him. He was wearing a silly vest."

"Not the little guy?"

"No, the guy who dove into the dry moat."

"Oh, yeah, him."

"I'd like to bring him with me. You haven't seen his best. He'd be great in Vice, a real asset. He's not stupid, despite appearances."

"Yeah, Gwen, I'd have to think about that. What's the second thing?"

"How firm are you about lying? I mean, was that just something you had to say? I'm asking because old habits die hard. Now I'm going to shatter the glabella on that target at a hundred."

"You can try, Gwen," Cindy reloaded, "But I'm going to fucking destroy the forehead boss on mine at a hundred. Winner buys drinks."

Nix had to call Steiger and have him put money in her account because Cindy liked strippers, country western bars, trendy appetizers, and expensive drinks. And Cindy could drink.

XXXVIII

Nix answered her phone, immediately saying, "Don't use my name. Don't use any names. Say what you want and keep it brief."

"It's me, Nix," Steiger whispered breathlessly.

"What part of don't use my name didn't you get?"

"I didn't use my name, Nix. Oh! Damn. Sorry, Nix, I mean, ahhh, Patty, sorry Pat."

"Say nothing else," said Nix, enunciating each word.

"Okay."

"That means say nothing, just listen."

"I am."

"Meet me at our friend's place. The place with the attractive cop on the corner. Do you understand? Say yes or no."

"How could I forget?"

"In twenty."

"Make it thirty. I have to go to the can."

Just as Leo was pulling out the keys to lock the front door of his building, Nix leaned on the Toyota's horn and didn't let up until Leo and Steiger stepped into the street.

"Get in," Nix instructed. Leo got right in the back, Steiger walked leisurely around and got in the front. Nix pulled out fast and headed for the huge rotary at the junction of routes 60,16, 1, and an on ramp to I 93 South. She drove around the traffic circle twice to check for tails.

Reasonably satisfied, Nix turned to face Leo and said, "I'll cut your nuts off if you let Steiger anywhere near a phone again. You're responsible for him and don't forget."

"I won't be responsible for Steiger," Leo said, head down, eyes up, "so why don't you just cut 'em off now. Save me the worry and you the trouble. I'm not getting paid enough to do any of this."

"This isn't about getting paid anymore," Nix was speaking to Steiger too, "This is about staying alive and out of prison. I counted on you, Leo, to be a stabilizing influence. What a disappointment. I think you're worse than Steiger."

"Stop it, you two," Steiger interrupted, "Nix, take that back and drive someplace we can talk. Leo, tell Nix about Sava."

"What about Sava?" Nix wanted to know.

"Sava filed anonymous complaints with the IRS and the FBI against Buffum....," Leo was only getting started when Nix cut him off, saying she knew all this.

"Maybe if you let me finish you'd find out that Sava, without telling us, filed something else. He filed a Whistleblower Complaint with the IRS, the GAO, and the Inspector General of the Treasury."

"So what?" Nix was still impatient.

"It wasn't an anonymous filing. He used his name this time so he could get the prize money."

Nix pulled over to the side of the road, braked hard, turned in her seat and said to Steiger, "I thought you said this guy was reliable. Didn't you talk to him about this?"

"Leo met with him first. Leo doesn't work in the building, like us. Sorry Leo. I arranged the meeting and both of us talked with Sava after he hacked Buffum's computer and dimed him out."

"Leo?" Nix asked.

"What can I say, Nix. He said all the right things. I even told him we didn't want him filing a Whistleblower Complaint, but then he went ahead and did so. I can't really blame the guy. Buffum was extorting him. He fucked him over big. He's got nothing else."

"What's he going to say, Leo?"

"He'll say whatever's best for him, Nix, like anyone."

"Then it looks like we're surfing, boys," a little smile touched her face.

"Surfing?" Steiger gave her a puzzled look, "Why would we be surfing?"

"Yeah," asked Leo, "we're looking at a ten spot for conspiracy and you want to talk surfing?"

"It's a metaphor," Nix explained. "Shit's going to happen, waves of it. Unpredictable waves of shit that we got to ride out. So, for now, while things are in a state of flux, we're gone surfing."

XXXIX

"You look tired, Gwen," the Fool stirred the ashes and threw birch bark and sappy split pine on the embers. The bark flared, the sappy wood spat and soon the Fool had that blue tinged flame he knew Nix could lose herself in.

"Oh, Charlie," Nix sighed, laying on the sandy scrub, sticking her shoes towards the fire, "I am so wore out from all kinds of shit that I don't think I can move from this spot. There's another bottle of rum in my bag if we need it. "

"You just relax, Gwen. We're having hot dogs and beans. I got a two-prong stick so I'll cook yours. And I got a cooler with ice, bitters, and lime juice. How 'bout that? If we had blueberry pie and ice cream we'd be all set."

"Sounds good, Charlie. Thank you, Charlie. I'm going to shut my eyes."

"You go right ahead, Gwen," the Fool got the Folly Cove rum that Nix brought and he liked so much. He also got a nice wool blanket for her from his tent and a canvas pillow. While he was doing so, Nix talked to him with her eyes closed.

"You're the only one who knows me, Charlie, even a bit. That's the truth and, unfortunately for you, that carries a price. I need a favor. I got this stuff in my head and it's not all making sense. It's turned to gobbledygook in there. Can you just talk to me in your Charlie voice while I try to get some shuteye? I don't care what you say, just talk, okay? But talk to me."

"Sure, Gwen," The Fool draped the wool blanket over her and tucked it in around her shoulders and she smiled. Then he built a wind break out of a tarp and two camp chairs, all the while going on about the wind and how the trees sough and the currents in the lake flow.

After a lull, the Fool asked whether she was too warm and if she knew on what side of a tree the moss grew? He told her there are underground springs that feed the lake and that the water is so cold and sweet and earthy that if you catch a fish near one of the springs it's likely to taste like it. He spoke in simple terms of the connectedness of things. He took comfort in the knowledge he gained observing the lake, the meadows, and woods and he shared this. He credited the lake and, of course, the fly rod with his hands having healed as fast as they had since he began staying there.

"I'll tell you what, Gwen, before I met you I had a low opinion of myself. I thought that my value as a person, my whole worth, was found in the opinions of others. How stupid is that? I didn't know any better. That was a mistake and you're the one who pointed it out."

"I did?" Nix mumbled, half asleep.

"Yeah, but what you said is I'm the only one I've got to live with so it's what I think that should matter most, not what others think, no matter who they are. Stan is my father and I know it. I know that like I know my left hand. I don't need the King to tell me that. I didn't even need Stan to tell me and I didn't need him to tell me he loved me because I know he did and he showed me every day. I loved him too, like a son."

"Um-hmmm," Nix fluffed the canvas pillow, such as she could, and turned on her side.

"Go to sleep now, Gwen. The rum's by your head if you want some. You're some kind of goddess to fuck ups like me and that partner of yours and who knows who else. I just know I owe you for pointing me in the right direction and loaning me your courage when I really needed it. I'm going to need it when the King comes for me, as he surely will. I ran from him once and Stan died. I ran from him once and look at me now. If I run from him again I'll be less than his slave. I'll be him, that's who I'll be. Dream of the angels, Nix.

XL

When Buffum woke up he realized his watch was gone. So were his shoes, his belt, and his glasses. He shouted for someone's attention and the rest of the lock up, mostly kids in gangs, warned him to clam up or else. He did until someone walked by on the other side of the bars. Then he popped up and demanded a phone call. They might have kicked him around for that but another person, an administrative escort, came in to take him to the phones.

Buffum had a phone number memorized for times like this. His escort took two steps back but could still hear everything he had to say, which was, "773-174 immediate at East Boston Police Station. Lock up. Monday arraignment, need counsel, need everything. Lunch for fifty at the station, with gratitude for service, immediate departure planned. Pick up immediate, my end in process."

Buffum was being taken back to the lock up when he stumbled and almost fell on his face. The escort helped him up and delivered him to the lock up. As soon as he was through the bars Buffum tossed the escort's cell phone to the leader of the gang arrayed against him and said, "Pick on me. Say you'll fuck me up. Now, goddamnit, aggressive, loudly!"

They were loud and threatening and Buffum cowered in a corner and whined when the escort returned and demanded his cell phone. Buffum denied knowing anything about any cell phone so the escort got a police officer and did a strip search of Buffum but they found nothing. The escort told him that unless he produced the cell phone he'd be staying in this cell with his new friends. Buffum sniffled, cried, and denied knowing anything about a phone and begged them not to leave him. When they were gone he smiled slyly and said in a low tone to the leader who'd caught the phone, "Want to break out?"

"Yeah," he answered softly.

"Give me the phone."

Buffum made a quick call, typed something on the phone and then had someone take pictures of a fat prisoner's naked ass and dropped it in the text que with the message, 'Want some of this, Boys? The Captain just had his!'. He hit SEND ALL and waited until he could hear footsteps on the stairs above and behind the wall. He gathered his cellmates around him.

"Do everything I tell you, when I tell you, and we walk out of here free men. You're going to crash the cell doors when I whistle, and not before. Strongest guys up front, right now, so you can crash them hard. Now back up and get ready. Not until I whistle."

As the footsteps and yelling grew closer, Buffum signaled the leader of the prisoners over to him, saying softly, "Sit next to me, we travel together. We walk out on the backs of everyone else. You got me? Once we clear the cell door, head left and take your second left. Go down the stairs one flight. The door ahead of you goes to employees' parking. We're going to walk, not run, through that door, over to a car and we're going to drive out of here. I have people waiting. Stay near, do what you're told and there's a hundred K for you, just for your help in springing me and you. You can afford to stay lost for a while on a hundred K."

"Who are you, man?"

"You don't want to know. All you need to know is that you aren't getting out without me, so stay close and watch out for me or there's no money."

"Fine by me. I don't want to know you. This is fast pitch, man. It's not my league."

"Right, and don't forget that."

There was a melee, as cops from the Detective Bureau and Vice collided with street cops and staff coming from the other direction. They quickly united and, consumed with a singular purpose, headed for the lock up where the disrespectful douche bags were. It hadn't taken long for the cops to figure out that the message came from the escort's phone and that phone was in the lock up.

A burly sergeant named Red was in the vanguard and held a big old-fashioned jailer's key. He was followed by a noisy horde of well-armed, ill-intentioned cops that, like a rush of Vandals, pushed against the iron bar door in which Red had inserted the key and behind which the prisoners waited. But the door couldn't be opened because there were too many enraged and screaming officers pushing against it.

***

Officers d'Orsay Juarez and her partner, Custanzu 'Sally' Salvatore walked in the back door of the East Boston Police Station and caught a glimpse of what was developing in the corridor outside the lock up.

"This don't look right, Sally. It looks wrong. What do you say?"

"There might be a good reason for these guys to be down there with their sticks drawn and tasers ready, d'Orsay, but I can't think of one. On the other hand, it could be what it looks like, in which case we got to ask ourselves, 'Did we see anything we saw?'"

"Any of what, Sally. Back up, we're going in the front door. I'm not going through another two-day deposition with twenty know-it-all, dickhead lawyers. I never saw a damn thing."

"Nothing to see, d'Orsay," Sally called, as he slammed the back door, "but out front, I forgot to tell you, there are four K O Pies trucks in the driveway. Somebody donated lunch. You can't get in or out unless you go through employee parking."

"No way! I love that Vietnamese chicken salad and what about the Piri Piri chicken?"

"My wife loves that too. Meat pies for me. Who do we thank for lunch?"

***

"Back up, you goddamn clowns," shouted Red, the burly sergeant, shooting elbows to ease the crush of angry cops behind him, "back the fuck up, you damn fools. Haven't we been through this before? You sound and act like a pack of hyenas? I spare no one and no rank. You in the back, the way back. Back up, back way the fuck up. That's it, now the rest of you donkeys, back the fuck up like they did. Okay, now, you guys behind me, back away from the bars. Get away from the bars!"

With the Sergeant's back turned, Buffum told his new friend gang leader to go quickly and turn the key. But his new friend hesitated, asking Buffum if he was going to whistle before he got back. Buffum paused a moment and then said smilingly, "I chose you from all of them. Would I do such a thing and waste you?"

So, his new friend ran low to the ground and turned that key before anyone could see him and Buffum whistled and the prisoners trampled him as they screamed and crushed the iron bar door against the unsuspecting cops. A melee ensued and as he said he would, Buffum climbed over the prisoners' backs and down the corridor to the stairs and through the door to employee parking where he found a Rav 4. With one photo of the VIN and a text, the little SUV unlocked and started up. Buffum figured he had some catching up to do, needed some rest, and thought it would be smart to lay low while things were hot. He slipped the escort's cell phone into the back seat of another car sitting at fifteen-minute parking. He drove off, getting lost in Eastie.

XLI

Sava never had trouble sleeping. That's what he told himself, but tonight was different. He had the feeling he was being watched. He reminded himself that it's the wise one that trusts his instincts, but wiser still is the one that tempers this impulse with patience. So, he lay back on the flimsy mattress over springs and reached for the vodka on the nightstand, taking a long swallow. He stood the bottle back up, locked his hands behind his head and wondered at his source of worry.

This afternoon he'd been called by an Assistant U.S. Attorney. She left a message with a number and a request that he come see her in the Federal Building, first thing Monday morning. Then there was a call from the Inspector General's Office and that person wanted a call back to arrange a recorded interview. Finally, a Secret Service agent named Bolgarov said for him to call back. No threats, no impatience, no anger, 'pochemu ya tak chuvstvuyu,' he thought, what am I worried about?

But he was worried and realized that there must be a threat he didn't know about, but for which there were clues. Quietly, he got out of bed and walked to the side of the window. He peered through a crack in the blinds to see if there was anyone there, lounging on the corner or hiding in the alleyway across the street. There was no one, but what he did see, to his surprise, was nothing outside the window, but on the wall above it, in his room. There was a tiny camera and it was focused on the table, chair, and bed he slept in.

It wasn't focused on him now so he composed himself and walked back to his bed and put his hands behind his head again, never looking up or at the camera. Then he felt his pockets, as though he was looking for something. He got up and took his jacket from the back of a chair and patted the pockets. Sighing, he threw the jacket in the pantry along with a shirt he picked up off a chair. Then he seemed to remember something and reached up on a shelf and came back with a pack of Lucky Strikes.

He grinned ear to ear, a Lucky dangling from his lip. Now came the search for a light, which he finally found on the table next to the door. He kicked his boots into the pantry in the process. At last, he could have a smoke. And if that camera had a microphone it could have heard him open the squeaky little pantry window, but it couldn't see him climb out because that camera couldn't look into the pantry.

The rooftops of Chelsea are the parks, playgrounds, and nightlife of the sky. The Russian Mafia traveled by rooftop, cellars, and sewers, like they were still in Moscow. It was they, as much or more than any group, that turned the rooftops into a transit system.

The Russian Mob subcontracted electrical work to Sava for special projects now and then. He got to know the gangsters well enough to have a drink and a word. Over time, Sava learned some of the routes over Chelsea and that came in handy tonight. Once through the window and onto the fire escape, Sava scurried UP. UP is the world above, where bars, clubs, parks, buildings, bridges, and gardens proliferate, fifty to a hundred-fifty feet above street level, looking down on the poor bastards on terra firma.

Sava decided to put a little distance between himself and the rooming house, so once on the roof he took the stairs to the third floor, walked across a failing raised bridge of shopping carts, tripping on the key cart, but catching himself before plummeting to his death. Hurrying into the next building, he took the elevator to five, got off, made his way over a narrow board and wire walkway to an office building where everything was closed except the roof.

There Sava found a steamy Russian café with tall glass windows, the smell of pastry, and a steaming samovar. He had a demi-tasse and vodka chaser and then two more chasers. He was finally able to light that Lucky, relax and think for a moment. 'Robho, what to do? I don't even know who is watching me,' Sava considered his options. 'Maybe I should go back and find out?'

So, once he finished the cigarette he retraced his steps, but crossed through the cellars to the building across the street from his rooming house where he could see what was happening in his room. From this perch looking down on his room, Sava chanced another cigarette and stared into the night until the light he left on in his room went off. By the dim light from the pantry he could see two men in longish dark raincoats and hats, gently ransacking his apartment, taking down the camera and relocating it in a dark corner where it would be able to look into the pantry and be harder to spot. They riffled through his drawers, flipping through the letters he'd received from home.

Sava had drawn some schematics for improvements addressing the condensation problems of refrigeration units. They studied these and other renderings, taking pictures. Sava also had a Greek Orthodox shrine in one corner that held a picture of his mother, his sister, and the risen Christ. They considered it indifferently. After placing a call they talked for a few minutes, turned the light back on, left the apartment and closed the door.

Sava scrambled to the first floor in time to see his two visitors get in a large black SUV and speed off. For what it's worth, he got the license plate number. It was Rhode Island or Virginia.

XLII

Buffum opened the blinds to the magnificence of the Berkshire mountains in Fall. There was a wonderful wash of colors on this cold clear day. "Ahhh," breathed Buffum, reassured that he was free, if not safe. There was a light, inquiring knock on the door and Buffum felt comfortable enough to say, "Come in."

"Your breakfast, sir. You left instructions with my predecessor of the evening before. Shall I set your table by the window?"

"Please," Buffum was impressed. His server brought fresh flowers.

"We have your sunflower seeded toasted pane with a savory cherry conserve, popover with fresh fruit, warm prosciutto and soft-boiled eggs, but may I first pour your coffee? The kitchen has brewed a robust Guatemalan light roast and espresso bean blend that I think you'll find sips well in the mountain air. Although you didn't request orange juice, ours is so fresh and good that I thought I might tempt you. I've also brought a bottle of mineral water from which you may refresh yourself during the day. Is there anything else I might bring or something you would like me to take away?

"Everything is fine, thank you, aaah?"

"Lazar, sir, thank you for asking. You received a call this morning from a Mr. D. He asked whether I might notify him once you've had your breakfast. May I do so in half an hour?"

"That would be excellent."

"Very well, sir. You also received a package this morning. I've brought it up."

"Thank you again."

"Very well, sir. Have a pleasant day and call the front desk if you require me."

Buffum sat at the table, sipping his coffee, and enjoying the view. The coffee was as good as described. He opened the package and there was a heavy-duty, thick antenna cell phone, fully charged. After breakfast it rang and Buffum answered.

"Hello?"

"We're piecing things together on our end. Can you give us anything to go on?"

"Not much until I know what the charges are," Buffum was playing this cool.

"We think there are overlapping interests here, two, anyway. We don't know what the charges will be but we know the evidence on which your arrest was based. It seems your computer...."

"What computer?" Buffum was alarmed.

"Your computer at work was hacked."

"How can that be? I run everything through that computer."

"Yes, apparently."

Buffum insisted, "It has the strongest firewall there is. Everything is encrypted. It's an IRS computer."

"The lack of fingerprints, traces, echoes, dead ends, and a dearth of any evidence of a hack itself leads us to consider it an inside job."

"Interesting," Buffum got up and began pacing, "who do you suspect?"

"Someone with direct access to your computer, permitted or otherwise. Can you provide us with names of those who may have had the means, method or opportunity to open your computer?"

Buffum was rattled and trying not to show it, "Not even IT has access to my computer. I run the whole office. No one even has a key to my office... except, that is, for the cleaning staff, of course, actually just one person."

"And who might that be?"

"It's not possible. He's a clueless Russian immigrant. They call him 'Porkchop'. He got caught trying to marry an underage girl. All he does is empty the trash."

"Someone copied your files and sent them to various government offices, including FBI, Treasury and, of course, the IRS, Secret Service and Inspector General. There was something wickedly playful in the way the files were arranged."

"There are two employees I can think of who might have it in for me. One is named Nix, Gwendolyn and the other is Steiger, Russell or Rusty, but they're Luddites, as stupid as the cleaning guy."

"Text us their particulars, including description, as well as those for Mr. Porkchop. Send it to the number associated with the contact 'Bob'. Please do that as soon as we hang up. Do not sign onto the internet under any circumstances."

"Very well."

"Do you have electronics on your person or in a bag?"

"I have nothing other than this phone."

"One last thing,... of a distressing nature."

"Yes?"

"The release of this information was clearly designed to ruin you personally, not our businesses. While we cannot know the workings of your office, we did become acquainted with some of the files that were forwarded to your employer and the various government agencies."

"Listen, you knew I trafficked in edgy porn before we were ever in business. You contacted me because I ran that kind of ship."

"There was one live stream in particular we would like you to address."

"And what would that be?"

"'The Girls' Room'."

"Oh, Pee Poo."

"We have a problem with live acts of any kind. We explained that we do not sanction live action pornography on our platforms. This was explained in exhaustive detail because that is a foundational principle for us. It, therefore, comes as a distressing surprise to find that you've engaged in it."

"Ahh, yes, and why I'm not just a market leader, but a market driver. I was out there when you brought me in. You knew what you were getting in me. The leopard doesn't change its stripes."

"Indeed, no one could dispute that. I think we agree completely."

"Good, and you benefit and benefit well from Pee-Poo. You'll notice I don't call it porn. I don't call it porn because it isn't. It's my largest subscription service and you take twenty-five percent."

"Nonetheless, this channel is prohibited under the terms of our agreement because it has live performers."

"But it's not porn. If I was broadcasting a simulcast baseball game would that violate our agreement?"

"We won't engage in hypotheticals. This is not baseball. You knew what we meant when you agreed to work with us."

"A vagina, now and then, I'll admit, but it's mostly the sounds of peeing and pooing with some girl-talk and narration. Only twice has there been sex in there. If you average the air hours of offensive incidents or language on mainstream media with 'The Girls' Room', I don't even think you can call my show pornography."

"Federal judges make those determinations, not you, Mr. Buffum, and frequency alone is not determinative. We are well aware of your program and certainly appreciate your business acumen and ability to extemporize, but that's not the point. The point is we do not sanction live action pornography, especially with amateurs. There is too much risk. We made that decision long ago. Even when the actors are fully aware and fairly compensated union professionals, this is a difficult thing to control."

"Control? There's no need for control. No one involved knows what's happening! What's to control?"

"From our perspective this channel is violative of all acceptable pornographic norms."

"Pornographic norms? I establish pornographic norms, whatever those are. That's me."

"Sir, not only is your program live action, but the actors are also unwitting, the filming is secret, and everything is non-consensual. To make matters worse, the action takes place in a ladies' room, which I think you will agree is considered by most to be a safe and private space for women. Some women may attend to babies and children there. Girls and others may use the ladies' room. The patronage is fluid but there is one common expectation of all and that is an expectation of privacy. Do you understand that this may be seen as an invasion of privacy, child pornography, and violative of essential civil rights? There are criminal statutes prohibiting the very thing you're doing."

"It's good fun is what it is and there's less skin, overall, in 'The Girls' Room' than in most PG-13 movies. I paid good money for that statistic. The audio is only rated R, Restricted. R is the new PG."

"Add to this that the actors are not compensated and you, sir, are going to need five hands to count your minimum mandatory at sentencing. On the high side, you will surely die in prison. There isn't enough money in all of pornography for us to run this risk, but now it seems we have. May I ask you a question? You don't have to answe."

"Shoot."

"Does it trouble you that you seem to have taken advantage of women who simply want to use the ladies' room? These are women you know and with whom you work? Isn't there something about this that bothers you?"

"Not in the least. As I said, it's simply good fun. I've asked myself how I'd feel if I was me on camera and I'd like to think I'd laugh right along. There's rarely any skin. Once in a while one of 'em will brag about the weekend and there are fart noises. Honestly, I don't know why the show is so popular."

"Sir, we're going to have to change your lodgings to someplace more remote."

"I'm in the mountains..."

"At the peak of leaf peeping,"

"Of course, understood, okay."

"We're thinking across the border in upstate New York. At four o'clock this afternoon a black SUV with Virginia plates will be parked outside the exit closest to the skeet shoot."

"Skeet shoot?"

"There's a dirt road used mostly by delivery trucks and heavy equipment. Head for the gymnasium but keep going."

"There's a gym?"

"Please don't go out except to meet the car. We'll settle the room."

"Very well, later on, then."

"We'll speak this afternoon or early evening, once you get to your new lodgings."

XLIII

Nix took Leo's credit card and ordered three pizzas and a six pack.

"Why'd you have to get beer, Nix?" Steiger complained, "A decent pinot noir wouldn't have cost much more. Really, if we have to drink something, why can't it be something that doesn't bloat me?"

Ignoring him, Nix pulled into an hourly motel on Chelsea St. in Revere and used Leo's credit card again to pay for a room because she could imagine what it would be like with the three of them trying to eat and drink in her piece of shit Toyota.

"Go right ahead, Nix. Use that card like it's yours. Don't be shy," Leo groused.

"Drop it, Leo. We work this out when it's over."

"Does everything you say have to end up with you telling one of us to shit or go die? I wonder about that, Nix," Leo shook his head.

"Give it a rest, Leo, I never told you to go die, but you should. Get inside the room. Steiger, follow Leo. I'll be back in a minute with the pizza."

"You didn't order a salad, did you, Nix? Of course not. Did you get thin crust or deep dish? Don't you think deep dish is too heavy for lunch? And get me a Dr. Pepper."

As soon as Nix got back, Leo's phone rang. It was a local call but he didn't recognize the number.

"Pick it up," said Nix.

"Ahh, you said we shouldn't..."

"We're surfing, Leo. We talked about this. New rules. Pick up the call and say, 'no names' and then ask what's going on."

"Hello?" Leo said tentatively.

"Leo, is Sava..."

"No names."

"What? Is this Leo?"

"What do you want?" Leo tried to sound cool, tough, and efficient.

"Know names or no names, Leo?" asked Sava. "Am confused. Which? I don't know no names, okay, but I know names, of course. Put Nix on phone."

"I mean don't use my name, Sava. Don't use any names."

"Why don't you say so?"

Nix took the phone from Leo, "It's me, what's up?"

"Many things, Nix, I mean...oops."

"Too late now, Sava, go ahead." Nix shook her head.

"I had visitors last night, serious men in long coats."

"How many?"

"Two of them come by. I find hidden camera in room, on wall, and pretend not to see. Then I sneak out pantry window and disappear like dust in dark. But I circle back in time to see them go in my room. They go through my things very, ahhh, deli, delica, ahhh, no, is deliberate, is how you would say, which is not good. These are professionals. I have plans and electrical designs for different machines and things, like condenser for refrigeration unit and airfoil system for aircraft that syncs all six flaps and brakes on wings and tail with one control mechanism. Is very good system with fuel savings in mind but is not what office cleaners would have in bedroom."

"Yeah," Nix lowered her slice, "I'm afraid you're right. They're going to think...."

"They are going to think that I am not cleaner but spy for pornographic competitor, like that."

"Who or what are we talking about?" Nix wanted to know.

"I don't know," Sava sounded worried, "I know it is not government. Government called me on phone, three of them, asking to make arrangement to speak with them about blah, blah, blah, not urgent. Government peoples in America are not so slick as these guys."

"So?"

"So, I think who can afford professional tough guys in long coats with secret camera? I think how much it cost to have this kind of mafia follow me around? Is much, no? Get me thinking if they are not some government they must work for pornographers that Buffum works with. Makes sense, no? Who has money to hire slick operators? This must be pornography mafia."

"Does everything around here have to do with pornography?" Nix wanted to know.

Leo and Steiger exchanged worried looks.

Sava leapt in, "Mr. Buffum is big shot pornographer and runs operation from IRS. He makes much money. I see secret files on computer."

"Really?" Nix sounded more interested than surprised. "I guess that would explain why those guys tossed your room. Where are you, Sava?"

"I don't want to say on phone."

"You said everything else on phone, why stop now?"

"Go to where I last see Leo and Steiger. Ask if they remember?"

"They remember."

"In half hour I be there."

"Half an hour then." She hung up the phone and said, "C'mon, we're going to Chelsea."

Steiger protested, "I'm not done and I have to use the can."

"You've got five minutes. Wrap it up."

"You mean to go?"

"Be in the car, Steiger."

Nix drove to the windowless Thai restaurant and got there in thirty. As they were being seated, Sava walked in.

"Hello, Nix, and hello, Steiger and Leo."

"Sit down, Sava, please," invited Nix.

"Thank you, Nix. It was nice to talk to you on phone. I have seen you at office but have heard more about you than I know."

"That's fine, Sava, someone order tea or something. Let's talk about you being rousted last night."

"So, I have looked at this from distance, ahh, different perspective. I don't think someone is out to kill me yet."

"Really?" Nix responded coolly.

"Why put camera back and hide? Why not wait in room until I come home and pok-pok, eh? Maybe is not so dangerous yet, but soon will be. I think these people are curious and want to know what is going on and then they will kill us."

"Us, Sava?"

"Nix, I am Russian. I may not tell the truth but I know it. This is life. If they don't figure out themselves or from Buffum or who knows, they beat it out of me. So is us."

Nix gave him a wry smile, "Thanks for cutting through the bullshit".

"Pozhaluysta, but I am not here to plan funeral. Like all people, I prefer you think I am virtuous but there are people I know who, once or twice, I do work for, now and then. These are good honest people but are terrifying at same time. I have never seen them laugh, except at someone's misfortune, last misfortune if you know. I would never want them as enemy. So, is not with eagerness I suggest we see Uncle Otto at the club."

"Who the fuck is Uncle Otto and what are you talking about?" Leo was scared and edgy.

"Yeah, why should we go see Otto? Who's he?" Steiger added.

"I am sorry guys," Sava gave Leo and Steiger a little smile, "When organ grinder is in room I am not talking to monkeys. Is decision time, Nix. They are scary people, but without them we are going to get killed by different mafia. You come see Otto with me and you have a chance. Is best for you to come."

"Who is Otto?" Nix wanted to know.

"Otto is maître di of Russian mafia. He decides if we get table."

"You don't fuck around, do you Sava?"

"Is only option. These Russians always want me to do something because I know electronics, alarms, and computer programing, we'll call it, but lately I stay away .... Mostly. I am not comfortable around people who kill."

"Smoking kills, Sava," Nix pointed out, "tuna fish and cheeseburgers too."

"Cheeseburgers?" Sava was crestfallen.

"Yeah, but they won't kill you tomorrow."

XLIV

Buffum sat in the back seat of the custom Suburban. There were newspapers, a small desk and lamp, a thick ply rug, an audio/visual library, and beverages, but no electronics. Buffum had been thinking about the morning call and allowed that he may have come on a little strong. Perhaps a more conciliatory tone was warranted. He could admit that the project, he would call 'The Girls' Room' that, got a bit out of hand. He could redefine it. Good word, redefine.

He could continue the structure but take it out of a ladies' room. No, not that. Buffum knew these things. It was essential to the success of the show that it happen in a ladies' room, someplace taboo. Maybe he could use a girls' locker room? No, no, no, that's insane, way worse. What am I thinking? Women's locker room, yes, but where? College sports, women's beach volleyball locker rooms, women's country club locker rooms?

Buffum was overwhelmed and angry with himself for having let TGR run so long before saying anything about it. He knew he looked sneaky, greedy, and untrustworthy. And what a time for this to come out, while he was scrambling for his life. Like it or not, he had to agree to end or drastically reconfigure 'The Girls' Room', but there was no time.

They were on the Northway and the sign they breezed by said, Saratoga Springs, Saratoga Raceway, Saratoga Lake, next exit.

"Are we almost there?"

The smoked glass divider came down and the driver said, "Excuse me, sir, did you have a question?"

"I wanted to know if we're close,"

"We are close, sir." And the divider went back up.

Buffum didn't like this. He didn't like that there was nothing he could do to prevent himself from going where they wanted him to go. As he was worrying about this the cell phone he had been provided began ringing.

"Hello?" Buffum answered.

The big black SUV took the exit to Route 9 North.

"Sir, this is the party with whom you were speaking this morning. I said I'd call you once you got to your new lodgings."

"Thank you but we're not there yet."

"You're closer than you think."

At the end of a long dusty road, a right turn and a long dusty road after that, the driver turned into a quarry.

The voice on the phone resumed, "There was a big strike and the quarrymen stopped work in 1929. This quarry is one hundred and twenty to two hundred and seventy feet deep and full of water. I'd like to be the first and, unfortunately for you, last to welcome you to your new lodgings."

"We can work this out!"

"We have."

XLV

Sava salsaed his way through the crowded streets of Chelsea. It was one of those small cities where you had to turn, cross, or sidestep every ten or twenty feet. The roads were narrow, the trucks wide, and the buildings cheek by jowl. Nix was having a hard time keeping Sava in sight. Leo and Steiger, buffeted by the crowd, dragged ass in the distance.

Sava hopped up on a loading dock platform and waved his arms above the crowd, signaling them to hurry up. He keyed a control panel and a small lift rose from a cellar hole. They piled into the elevator and the noisy doors shut. They were in darkness until the elevator stopped, the doors opened and the lights turned on in a vast cellar.

"Where are we?" Nix was checking out the underground space.

"I'm taking you," Sava explained, "in, ahh, not direct way to Otto. It has to be this way for now. We go through grey door ahead. Is very good, and now this other elevator. I have special key. Others have too. Is Chelsea thing. We go beyond penthouse."

The elevator dinged and the doors opened to a warm Western sky. The sun was still muscular on the horizon, retirement barely nibbling at its edges.

"Sava," Nix gasped, "where are we?"

"Here is called Up."

"Up? It's magnificent."

"Yes," Sava smiled, "the world up here is Up. Look around. Chelsea is small, nowhere to grow but up. So, for many years the people have their rooftops, each one special, some gardens or shrines, some arbors, some chickens and goats, each individual among rooftops. Many have specialties like fig trees, still for making liquor, Korean barbeque, wine grapes, solar array, communications, pigeons, bocci, tennis, you name.

Each one with easements to do this or that or pass and repass on some part of one roof or many rooves. Each one with regulations governing behavior and business. Is more complicated than United Nations. We have kosher rooftop with black bread and butter. You obey that law there. There is UP for Islam not far from there and funny thing is you can get from one to other and no papers. I go to Greek Church in UP," Sava smiled.

"One day, years ago," he continued, "two rooftops get together and build a bridge so they can be closer and share whatever. Some others do the same. No surprise, the Russian mafia takes notice. They have Up tenancy too, so they know everything and see a profitable future for themselves in sky. Before too long the mafia goes to every rooftop and says what you might expect and after some broken teeth and minor, but timely, explosions, they get agreement to construct a rooftop to basement transit system through downtown Chelsea. They even get state funding."

"And this is UP?" Nix was looking at all the rooftops around them, some higher, some lower, all with people scurrying about, delivery drones and kites in the air above every roof, scooters going too fast for roof to roof travel, and bars and restaurants starting to fill.

"Come with me to other side. We have to go," hurried Sava.

On the other side of the building, behind the air conditioning system, hanging in the air was what looked like a Quonset hut with solar panels covering the roof. Below this was an attached pellet stove as big as a Buick that ran several hot air heaters, keeping the Quonset hut in the air. Below the heating element was a platform with seats for fifteen. The platform and Quonset hut fit snuggly between the two large mixed-use buildings. The whole system was attached to steel cables on the sides of each building, allowing the platform to act as a mobile elevated bridge servicing both buildings.

"Is called a 'Floater' and is very economical. Other advantages too," Sava led the way.

They got on the platform and Sava told the Captain they wanted to get off on the fifth floor, other building, and they all needed transfers.

The Captain fussed, pushing and pulling the controls to 'Down/Slow'. As the contraption finished rattling and started to descend, the Captain complained, "Everybody needs a goddamn transfer," as he sent them to Sava's phone.

They got out, walked through the building to an intra-building bridge, paid the toll, crossed to the next building, and took a floater from there to the roof.

This was a well-appointed roof, with shrubbery and trees and, off to one side, near an exit, a tall glass and steel enclosed bar called 'Doroga V Ad'. The windows were steamy and house music thundered.

The Americans sat together in the lounge while Sava went to find Otto. Finding him in the bar, Sava began telling Otto his troubles when Otto hushed him with one hand and took out his ear plugs.

"I'm hard of hearing without this fucking music. Step outside."

Sava got the others from the lounge and they walked towards a small, open air, walled garden. "Before we get there," said Sava, "only Nix or I should talk. Is important, okay? And look intelligent if you can. Here's Otto now. Hello, Otto, these are my friends. She is Nix, you met the other two at the cafe."

Otto nodded.

"So," Sava began, "there is this sonofabitch who was, let me speak Russian..."

Sava explained everything to Otto and Otto said, "I can see you are in trouble, but I am not. What are you doing here?"

"I was thinking, Otto, that your friends might help us stay alive."

"Why would they do that?"

"I could begin doing business with them, more regular from now on."

"You have not been dependable, Sava."

"But I will."

"Those are words. Words don't butter bread."

"Okay, Otto, here it is. This guy, not important who, had porn sites he ran from the IRS Office in Boston."

"From IRS office? In Boston?"

"Da, is brilliant. Most secure computer system on earth. Their firewalls would pick up the tiniest fart in the ionosphere and squash it. It is sneaky good idea but I am afraid that the operator of these porn sites will not be long for this world, poor man, if his associates find him. He may have had his last black bread and onion, but the business is big money-maker, Otto. I have the numbers for you, and the location is unbeatably secure. I know this first-hand and you know I know these things."

"Pornography is bad money," said Otto, "but let's say, for argument sake, that the people I know could be interested. What is to stop them from just taking this business from you and running it? I only say to say, but they will ask. "

"Let me speak Russian again to Otto?" Sava asked Nix. He told Otto that the secret to success was the location of the transmission of the pornography. That said, he asked how will your friends and mine, to be truthful, good friends, access this wonderful IRS computer system with state-of-the-art protection from prying eyes, Otto, prying eyes? Because, Otto, I have access and so does Nix and one of Nix's monkeys they call Steiger. How much is that worth to our friends, hmmm? Sava explained that the whole operation was run by one man who cobbled together different websites and private channels. He told Otto these subscriptions were not expensive and there was no overhead because nothing was produced. Even the office space is paid by the federal government.

Otto said he understood and wanted to know more. He said that even if everything Sava said was true, what made this porn site different from thousands of others? That's when Sava told Otto about 'The Girls' Room'. He explained that it was a passive feed from a ladies' room in the building. Otto laughed, saying he'd seen it and thought it must have been produced because it was so ridiculous. Especially, he said, the woman who can pee standing up, mouthing off with her left leg on wall.

Sava hushed Otto, telling him that this part is secret and the woman standing next to him is the woman who does this, but for Otto not to say anything because she doesn't know anything about it. Otto glanced at Nix and his eyes widened.

"Sava", he said, "is Ramrod. I have her T shirt."

"Udivleniye, Otto, she doesn't know she's Ramrod. Is cekpet, say nothing."

"Ah, Sava," Otto fit a finger in his collar and stole another look at Nix, "I think the people you want to see would like to see you and your friends. Wait in the lounge while I make a call and arrange for an escort. I will have someone come by to get you refreshments and caviar."

"Thank you, Otto, but these are Americans. Caviar would be waste."

"It cost me nothing. They don't eat, I feed to cats. Hebeca, this fucking music is going to give me ear cancer."

XLVI

Chief Cindy Beauchamp was having a bad day. Her second in command, Captain Wilkerson, Frank, as she knew him, had been indicted by the Massachusetts Attorney General's Office. She heard there was a similar indictment coming down from Rhode Island later today, different victim. Both could end up in federal court. Cindy had a bottle in her left lower drawer, Johnny Blue. It sat there untouched through her brother's suicide and her mother's cancer. She lived by rules, but she knew, being human, that rules get broken now and then.

So, Cindy cracked the seal on the Johnny Blue, took a sip, then another and knew, as she reached for the phone, that opening the Blue was the best call of the day.

"Yeah, Gwen, listen, I got that opening I told you about. Uh huh, you'll be reading about it. No, even worse. There's another case in Rhode Island. Here's the thing, I'm offering you the job of Lieutenant, top grade. If things work out you'll be Captain in a year. Salary is seventy-five and I haven't got a penny more. I know, but as far as I can tell, you ain't going to be working there much longer. Of course, it's just what I think, but you were made for police work, not that tax bullshit. No, you don't get a car. You get a car when you become Captain. I don't know, a Ford something. Just hear me out. No, but if you come here I let you lead the Zimochowski murder investigation into Ronald Overbee, a/k/a, the King. No, Gwen, I can't use Steiger, I'm sorry. I have thought it through and wish I could, but I've got limited funds and have to rebuild carefully. No, I'm glad you want to think about it. Take a couple days, but no longer. Think about Zimochowski. There'll be a news conference and I've got to put out something positive so I hope you say yes."

Chief Beauchamp got up and got a paper cup from the water dispenser and put it on her desk. She didn't want anyone to think she was drinking from the bottle, as she tipped it back again. The pain in her neck was fading. The muscles in her back relaxed and she could sit a little straighter.

XLVII

Blindfolded at times, soaking wet from walking under Mill Creek and Island End River, and now dizzy from staring down on the Box District from UP, neither Nix, Leo, nor Steiger had any idea where they were, how they got there, or how they were going to get back.

They were led to a dingy looking bar on a neglected corner of an ordinary looking rooftop.

"Wait here," the escort directed as she left for the bar.

Nix said, "Steiger, take your hands out of your pockets and don't slouch. Look serious and Leo, try and look a little taller."

"Christ, Nix, I've been trying to look taller my whole life. Don't you think I'd do it if I could?" Leo turned his back on her, "What a thing to ask."

"I'm nervous, okay?" Nix wished she had a cigarette although she'd quit years ago, "I'm nervous because it all comes down to this. These guys don't help us, I don't know what we're going to do. We're out of running room. Let's say those slick guys that rousted Sava pull a gun, so we pull a gun, then someone gets shot. We don't want that. Those are shitty odds for us. Even if we win the first encounter; they get replacements in an hour. What do we get?"

"What are you talking about, Nix?" asked Sava and Steiger in one breath, "We don't have guns."

"I've got my Glock."

"Get rid of it," Leo urged. "These Russian thugs will kill us if they find you with a gun."

"I don't think so, Leo," Nix checked her shoulder holstered gun, "I think the opposite. I think people who go begging get scraps."

"I was telling Sava that the other day," Lèo smiled, "right, Sava?"

"You were trying but it made no sense the way you said whatever. I agree with Nix, show of strength. They never said no weapons, so... why give them that?"

Before they could argue further, the escort popped her head out and motioned them in.

Sava walked in first, with Steiger and Leo behind him and Nix trailing. She stopped and watched the hugs and kisses and Sava's fawning and flattering. Half of her was embarrassed for him, the other half was wondering what they had to celebrate. Who is he, she asked herself, which made her ask, who are they? I know nothing about these guys except they're Russian. So, she hung back and waited for the greetings to exhaust themselves, noticing a man in the shadows at a table with the light off.

Sava walked back, a big fake smile on his face, "Nix, I would like for you to meet Mr. Androvski, the old friend I told you about. The gentlemen with him, ah, is his associate."

"Tell me, Sava, does Mr. Androvski's associate carry to business meetings? If so, is it by design?"

Before Sava could respond, Leo pointed to the 'associate' and asked, "Hey Muscles, didn't you go to Medford High with my sister Gladys, Gladys Ianetti?"

Sava jumped in, "I told you stay quiet, Leo. Only Nix and I talk."

"Don't tell my man what to do," Nix didn't bother looking Sava's way, "They don't belong to you. Go ahead, Leo."

"Well, did you?" Leo wanted to know.

The bodyguard looked over at his boss, who shrugged.

"How's Gladys doing? I took her to prom. She was such a nice girl, too nice for me. Tell her I said hi."

"Who says hi?" prodded Leo, adding, "Wait a minute. Don't tell me. You're Gus, you're Gus Miekewicz, the Polish Plow, Captain of the football team. How are you, Plow? It's Leo Ianetti. Didn't you sign with...."

"The Giants. Didn't work out. My coordinator hated me. And I gave another guy HGH, like that's a crime. Then it was all sign this and sign that. Now I'm here."

"That sucks, Plow."

"It's okay. I feel better."

"Mr. Androvski," Nix turned to him, "now that our associates have caught up I suppose we can get acquainted. My name is Nix and I work at the IRS. My boss ran a porn subscription service through the IRS computer system. I have control of that system now and I have a business proposition I'd like to discuss."

"Nice to meet you. You may call me Mikhail."

"Thank you, Mikhail. You may call me Nix. Tell me, Mikhail, why is it necessary for Gus to have an extra three pounds under his left arm? Do I detect a lack of trust or are you afraid that I wouldn't take you seriously?"

"Not either. You are my guest, Nix, and the last thing I want is for you to feel uncomfortable. I'll have Gus put it away and hope we don't need it, ha-ha."

"Have him keep it. I'm keeping mine."

A short bark of laughter broke from the table in the dark. Whoever was there turned on a weak light or he may have cursed the darkness.

"Come over here young lady," said the voice in the shadows, "Watch your step. My name is Andrei. My son in law, Mikhail, is a handsome man, wouldn't you agree?"

"Yes, but not my type, Andrei. I prefer something harder."

Andrei was so old that when he laughed you could hear the rattle in his chest. When he was able, he said, "You are very funny and have my sense of humor. I can't use mine anymore because I'm told it's cruel and offensive. Take a seat."

"Thank you, Andrei."

"What do you want?"

"We need protection. We just created a gap in the supply of electronic subscription pornography. Certain people don't like that, and I'm not talking about the guys with twenty bucks in one hand and their dick in the other."

Andrei laughed again, coughing into a crisp white handkerchief.

"I'm talking about the money behind porn," Nix continued, "It paid Sava a visit. No rough stuff but they put a camera on him. We need some push back, not violence, just a message. We could even consider this to be the opening of negotiations or establishing lines of communication. Looking forward, we're going to need help with the transaction and I was wondering, Andrei, if you might be the right fit?"

"I meant, what do you want from the bar."

"I'm sorry, Andrei, I got ahead of myself. I'll have what you're having."

"Oysters, black tea and pepper vodka, fresh Russian black bread with cow's butter, red onion and Kosher salt?

"Double Makers, crushed on the side, but I'll have oysters with you."

"Glad I asked. Let's get a drink and see if there's anything we can do for each other."

XLVIII

The King was ferried to courthouse after courthouse. He was arraigned on all his new charges, his defaults were removed on the old ones, a capias was lifted and dates were set for everything, including the financial neglect of two ex-wives and all four children. When he was done with his last set of charges, in Central District Court in Worcester, the Horseshoe Falls police van left him in the parking lot with a paper bag of toiletries, an empty wallet, and a broken cell phone. The King decided to hitchhike his way from the Worcester Courthouse to the Faire, seemingly unaware that the place had burned to the blackened ground. He should have known, having been the one that burned it.

His Highness made it all the way to the Faire before realizing his mistake. Falling to his knees and looking up at a blind and deaf sky, he screamed, "Where hath my Kingdom gone?"

After requisite lamentation the King composed himself, looking for a fig or cedar tree under which to catch his breath. Spacing out in the direction of the front gate of the parking lot, he hollered, "Hallelujah!" as he saw the pay phone.

Under the hot sun the King walked all the way to the front gate, only to discover that he had no change. Fighting back tears, he walked back to the scorch prints of the Faire under the same sun and stopped at the burnt-out husks of the Snow Cone mobile, Ice Cream truck and the remnants of Taco Tonite. He kicked around in the dirt below where the service windows would have been and this yielded a double handful of coins. He walked all the way back to the pay phone, same sun, before discovering that the phone was dead. It didn't even have a receiver.

The tentacles of self-pity reached out to welcome him but the King fought them off. Still, he only wanted to cry. He sat down on the hot pavement and wondered why bad things happen to good people. He decided to put some distance between himself and what had been his eponymous Faire, his Camelot. More by habit than choice, the King took out his cell phone and, what do you know, three bars and a static beep. "God hath not forsaken me!" the King screamed into a wind that suddenly kicked up.

Forcing himself to think, he checked his Contacts for the Queen's number. He'd never dialed her number, knowing it only as number 2, but this function didn't work. He hit Contacts over and over but only one number came up.

"Goddamn, I gotta call the fuckin' Blacksmith for help," the King shook his head and hit send.

"Hello?"

"Hel...Is that you, Diane? Diane? Hello, Diane? Is that you?"

"Ahh, no,... this is Clara."

"Clara? Sounds like you, Diane. Doesn't sound like Clara."

"Don't mention that bitch Diane's name around me. She's only Queen because she's old as fuck."

"Okay Clara, bring it down a notch. Diane's the vainest woman I've ever met and would sooner die of face cancer than hear herself called old. Anyway, I'm out of jail and need a ride. Come pick me up at the Faire."

"At the Faire?"

"Don't ask. Hey, quick question, where am I living?"

"I'll tell Diane you called."

"Don't hang up. Please, don't hang up."

The King redialed and the Blacksmith answered, "Hello, who is this?"

"It's the King."

"The King! King of what? There's nothing left. Excuse me for a moment. Good-bye, Clara, good-bye. I had to say good-bye to Clara. What do you want?"

"I need a ride from the Faire to where I'm staying."

"Why are you at the Faire?"

"Never mind."

"Did you bury money at the Faire?"

"What kind of question is that?"

"A good one," insisted the Blacksmith.

"Think, Blacksmith, would I be calling you for a ride if I had money? I'm coming from jail, where I was taken right after the fire started. I didn't realize...I didn't think it was going to be this bad. My trailer is gone. There's nothing left."

"No, there's nothing left," agreed the Blacksmith, "Now we live in FEMA motels with drug addicts, pimps and prostitutes. Thank you for burning everything down."

"It wasn't me. It was that IRS bitch and the Horseshit Police."

"Don't tell me," the Blacksmith yelled at the phone, "I was there. I think you wanted to burn the place down. That's the way it looked. Everyone told you not to fire the catapult..."

"Trebuchet."

"Gesundheit. Everyone said the tent had to come down first. Any moron would know."

"Not this one." The King smiled on his end of the call.

"You were warned, over and over, while you were sawing through that twisted hemp rope with that never sharp sword blade. That took time, time enough for anyone, I don't care how stupid, to realize the risk of fire. Why I say risk, I don't know. It was a certainty. You wanted a fire, King, and you got one."

"Come get me, Blacksmith. I don't know where I live and I haven't got a red cent."

"You brought this on yourself, King. Why'd you have to share it with the rest of us?"

"I never meant to."

"You never thought of us. You never thought of Diane, that's for sure. You never consider anyone but yourself."

There was crying in the background on the Blacksmith's end, now weeping, with heavy sobs.

"Who's that?" asked the King.

"Nobody."

"That's a woman crying."

"You'd know that sound, wouldn't you, King? It is only Clara."

"You just said good-bye to her."

"She's back. Don't be sad, Clara. I have to go, King. Clara is upset you called."

"Don't hang up."

XLIX

Buffum was dropped in a quarry, weighed down by a canvas tool bag stuffed with twenty-five-pound gym weights. Screaming silently as he raced to the bottom, the bacteria and tannin laced quarry water forced its way up his nose and into his lungs, down his throat and into his stomach. The bubbles became fewer. Rushing into deeper, darker waters, he silently coughed, breathing in water as he ran out of air.

He fell past the fishes, dead eyes seeing nothing as he passed into the thermocline, which steered him ever closer to the ledge below. There was a twenty-foot chain attached to the weighted bag on one end and fifty feet of three-quarter inch twisted rope around Buffum's legs and ankles at the other. If that rope had been a little thicker, or the chain ten feet longer, Mr. Buffum, or a vestige of him, might have rested just above the quarry ledge for the sliver of a half-life of Uranium 235. But there was a rusty shopping cart hung up on a dead tree limb sticking out of the side of the quarry, below the surface but above the ledge. That three-quarter inch rope rubbed and frayed against the rusted shopping cart and in only a matter of a day and a half a bloated Buffum popped to the surface before anything had a chance to take more than a bite or two.

***

The ornithologists were not as boring as everyone believed. The Bird's Eye Seniors got a late start this morning. Last night the bus got to the motel later than expected. The restaurant across the street, which they all loved for the popovers, was no longer serving dinner. They had to get Ubers to Caroline St. in downtown Saratoga Springs and spend more than they'd budgeted.

"But hell, life is for living," said Ernie, a retired CPA, and Secretary/Treasurer of the Bird's Eyes. He figured that if they didn't order pre-dinner drinks or anything from the top third of the menu, they could afford to order eight bottles of the Robert Mondavi Sauvignon Blanc.

It was unanimous and when the wine was done the earlier pledge of moderation was too. All of them were dragging today. Phyll and Bill trudged through the woods. Not only was it a little cool for shorts, their legs below the shorts and above the socks were all cuts and scrapes from the brambles, vines, and grasses. Phyll had the trail map and told Bill the quarry should be less than a quarter mile due West and sure enough, there it was.

They sat on a fallen pine tree and Bill pulled out their bird book. They'd done well today, cataloguing most everything on the watch list. Phyllis spotted a Northern Harrier not half an hour ago, taking off a lot of pressure.

"We keep going like this, Phyll, and we'll be eating for free tonight."

"Don't jinx us, Bill," Phyll took off her safari hat and wiped her face with a kerchief, "we still need a Short-Eared owl and a bobolink. The bobolink favors fields and grasses so..."

"Take a look, Phyll," Bill pointed up, "at eleven o'clock. There's our Short-Eared owl and it's heading right for the quarry. This is our lucky day."

L

The Queen tried to take a shower but this was one of those motels where whoever gets there first gets the water.

"Fuck you, Smitty," she called across the room to the Blacksmith, "I got to go get the King and you didn't leave me any water."

"Good, I don't like him. I like my scent on you," the Blacksmith breathed in deeply through his nose.

"You're a butt sniffing dog of a human being, Smitty. Normal people don't go around leaving their scent on people. You're nothing but a big-dicked moron."

"Why do you have to go? There's no more Faire. All of that is over."

"He's my husband, goddamn me, don't you understand that? You got to move back in with Clara."

"I can't do that. She won't have me. I left her for you."

"Go back. Say whatever you must. Do it."

"No way, I won't."

"Then you're going to die, Smitty, sure as shit, and me with you. The King has killed before and he'll kill again if you choose to ignore me. God have mercy on your ignorant soul."

"What do you mean, God have mercy on my soul? I'll tear him to pieces."

"You're a dead man, Smitty, and I'm not far behind. Maybe we can have a joint funeral and save whoever has to bury us some money."

"I'll tell Clara you had a witch cast a spell on me and I was helpless."

"Whatever it takes, Sweet Cheeks, just don't be here when we get back. It's going to be hard enough explaining why your shit's here."

Diane got in her car, putting on her make-up as she raced down the back roads to the highway, where she plucked and penciled until she saw the King walking on the soft shoulder in the opposite direction. She did a two-lane drift to catch an exit, hopping back on the highway in the King's direction. Pulling ahead and parking in the breakdown lane, she leaned on the horn until the King realized someone had stopped for him. Then he jogged over.

"Hey, Diane, I didn't think anyone was coming. I've been through some shit."

"I know, right?" Diane agreed, "Get in, Honey. Let's get you home and us to bed."

"Sounds good, Diane. You're just as pretty as I remember."

"It hasn't been a week and I visited you in lock up on Wednesday, what's up, Majesty?"

"How I've missed my name, 'Majesty'. That's not anything like the names they called me in jail."

"Is there something I can do for you, Hon? Something you want to ask me? C'mon, out with it."

The King put up faint resistance before asking, "Would you, my Queen, happen to have a little sip of something that has been distilled? I just need enough to settle my jangled nerves and kickstart my gut bacteria. Maybe something strong enough to kill this itch I have everywhere. And I'd be beholden if you'd front me a bottle of Turkey from the mom-and-pop liquor gun store? It'd help me settle back into freedom. I think I got a dose of PTSD from jail and have to drink it down to a manageable level. So..."

"For starters, Ronnie, I have a big roach in a mint tin in the compartment and this car has a cigarette lighter, so go to town. Let's see, my nephews used the car last night so, aah, reach under your seat and feel around for a bottle of tequila. They always leave something. Check the back seat too."

"I found two beers under my seat and another in the back. That's three in all, want one?"

"Go ahead, be my guest."

"Ooow, damn, must be what God tastes like...... Sweet Jesus in Heaven."

"My King, my liege, bearer of the Royal Scepter, welcome home."

"So, where are we living?"

"That's a funny story," began the Queen, going on to say that when they got to the fleabag motel the FEMA people only wanted to give her a single but the

Queen told them she was married to King Henry and he would be right along. The next day they came back to check and she wouldn't let them in.

"Good," nodded the King.

"Except they said they'd be back, unannounced, with a key, and if there wasn't evidence of my husband living there I'd be bounced out on my ear. All I can say is bless dear Clara's heart."

"Clara, the Blacksmith's Wench?"

"She's not no man's Wench, King, she's her own. Anyway, Clara offered to move some of the Blacksmith's stuff into our suite so I can fool FEMA. This way I'm ready any time they come, whether I'm there or not. Of course, now that you're here we won't be needing that stuff. It's so good to have you back, Hon."

"The sooner it's gone the better,"

"I couldn't agree more. You must be starving. We got a suite with a kitchenette. How does tuna casserole grab you? I'll cook."

"Thanks, Honey," the King drained the first can and popped the second." Have you seen Agent Nix or her partner nosing around?"

"We're spread out across three motels and a campground. I haven't seen her but that don't mean she ain't around."

"What about the Fool?"

"What about him?"

"Has he been spending time with her?"

Happy to distance herself from the King and his suspicions, the Queen said, "He's out at the campground and I think he's seen her. Why do you want to know?"

"No special reason, Di. Does the Fool seem different?"

"Since you mention it, yeah, he does seem a little different, surer of himself. I went to the campground to get him to hook you up and I found a woodsman. He's catching fish, cleaning and eating them, making fires, and walking in the woods."

"Are those the only troubling signs?"

"Mmmh, I don't know if you'd call it a sign, but never before have I looked on the Fool as a man."

LI

Andrei and Nix walked out of the bar arm in arm. Nix let it look like he was leading and Andrei appreciated that.

They walked off the terrazzo deck to the pebbled asphalt roof, "Let's stop here, Nix, and look at the moon. It's our nearest neighbor but we know almost nothing about it. Half of it, the dark side, we've never seen. Funny to think that way about something we've grown up looking at, something we think we know."

"What's the moon got to do with anything?"

"The moon is a mystery, Nix, and unlike the moon, you are exactly what you seem to be. You, all of you, Sava too, are amateurs. The only saving grace is you seem to know it."

"Am I supposed to be impressed by this deduction? Fuck sake, Andrei, I know we're not gangsters. Steiger and I work at the IRS. We stumbled into this. The IRS isn't a gangster shakedown organization, not in the traditional sense. I like to think we're more of a collection agency with prison terms on default. Of course, we're amateurs."

"I like to know who I'm dealing with and you should too."

"Come on, Andrei, I was starting to like you. Why are you acting coy?"

"You should know about me. We are not a real mob." Andrei sighed.

"Whaa?"

"It is a funny story. I was an active mob soldier for many years, vice mostly, shakedowns, of course, and a hijacking every month or so. I have a pedigree: Gambino on my father's side, fuckin' Genovese on my mother's. I spent my entire professional life trying not to look like a mobster. Then I retire from somewhere and get moved here to live out my life. But in retirement I would sometimes pretend to be a Russian mob boss. I did this with a couple of friends who were wise guys in their day but are just old men today. After one loud and threatening exchange in a diner I get an envelope full of cash stuffed in my pocket from the owner. Pretty soon the whole neighborhood is feeding me. I pinch myself. Is this a dream?

"But, of course, there are real gangsters in Chelsea, Nix, not only the make-believe kind. East Side $ has its paw prints on everything. They are the elite gang and keep a lid on things so no one kills the cow. The Tiny Rascals are right behind them. They're young and dangerous."

"Tiny Rascals?" Nix was incredulous.

"I know, it's mostly Asian too, so try and figure that out. Just don't underestimate them. They are disciplined and strike in synchronized small groups, probing in multiple short but ferocious attacks, when and where they're least expected. But there's peace between both gangs right now, though they spat through proxies. I am afraid of the real gangs so I go and tell them that everyone thinks I am a Russian gangster with the Russian mob. Both of these gangs tell me not to worry. They let me know we have our uses."

"Uses?"

"There are three things that all real gangsters value. The first is information, for obvious reasons. Then there must be lines of communication between gangs in order to avoid misunderstandings. Lastly, there must be dispute resolution that is fair, agreed upon, and doesn't leave bloody messes. We provide these valuable services for the real gangs of Chelsea. It's like diplomacy. In exchange, the real gangs allow the so-called Russian gang, my gang, to run protection for Up commerce and transportation in Chelsea."

"Ah, passive income in tolls, protection and maybe some UP rentals, that's what I'm seeing. You are a clever man, Andrei."

"Thank you, Nix. The secret to success is finding a need and filling it. Now you know about me. Tell me about yourself and how you got involved in this?"

So, Nix told Andrei that Buffum was a dick and they were getting back at him and in the process discovered that he was an even bigger dick than they thought. Andrei asked her what she wanted out of this and Nix answered truthfully, "Andrei, we'd like to get out of this unharmed. If you can manage some money, that'd be great."

"What are you looking for financially?"

"Twenty grand for Leo and a lifetime subscription to Barely Legal for Steiger. That ought do it."

Andrei started walking again, "And you?"

"All set, Andrei, but I hope I can call you a friend. It wouldn't be bad to have a connection with the Russian mob."

"Of course, we are friends, but listen, I'm going to make a great deal of money shopping that porn site. Do you know that?"

"I figured."

"You ought to get a piece."

"I got my standards, Andrei. They're nothing to brag about and don't feel insulted. They're low, but there are some things I can't do. It's personal. Get me a steak at Sinatra's and a seat at the high rollers' table at the casino some night when everything is over and we'll call it square."

"Okay, Nix, I tried, but I have something else to discuss with you. I have three daughters around your age. I don't understand them either. They are wonderful girls who, with their children and their mother provide meaning for my life. I raised them to be naive to people like me. They are American women now and all married, tre tirapiedi, Stupido, Bel Ragazzo and Balbuziente."

"You've lost me, Andrei."

"We live such a short time, Nix. I want everything to be perfect for my girls but, unfortunately, they have married morons. You met Mikhail. How can I die and know a fool will be running things?"

"You have to just let things go, Andrei. They'll work this out or they won't. When you're dead you can't interfere in their marriages any longer. You did your best and now it's up to them. That's how it works."

"I know, I realize, but..."

"No 'buts', Andrei."

"But I'm going to send you three hundred grand to do with as you please, no strings except I'm going to give my girls your information. They are to call you if one of these ragazzi sciocchi give them any trouble. You will straighten out these boys like you are my right foot from the grave."

"Why me?"

"I am a good judge of character. You don't love money over honor and you don't take money without obligation. I trust that, not you. Now that we've settled this, I will take care of this pornography problem. I have a good idea to market this and it involves Steiger, but first I have to tell you something. One reason the pornography that came from the IRS was so popular is because there was a live stream from the ladies' room next to your offices."

"Next to our offices? A camera? What are you saying? How do you know this?"

"Sava told Otto."

"I use that bathroom."

"They say on this live stream your name is 'Ramrod'."

"It's what?"

"Ramrod, Nix, but I will destroy any remnants of that live stream and make certain it does not get republished or sold with the rest of the pornography. It will reduce the price, of course, but I will not see you dishonored. We can rejoin your friends whenever you like or stay here if you'd rather."

"Ramrod?"

"Yes, Ramrod. Try and forget about it. I've learned about the stars since I retired. Not so much about them as about us. When I look into the night sky I realize that we're nothing more than shrieking chimpanzees defecating on our dinner plates. What do you think, Nix? Nix?"

"In the ladies' room, Andrei, I would do this certain thing, a funny routine to make the girls laugh. I would sometimes pee standing up. Oh, Lord, is that what they broadcast?"

"I have not seen this offensive material, nor would I witness it voluntarily. However, I am told that you have an uncanny ability to pee while upright, as though you are a man, and so I can say with some assurance that...."

"Oh damn, I knew it! I just knew it!"

"Yes, this man Buffum is evil, evil and unscrupulous. If he hasn't been eliminated yet, may I suggest he be fed to the Tiny Rascals?"

"Let me digest this for a moment? Was there audio on this live stream?"

"I understand, yes, and there was narration, I'm told."

"Oh Andrei, I would talk as though I was a man when I would do this. I would swear and spit and pretend to scratch my nuts while I talked about my bitches. I would tell the girls in the bathroom to 'get over here and wet my giant dick or I'll slap you in the face with it'. How humiliating, how embarrassing."

"Yes, and this man, Buffum, used a picture of you from the back with your left leg up on the bathroom wall to silkscreen on tee shirts."

"What!"

"Iddu deve more, Nix."

"Yeah, whatever that means, but tee shirts? Tee shirts with me on them?"

"They are the biggest seller on the website, I'm told."

"Website! Did you say 'website'?"

"Se, this is a big operation from what we can tell. It traffics in your dignity."

"Yeah, it traffics in my dignity. That's one way of looking at it. Can you get me a couple of those tee shirts, Andrei?"

"Of course, do you have a color preference?'."

"Green will be fine, thank you, Andrei."

"Shall we go inside now? You have made my evening, Nix. You remind me of myself as a young man."

"I must remind men of something. They don't stop chasing me."

LII

The Queen pulled into the Top Hat & Tails Motor Inn and parked next to the dry, leaf filled swimming pool. The King got out clutching his bag of toiletries. The Queen held the Turkey by the neck in one hand as she turned the key in the lock with the other and hip-checked the door open. It smelled like a zoo.

"Holy crap, Diane, this place is funkier than a tin roofed jailhouse."

"I know, right? I got to tidy up."

"I'd say."

"If you do you can find someplace else to stay."

"I'm not saying nothing."

"No, you ain't, Majesty, so why don't you clear off the table and pick up some of those clothes and put them back in the bedroom."

"I got to have a sip of Turkey and take a shower before I do anything. I got to get the stink of stir off me."

"Clear the table first and take the clothes with you on your way to the bathroom. Is that so hard to do?"

"No, not hard, but what's a Tiparillo doing in the ash tray and why are there are two coffee cups on the table."

"I had a few friends over but I went to bed early. Couldn't tell you who smoked and drank what, but I'll tell you one thing, FEMA wouldn't think just one person lives here."

"That's for sure," agreed the King as he walked over the clothes, tipping back the Turkey on his way to the bathroom. "Smells like the circus is in town," he called over his shoulder.

The King stood under the dripping showerhead and shouted, "How do I turn on the water, Diane?"

"Did you turn on the faucet?"

"Yeah."

"Is there water?"

"No."

"Then the shower's out of water."

"So, what do I do?"

"You take a shower later. That or you go see the Fool and jump in the lake."

The soapy King stepped out of the bathtub, damp from the drippy showerhead. He tried to wipe the soapy residue from his body with his hands. This wasn't working so he looked for a towel, all the while encouraging his moody penis to take a greater interest in its surroundings. There were no towels in the closet and none on the hooks near the vanity. He checked the laundry basket but everything in there was too dirty. That Clara sure is clever. There was even men's underwear, socks, and tee shirts in there. The King was trying to think of the word authentic, but it wouldn't come. Then he noticed there were two toothbrushes standing in a glass next to the bathroom sink but again, no towels. A man's clothing littered the bathroom floor.

"Nice touch, my Queen," the King smiled.

Skinny and naked with his little pot belly, the King wandered out of the bathroom to the bedroom, shouting for the Queen to tell him where he could find a towel?

"You can look for one just as easily as I can."

The King couldn't find one anywhere and was getting steamed, "Goddamn it, what kind of place doesn't give you towels? Guess I'll have to improvise," the King pulled back the bedspread and pulled off the top sheet and was about to dry himself with that when he saw a used condom stuck to it. For a moment he thought that this motel must have a terrible laundry service, but that was only for a moment because there was another condom stuck to the bottom sheet and this one was wet and gooey.

"Get your ass in here, Diane, and start explaining."

The Queen, gifted with a strong sense of survival and unwilling to further pique the King's ire, hurried towards the bedroom, reaching down to grab a long-handled, hard-plastic whiffle ball bat along the way.

"What can I do for you, Majesty?"

"You can explain this to me, right now!"

The King held up a flaccid, drippy condom.

"Oh, that. What do you think? Do you think that's mine?"

Before the soapy King could say 'yeah' the Queen stepped forward and swung the bat in a long arc like she was reaching for a low outside ball to drive to the opposite field. Just before she was to connect with the King's droopy scrotum she torqued her wrists, adding another five to ten miles per hour to what was a fast bat without it. The King dropped to his knees like he had been shot in the back. Eyes wide, the instant of pain frozen on his face, a falsetto squeal escaped his lips before he buckled and fell motionless on his face. Grabbing her keys, purse and phone, the Queen sprinted to her car and skedaddled in a cloud of dust.

LIII

Feeling cooped up and uneasy, Sava worked his way down from UP to walk the real streets of Chelsea. There's comfort to be found on terra firma, but he had his doubts that it could be found in Chelsea. At street level it was claustrophobic. A wall, a sign, the ass end of a truck assaulted Sava's every view. There's no comfort in that. There was none in the smell at ground level either, a smell that hung on everything. On rainy days they called this place Chelstew. Truthfully, there wasn't anything suggestive of comfort about the firmament of Chelsea. But ever the optimist, Sava observed that there is less far to fall down here.

Crossing and re-crossing the street, darting glances at reflections in the windows, Sava made his way to Tony's News, where he could get an espresso. Sava had a few dollars in his pocket and thought about buying the Racing Form. But when he got to Tony's the first thing he saw was the headline of the Boston Herald: LOCAL TAX MAN KILLED IN NY QUARRY.

Sava didn't finish the article before calling Leo who, before Sava could utter a word, said, "We know. See you in half an hour at the coffee shop."

Steiger said, "I'm not going to drink that swill. I'm not even going inside that coffee shop. It's for gibrones."

"Why are you worried about the fucking coffee?" Leo asked angrily, "The fucking coffee is fucking irrelevant. Did you read the article? Buffum was bound and drowned in a quarry in New York State. What's important here, Steiger, is that we have killers on our trail, honest to God killers. Who do you think these gangsters are going to kill next? Have you thought about that?"

"Of course, Leo, don't get hysterical. Just hear me out. The coffee and the killing are separate issues. We have to meet Sava someplace. Coffee shops are a great place to meet for any number of reasons. We can meet at any coffee shop. So why, for heaven's sake, can't we go to one that has decent coffee and where we might be able to get a blueberry scone instead of some doughnut? I don't understand your decision making."

"Get in the car, Steiger, and stop talking."

"Get in the car! Get in the car! You're irrational, Leo. Why can't you see these things separately. Good coffee and meetings aren't mutually exclusive."

"Get in the car and call Nix."

"I'm not calling Nix. She treats me like a fool who needs minding. You call her, Leo."

"I'm driving. Don't use her name or yours. She knows your voice. After she picks up you tell her the missing man was found dead. That's all you have to say. Have you got it?"

"Yeah, I've got it. I'm not an idiot."

"Jury's out, Steiger. Make the call. Prove me wrong."

Nix picked up but didn't say anything. Steiger started, "The missing man was found dead." He hung up.

"What did she say?" asked Leo.

"Nix? Nothing,"

"Nothing?"

"I hung up."

"Why'd you do that, Steiger?"

"I was done talking."

"You were supposed to wait to see if she had anything to say. Call her back."

"No, that's an admission that I fucked up. I won't give her that."

"Call her back, asshole. This isn't some kind of game."

"Yes, it is," said Steiger as he hit redial, "you just don't know it."

When the call engaged and the phone stopped ringing, Steiger said, "I'm sorry I hung up, Nix. Leo never told me to wait for a response. He seems to think I should have known one would be coming. We'll have to agree to disagree, I suppose. Anyway, is there anything you wanted to say? Hey Nix, are you there? Nix? Leo, the line's dead."

"Hang up the phone, Steiger. End the call."

"Want me to call her back again?"

"No, stay disconnected. Fuck me, I have to say good-bye to my nuts."

LIV

Nix couldn't see any advantage to speaking with Steiger. Afraid he may call back, she turned up the volume on her shitty car radio. Eric Burdon and the Animals were wailing 'Monterey'. She floored it on a downhill, threw it into fifth and kept the pedal down.

'His Majesty, Prince Jones, smiled as he moved among the crowd. Ten thousand electric guitars were groovin' real loud-yeah'.

She broke ninety but heard a tick, felt a shudder, and smelled oil. Backing off, she checked her rear view and saw a black SUV a thousand feet back, shadowing her moves, though the distance between them wouldn't warrant it.

Realizing she'd hit a tail, Nix continued South at sixty-three miles per hour as she decided how best to lose it. But as she was laying this out in her head she saw another car behind the tail, a Ford something. It had out of state or dealers' plates and kept the distance constant between itself and the tail. Ah-ha, she thought, I'd do a double tail too on a long straight highway like this, not many off ramps. 'Let's see what they do now', she mumbled to herself.

Nix pulled off the highway onto the long ramp of the Massachusetts State Police Barracks in Canton and watched the first tail continue South. The one behind managed to pull over on the shoulder, further back, and pop the hood, which was fine with her. She parked behind the barracks and walked around to the front and buzzed her way in, showing her Department of the Treasury ID and badge.

"Excuse me but may I speak to the desk sergeant?"

"I'm the desk sergeant, ma'am, Sergeant Wilansky. What can I do for you?"

"Thanks Sergeant, I'm Agent Nix with the IRS, Investigation and Enforcement, Boston Office. I've left my weapon in the car. While I was traveling

South the last few miles, fewer than five, I was repeatedly boxed-in and harassed by a black SUV, Virginia plates, and a Ford sedan.."

Nix left the impression that two vehicles were trying to scare her away from her investigation of King Henry's Faire. She saw skepticism creep across the sergeant's face so she told him there were thirty million dollars at stake.

"Thirty million owed by a flea circus?" questioned the sergeant.

"Over ten years with penalties and interest, compounded annually, yeah. These renaissance fairs are cash cows. I don't care how shitty and dirty they look."

"Who'd have guessed. What would you like us to do?"

"Could you have a couple rock hard state troopers, handsome as yourself, go monkey on those clowns so they learn that Massachusetts doesn't tolerate intimidation of state or federal law enforcement officers?"

"I'd be happy to have a couple of troopers educate these motorists for you, ahh..."

"Nix, Agent Gwendolyn Nix, and what a gentleman you are, Sergeant Wilansky. Thank you so much. May I go out the back door? My vehicle's parked there. I'll just take your access road over to Horseshoe Falls. That way they won't see me leave. Here's my info and thanks again. That's my personal number on the bottom."

Getting into her car she shouted, "I think that maybe I'm dreaming,....... MONTERY!"

LV

The King was so hurt and angry he said he wanted to kill someone. For most people, saying you want to kill someone and doing it are completely different things. Not so with the King who, having killed, knew the difference. So, when he said he wanted to kill someone that's what he intended to do.

But here he was, stuck in a hot funky room at the Tits & Tail, which is what everyone called the Top Hat & Tails, not a cent to his name and an empty bottle of Turkey staring him in the face across the dinette table. He walked angrily down to the Blacksmith's unit, palming his nickel-plated revolver.

"Blacksmith, open up or die like a dog."

"Who's there?" answered a woman's voice.

"Open up!"

"If you're the King and you're looking for the Blacksmith, maybe you ought to be talking to Her Majesty. He says she cast a spell on him and stole him away from me."

"Is that you, Clara?"

"Of course, it's me. Who do you think would be talking to you through my door?"

"I don't know and I don't care. That Blacksmith has to die and I got to be the one who kills him. Where is he?"

"The Queen drove down here in a cloud of dust and yelled for Smitty to make himself scarce because you were on to them. So, no one was under no spell. That was all bullshit, wasn't it?"

"We ought to have sex right here, right now, Clara, you and me, revenge sex."

"Just the thought of it makes me sick. It sounds like the cure is worse than the punishment. I mean, I'd rather eat glass, Your Highness. Why don't you leave before I call the cops?"

"Before I go, Clara, did you talk to me on the phone this morning?"

"Ugh, no, I didn't, okay? The last time I talked to you was the day you burned down the Faire. Now scram, I've got things to pack."

"Goddamn, where's that fucking Blacksmith?"

"We're not going through that again. I just told you. You're not carrying, are you, King? The Queen told Smitty you would if you could. That would be stupid. You just got out on bond. You're not allowed to carry."

"How about I put one through the door so you find out if I'm fucking carrying," the King pulled the trigger but the gun only clicked. "Motherfucking gun will shoot my dick and nothing else."

"I'm calling the cops, King. Here I was, feeling sorry for you because my man has been laying the lumber in your wife, but no more pity from me."

"I don't want your fuckin' pity, Clara. I want that Blacksmith's nuts."

"I'm getting my phone and the po-po is coming for you."

The King saw a shiny red scooter up on its kickstand at the back door. The key was in it.

"Okay, Clara, I'm leaving. You don't have to call the cops. You're right, I have some things to think about. I'm going to go back to Diane's unit and cool off."

The King saw the curtain pull aside and heard Clara say, "I hung up. You're doing the right thing, King. Trust Jesus and I'll remember you in my prayers."

LVI

Nix enjoyed the woods, hills and valleys that peppered her view as she drove the country roads into downtown Horseshoe Falls. She pulled over at the Athena because Lesous, the pizza chef, was sitting on a stair out front. She stepped from her car, engine running.

"Hey, Les, you haven't called."

"Les?"

"You're Les in my head, Lesous."

"It's nice to know I'm in your head but there are other rooms I'd like to visit."

"I'll see if I can get you a visa."

"Do you know what I have in my hand, Gwendolyn?"

"No idea."

"It's the fifty-dollar bill with your phone number."

"It is, is it? Let me tell you something about that number. You can stare at it all day long and it's never going to call itself."

"I've been trying to find a way to ask you to come to my house for dinner. I want to suggest an Adriatic salad with fresh off the boat shrimp and calamari and fresh mint, young briny olives, a local goat cheese with my own freshly baked rustica, and sour lemon orzo soup that my mother showed me how to make. I also have a wine from my village you will enjoy. Finally, I thought I'd bake a lemon cake that we can enjoy al fresco with the mosquitoes."

"What do I have to do for this, Lesous? I'm a fly to your spider. Where's your web?"

"Exactly two miles down the road on the left. Police wouldn't let me drive one night. How is Monday? On Monday, the pizza joint is closed, so, any Monday."

"Things are hopping on my end, Les. Can I call you Sunday?"

"I'd like that, Gwen."

Nix sped off to check on the Fool, who'd been busy with his campsite. There was a lean-to, now with an air of permanence. He'd insulated the tent, inside and out, and built a bigger and higher stone firepit just outside. He had stores of fish pickling, others drying on racks in the field and fish chowders in mason jars. There were boxes of apples and paper bags with green onions and mushrooms. The Fool had taken to this physically active life. Most telling of his presence were the well-worn paths to the lake and the timber trails. Nix parked at the Welcome Center and hiked up.

From the lake the Fool watched Nix cross the field in a nice pair of low heels.

"She doesn't learn, does she," he asked himself as he gathered his pole, basket of fish and bait box and made his way up the hill to his campsite. When he got there, Nix was seated before a pile of grey embers, both shoes off, massaging her feet, a bottle of Folly Cove rum at the ready.

She smiled and said, "Why don't you fucking boy scouts put in a road and a sidewalk on this goddamn hill. I tweaked my back getting here and my feet are killing me."

"It's nice to see you too, Gwen. Maybe if you wore the right shoes instead of cursing the boy scouts you wouldn't be in such an awful mood."

"Yeah, right, nice to see you too. How you been, Charlie?"

"I'm okay. This life suits me."

Nix sat up, hugging her knees, "This Walden Pond, deep thoughts Taoist kind of life doesn't pay much though, does it?"

"Your point?"

"FEMA is going to shut this site down any day now. Winter is around the corner."

"Yeah?"

"You have to stay ahead of things, Charlie."

"Don't you think I know that Gwen? I got things to worry about before winter gets here."

"Like what?" Nix pushed him.

"Like the King coming for me."

"I came here to tell you he's out on bail. You can stay at my place, I suppose. There's no furniture."

"I figure he'll come nosing around and ask me about that night at the jail with you."

"I can't be here all the time but...."

"Thanks, Gwen, but I can fight my own battles. I have to. I don't want to start thinking like the old me, who always found a reason not to do something."

"He's a bad man, Charlie, and he's desperate."

"And he's crazy on the booze and drugs, too. Don't you think I know it? I know him as well as anyone. I know he's going to come here to try and scare me and he probably will. But I know there's really not much he can do. If he kills or kidnaps me, they'll catch him. If he lays a hand on me, he's back in jail. If he threatens me, I'll call 911 or Victim/Witness Assistance, after I hit him with my pepper spray. King hates pepper spray and back to jail he goes. There's not much he can do and he'll know it."

"You went and thought this out on your own?" Nix watched him breathe life into the fire, "So, I guess you've sized the situation up and you're prepared for what's coming. Pass the rum, will you, Charlie, and tell me how you're going to call 911 without a phone?"

"Here you go, Gwen. First sip is the best. There's a phone at the Welcome Center."

"Life in prison, Charley. Ahhhh, you're right about that first sip. That phone's too far away. You'll bleed out before you get there."

"As long as the King doesn't feel trapped, people are safe, and by people I mean me. So, whenever we talk, I'm not letting on that I remember much or that I've decided to testify against him in the murder trial of Stan."

"Even talking to him is a dangerous move, Charlie."

"I know better than anyone that he's evil and no good. And I know he is not to be trusted. I'm not going to let him know what's up. Guess what's for supper, Gwen?"

"Don't know, let me think. Ah, fish, that is, unless we're having fish."

"You're right again, Gwen. I'm throwing these spuds in the ashes and the onions too. I got a rhubarb salad and greens. What do you think of that?"

"You surprise me so often that sometimes I don't get surprised. You didn't mention dessert."

"Now that's a surprise," Charlie smiled his Charlie smile, "I was keeping it a secret but I got us a strawberry rhubarb pie from the supermarket and I got a spray can of whipped cream for on top."

"Thank you, Charlie. You really pulled out the stops."

But as the Fool started to tidy up before starting dinner an older model American sedan turned into the campground in a cloud of dust and lead footed it to the Welcome Center. It was the Queen's car and she pulled it around back so it wouldn't be seen from the road. Nix and the Fool heard a door slam and a series of profanities followed by a cascade of obscenities as the Queen fought her way up the hill.

"Fool," she cried before stumbling and falling into a gully full of briars. They stuck everywhere on her clothes and even in her hair. Dusting herself off and picking off as many as she could, the Queen continued, whimpering a little under her breath, "This is the worst day of my life, and that's saying a lot. I'm going to die in a gully wearing a skimpy housedress covered in burs. I'm not even wearing make-up. Fool!" she screamed.

"Your Majesty," the Fool feigned a bow.

"Cut the shit, Fool, you have to run."

"What do you mean, I have to run? How's your ankle?"

"Hurts like the devil. I think it's sprained," she winced, "You have to leave. The King is free and he was asking about you."

"I expect him, Queen, but thank you."

"Yeah, but this time he'll be worse than ever. He thinks I'm sleeping with someone else and he's lost his mind about it. He tried to kill me. He'll try to kill the Blacksmith. If he can't find him or me, he'll come after you. It's how he thinks. I don't intend to stick around so you better get ready."

"Where are you going to go, Queen?"

"Call me Diane from now on or don't call me anything."

"Where you going to go, Diane?"

"I don't know but a hole in the ground would be better than him finding me here."

"Come over to the campsite and see someone you know. I'm making supper. You'll like it."

"You're all grown up and I can't call you Fool anymore."

The Fool had her lean on him to take the pressure off her ankle, "Call me Charlie then. It's my name."

"I know, right? So, Charlie, it sounds funny, doesn't it? Charlie. Is the King armed, Charlie?"

The Fool assisted Diane to the campsite, telling her, "I'm not sure but he was carrying a little six shot revolver before he went to jail. It was the gun that got me in the hands."

"Yeah, after grazing his brain."

"That's the one. Do you remember Agent Nix?" The Fool pointed to Nix, sitting by the fire sipping rum.

"What's she doing here?" asked Diane, not acknowledging Nix's presence.

"She's my friend and you'll like her too. Especially where you have something in common."

"What, she hates the King? Get in line. Nobody could hate him more than I do," her hand went to her throat, her other arm covered her breasts. "I married him."

"I'd hate myself if I were you," Nix piped in and a heavy silence fell. Things could have gone sour. I think Diane's sprained ankle tilted things towards a peaceful reply.

"I do," Diane smiled privately and sad-laughed, "On our wedding night the King had sex with a Wench whose head was in a bush below our motel window. I saw them from the room and started crying and then hollering from the balcony. When he got back to the room he said he thought she was me. He'd gone out for ice. But I stayed with him after that and after every other time. I must be the dumbest bitch there is. "

Nix propped herself on one elbow and said, "If we're limiting your 'dumbass bitch challenge' to interactions with the King, you win. I don't know him like you do, honey, but if this challenge is open to any douche bag girlfriend, boyfriend, husband, or relative, I can give anyone a run for her money for most humiliating, desperate and stupid behavior."

"I know, right, but I'm from Kentucky," Diane sat down next to Nix. "And our idea of humiliation is probably different from anyplace else in the lower forty-eight. It cuts to the bone. Where you from? You might need a handicap or we might need a judge to resolve this."

"Let's try first."

"Okay," Diane got comfortable, "I married our King when I was just a girl. Life at home was hard back then..."

"When was that?" asked Nix.

"When was what?

"When did you marry the King?"

"I wasn't underage, if that's what you're driving at," the Queen got huffy, "We got married on my sixteenth birthday, September 16, 2010. My parents signed a waiver."

"Are you sure of that date Diane?"

"Yeah, I'm sure and nobody forced me and we didn't have to either. I'm embarrassed to say that I wanted to be a queen. How stupid is that? I wanted to live a fairy tale life where women would look up to me and men would obey my commands. I gave up everything that might have been and for what, to be the Queen of King Henry's Freakin' Faire?"

"I mean are you sure of the date you got married?"

"Of course, I'm sure. It's my birthday."

"So, you were saying life was hard back then."

"Yeah, it was hard. That's why I married the King. That and being the Queen."

"Well, that's all terribly sad."

"What! Did you just say...? Are you fucking....?"

"My turn," Nix's eyes narrowed. "When I was twelve, not quite thirteen, my father brought me to the bathroom, took down my shorts and undies and plucked the few pubic hairs I'd sprouted. When he was done he smiled up at me and left to meet the men to whom he sold me. Best two out of three, Diane?"

"Oooww-wee, Nix, your own Daddy. Not even in Kentucky, girl. I can see where this is going. We don't need a visit to Terror Town. I've lived on the outskirts and never wanted to shop Main Street. You win. Your own Daddy, huh?"

A silence descended. No one knew how to move on. That's why they could hear a tinny whine in the distance, like a buzzing bee, growing closer. There was a backfire and Diane jumped. Charlie said he'd check and see. He poked his head up and saw the King on a little red scooter trying to make it up the hill.

LVII

Leo and Steiger parked behind Leo's cousin's funeral parlor in the North End. They walked down the hill to Causeway St. and over to the coffee shop that Steiger hated. He thought Leo did this to spite him.

"I don't care what you think of the coffee. I don't give a shit what you think at all. Until you start carrying your weight, I'll make the decisions."

"I'm not carrying my weight? Did I hear you right, Leo? What about my ass?"

"What about it?"

"C'mon, Leo, it's our early warning system. Haven't I demonstrated that? Without my ass we'd probably be in a hospital bed too."

"Don't say stuff like that, Steiger," Leo clasped his hands. "Think about where we're going. Poor fucking Miekewicz could have bled out. We could be on our way to his funeral instead of the hospital."

"Yeah, you're right, Leo. Look at my face. Do I look despondent?"

"The fuck are you asking me, Steiger?"

"Can you see grief or sorrow on my face?"

"There's something wrong with you, Steiger."

"People say that but nobody ever does anything."

"Here's Sava," Leo walked ahead. "Thanks for coming, Sava, and thanks for letting us know about Gus. We can skip the coffee if it's okay with you. We'd like you to come to the hospital with us to see how The Plow is doing."

"Sure, that is fine. But I don't have any classes today so if my ankle bracelet shows I'm not at my rooming house, work or school for so many minutes, you will have to talk to my probation officer, Mr. Hakeem Joseph, who doesn't like me too much."

"No problem," Leo assured him.

"He will ask what I was doing."

"Miekewicz is at Mass General, right down the street. Steiger will tell this Joseph guy that the IRS wanted you to get a flu shot or something."

"Is that where I go for that?"

"He's not going to know."

Sava's face soured, "Don't you have a better lie?"

"It'll work fine. Hospitals are used to working with HIPPA. They won't answer any questions or give out any names."

"That sounds good," Sava seemed relieved, "but who is HIPPA?"

"He's the one who won't say shit about you."

"Thank him for me."

"Sure."

They used the Visitor's Entrance to Mass General and asked the woman at the reception area where they could find a Mr. Miekewicz? She looked at her computer screen, over at them, and pushed a button. A Boston police officer came out and asked them what they wanted with the patient. Leo told him they were friends of his so the police officer said that if they were friends they wouldn't mind presenting ID, being frisked and then escorted. They agreed without complaint and were brought to the room. There was a security guard sitting outside the door. He checked their IDs, frisked them again and eyed them suspiciously. Reluctantly, he let them in.

"Hey, Gus," asked Leo.

"Mmmpff..."

"You awake, Gus?"

Gus looked around and tried to move, "What down is it?"

"You're in the hospital, Plow," informed Leo.

"Huh, I'm where?"

"Mass General, Gus, you're in the hospital. What happened?"

"What happened?"

"We're asking you, Plow. We weren't there."

"Oh, yeah, in the hospital." Gus seemed to be falling back asleep but then all three hundred and forty pounds of him started thrashing and screaming, "My fucking hand, they cut off my fucking hand, oh, Jesus Christ, they cut off my hand. Help me God, Jesus, my hand."

The guard burst in and told them to leave immediately or he would call a police officer. Rattled and scared they headed for the elevators.

"Who cuts off hands?" asked Steiger as they poured out a door to the sidewalk.

"The Plow looked half dead," Leo was shaking his head. "Did you see the giant bandage where his hand ought to be? Good Christ, he said they took it off."

"I need drink. Where is bar?" Sava was paler than usual.

"The Red Fez is just up Cambridge St. No one is going to be there now. I need a stiff one too," Leo was paler than the belly of a slug in winter.

LVIII

Andrei let the phone ring until Nix finally answered.

"Gus Meikewski had his hand cut off by the people who killed that pornographer, Buffum."

"Hey, Andrei, what do you say? I'm kind of busy just now."

"Only got a minute myself, Nix. I sent the Plow to let them know I was in a position to get them what they wanted. They never even talked to him. They cut off his hand instead. They said they don't pay for what's theirs."

"Oh no, Andrei, I hear you but it's getting tense here. We have an issue at the moment."

"I'm just about done. These guys, Buffum's associates, went to East Side $ and said something. I don't know what but the Tiny Rascals won't speak to me either. I won't make it through the night, Nix, and I never got that three hundred K to you. I'm texting you a mooring number in Gloucester Harbor. The boat's name is 'Squam'. There's half a million in gold in a secret compartment beneath the head. Keep three hundred. Save two in case one of the girls has trouble."

"Andrei,...."

"Ah, Nix, the floater's here. Too bad. I'll have to say good-bye. Don't ever sell yourself short, Nix. You've got chops. Your name, not even your existence will be made known to these people, I give you my solemn, dying word. Go to my funeral and introduce yourself to my wife and wonderful daughters and tell them I was your friend, but not in that way. Have a good life. I'm throwing this phone out the window, then I'm following it."

LIX

I was standing on the top of the hill watching the King get up, start that motor scooter, race the engine and travel about ten or twenty feet before falling off again. He'd cuss and grouse, get up and make the same mistake. That's when I heard Gwen say into her phone, "Andrei....Andrei...". I didn't know anything about anyone named Andrei but it sounded like a lot was going on wherever he was. I was too busy with the King to say or do anything for him.

Finally, the King seemed to be done with the motorbike, getting up this time and kicking it until he fell to the ground again. Of course, all he was wearing on his feet were the white cotton socks they must have given him in jail. Both of his socks were now bloody and dirty and, I'm guessing, the feet within, but he didn't seem to care. I've seen the King every kind of fucked up. He's like the undead the way he fills his life with nothing. But when he gets into PCP and bath salts, something happens and the trouble is always supersized.

Still standing at the top of the hill with Gwen and the Queen crouched behind me, I watch the King popping some pills as he struggles up hill, leaving bloody sock prints in the dry grass. That's what PCP does to this King.

"Where do you think you're going, King," I asked him politely enough.

"That not any of your business, Fool. You'll get out of my way if you know what's good for you."

"I live here, King, so it is my business. This is my campsite, not yours. You ain't welcome here. Why don't you scat!"

"Don't you scat me, boy."

"I say begone, Your Majesty."

"Whatcha gonna do if I don't, Fool?" The King reached for his six shooter and aimed it at my head, raising it slightly before pulling the trigger. Nothing happened except a click.

Standing up, brandishing her Glock, Nix said, "If you're going to pull a gun, Overbee, it ought to be one that's loaded and functional, like mine. I wish I'd shot you dead before you raised the barrel, but the day is young. Now, hold the gun by the barrel only and place it on the ground at your feet. Anything else and I will shoot you in the face. I'll shoot to kill. Hear me, Majesty, shoot to kill."

The King turned the gun so the business end was facing him, holding it by the barrel. Nix released a half sigh and said, "My gun is aimed at your forehead and I can tell you, King, I don't miss this shot at a hundred feet, let alone fifteen, but there's a first time for everything, isn't there? You might get lucky, or me sloppy. Who knows? It is your call, King, but in the meantime my site stays on your forehead and my finger on the trigger of this Glock. Did you know that my Glock has a pressure safety? It's in the trigger. Ironic, isn't it, safety in the trigger, Now drop the gun and back up twenty paces, Your Majesty."

"Ten."

"The soft safety on this gun don't bargain," Nix's face was rigid.

"Twenty it is, Miss Bitch."

"Good, now empty your pockets. That's good, now take your pants down and turn your pockets out."

"Never. Not for you, bitch, not for anyone."

"You will and you'll pull up your shirt."

"How will you make me?"

"Charlie will."

"The Fool? He's my boy. You can't make him do nothing, especially to me. And if he tries he'll only get hurt."

"You can't win, King," Nix was unwavering, "Charlie, check him for weapons."

I told the King to reach for the sky. I've always wanted to say that. The King smiled. He wasn't taking me seriously. He said, "Touch me, Fool, and your life is over."

I held him by the hair and punched down on his kidney five times and he dropped like the dead. I was going to check on him but Nix said, "Wait a minute. That boy's got some snake in him."

She held the Glock to his temple while she tried to get a pulse.

The Queen said, "Pull the trigger."

Satisfied he was alive and to humor the Queen, who was now saying, 'Give me the gun', Gwen told me to tie the King to the timber sledge and drag him to camp.

He was so light I could have carried him but the Queen insisted he be tied. She was terrified of him until she saw how limp and unfocused he was. She had me tip the sledge up and brace it with stout branches so that the King was in an upright position, eyes blinking. Even then she was tentative, but as she got used to him being tied there she loosened up a bit. Finding a rag, she reached over and gagged him. Then, for the first time since His Highness arrived, she smiled.

The potatoes and onions were ashes. I took out some bread and butter and made coffee and heated up a fish chowder. The Queen was hungry and devoured it right in front of the King. Nix and I had a moment alone and she said she was going to take the gag off the King and ask him a few questions, but as soon as she did the King started in.

"You fucking bitch, Diane, sleeping with that filthy Blacksmith, again, and lying to me about it."

I built the fire and was tidying up here and there so I'd have an excuse to eavesdrop.

The King continued, "I don't give a shit about you, Diane, and never have. I needed you for the show, okay, and you did that fine. It was everything else you did that sucked. And the worst of it, Diane, the very worst part was I had to sleep with you. That was hard."

The Queen, that is, Diane began to say something but then her shoulders rose and slumped. There was a hitch in her breath and she sobbed, "Wasted, my whole life has been wasted," she pointed at the King, "wasted on you. Won't you please give me the gun, Nix?"

"One more thing, Diane," the King was grinning, "I've had sex with every best friend you've ever had at the Faire. How about that? Know what else? I let that sissy brother of yours suck me off and then I took all his money and told him I was telling you."

"You, never!"

"Oh, that's right. So sorry, Di. He's no longer with us, is he. What is it killed him, suicide?"

"Stop it, Ronnie."

"You're just like your hillbilly Momma who fucked the oil man."

"You killed Stan Zimochowski, Ronnie," the Queen was suddenly cool. She took a moment, "You told me so. You told me over and over. You threatened me that way. You bragged about it. You intimidated me. You're a murderer. You're a fraud. I know lots of terrible things you've done. You've stolen from everyone at the Faire, for years. You're a liar and a thief and a murderer. You're a rotten husband and the worst King a Queen ever had."

"Is that all you've got, Diane? Why don't you repeat it for Agent Nix, in case she didn't get it all."

"I heard her just fine, Mr. Overbee," Nix told the King.

"Good for you, Agent Nix. It's too bad you can't use it against me."

"Why can't I do that, Mr. Overbee?" asked Nix.

"Because me and the Queen are husband and wife, Agent Nix. This is Massachusetts and neither spouse can testify against the other. That's the goddamn law. You ought to brush up on it. I knew one day things would come to this. That's why I went to the Legal Clinic and asked them and they told me, like I said, neither of us can say shit about one another unless the other one says it's okay and it's not okay, you bitch, Diane. Go ahead and cry your fuckin' eyes out. I hope you cry forever."

"I see, Mr. Overbee, that you know the law," Nix was cool. She found a piece of sweet green grass and stuck it in her mouth and rolled it around.

"Damn right, Agent Nix. I prepare for treachery."

"Clearly, but this isn't your first marriage, is it?" asked Nix.

"You probably know it's not. It's no secret. Why ask?"

"What happened to your last marriage?"

"Divorce, Nix, this is America, not Iran."

"When did that divorce happen?

"I don't know, before I married this version."

Fresh crying. More sobs.

"I got divorced too," Nix moved closer to the King, "also in Massachusetts. We used the same lawyer because we had so much money to fight over. One thing the lawyer told us is that once the divorce is allowed we'd have to wait ninety days before the decree became final. He told us this in case either of us wanted to get remarried. Fat chance of that, but if I did want to get married again, well, it wouldn't be legal unless I waited ninety days from the allowance of my divorce. Is any of this sinking in, Your Majesty?"

"Tell me why I should care about anything you have to say? I don't give a fuck about you."

"Maybe you should give a fuck about the fact that you married the Queen only sixty-two days after the Hearing on your divorce. That was twenty-eight days too soon, Your Majesty."

"So what?"

"You were still married to your second wife when you married the Queen."

"Get to the point, Nix."

"Aren't you listening? You were never married to Diane because you were still married to your second wife when you and Diane tried to get married on September 16, 2010."

The Queen gave Nix a look and started screaming at the King, calling him a rapist. She cried, "I was only fifteen when you put that thing in my fanny, you pig! It hurt so bad. I'm going to tell everyone everything you ever did to me. I'm going to tell the cops what you told me about killing Stan Zimochowski."

The Queen seethed and grew red in the face, but then it dawned on her exactly what Nix was saying and she grew calm and, looking at the King, said, "You're not going to get away with it this time."

"What she means, Overbee," Nix explained, "is Diane's going to tell a grand jury how you bragged about killing Stanley Zimochowski and how you told her you did it. We don't have to worry about that pesky Massachusetts marital privilege any longer, Ronnie. We're going to get to hear everything that you ever said to Diane and also what you did and so will a jury. Hey look, your ride's here."

A cruiser followed by an ambulance pulled into the campground. The cruiser parked at the Welcome Center and the cops walked over while the ambulance powered its way up the grassy slope to my campsite. We had to cut the King from the sledge. It didn't look good, but these folk didn't know the King or, for that matter, the Queen.

The EMTs took his vitals and, of course, they were whatever the result is for 'Incredibly Fucked Up' with two lacerated and broken feet. The cops took the scooter and the Queen told them it belonged to Clara, one of the Wenches at the Faire. They paid closer attention at this information, planning on returning it tonight.

Gwen told them she was the one who called and the man we just cut down was named Ronald Overbee a/k/a King Henry. She mentioned that the King was out on bond when he threatened us with his six shooter, tried to shoot me, and unconditionally threatened to kill the Queen. She added that the King was the murderer of Stanley Zimochowski and that he had sexually molested the Queen when she was only fifteen. I think she added the last bit to resolve any doubts the cops might have had about who they ought to arrest.

The Queen walked down to the Welcome Center with the aid of the policemen, what with her bad ankle and the trauma she suffered dealing with the King. Gwen and I sat down with the bottle of Folly Cove Rum, facing West so we could catch the sun when it decided to finally sink. We drank lightly until sunset and then built a raging fire to chase away the night and scare off all the demons we let loose. Then we both fell asleep with the sun still a sliver on the horizon. It had been a busy day and a lot happened.

LX

Steiger drove slowly in the pelting rain. The wipers worked perfectly except for a broad swath on the driver's side at eye level.

"Nix, this rain is terrible. I'm going to get in an accident."

"Don't be chary," Leo needled from the back seat.

"It's funny that you say that Steiger," Nix responded, "I was just going to tell you to speed up or we're going to be late."

"I can't do that, Nix, not in this weather."

"No, I suppose not," said Nix from the passenger seat, "but if I reach my left foot over and step on your right foot, I'll bet you can."

"I can go a little faster."

They got to the funeral home when the line was starting to build. Without an umbrella they were soaked by the time they got in the door. Enough flowers to bury a pharaoh surrounded the casket, which was mercifully closed. It had been a long fall. Old ladies with big hair and black dresses sat in a cluster speaking in a Sicilian dialect, which anyone there would tell you is to Italian what Polish is to Portuguese. Their old men wore dark suits and ties and stood nearby, backs against a wall, uncomfortable in their best.

On one side of the funeral home stood a group of Black, white and Latino thugs wearing clean T shirts and their best jewelry. Most of their ink consisted of compasses pointing East and the $ sign, but hand signals, prison laments, naked women, and panther tears were also well represented. They laughed and talked among themselves, not disrespectfully. On the other side stood the Tiny Rascals, mostly Asian and all of them wearing tight black pants and snug black jackets over white tee shirts. Most of them were unsmiling and they didn't pretend to be at ease, but they tried to be respectful.

Nix asked Leo and Steiger to each take a side of the room and see if anyone was checking her out. Then she went to cut the line.

"Hey, lady, you can't cut the line," said a still soaked middle-aged woman.

"Oh, I'm sorry. I didn't mean to cut."

"You didn't, huh?"

"No, I did not."

"But you did and since then, up to this very moment, you're still cutting."

"Oh, I see," Nix conceded, "you thought I was cutting in front of you. I was here before you but I received a text, I'm sorry to bore you, a text that my flight was cancelled. I needed my boarding pass from my raincoat and I went to get it. I'm going to try and change my flight and book a room in case I can't." Nix smiled and turned around to face the casket.

"I don't care if you're fuckin' Santa Claus and you're on your way to Poor Town. Get the fuck behind me."

"Who's behind you?"

"Some pussy, how would I know? That's your problem."

"Let me just sneak in behind you then. Excuse me, sir, will you back up a few feet?"

"There's no room," said the man stuffily, "It's jammed all the way to the door."

"I feel that you're too close. My friend and I don't feel comfortable. Do you understand?"

"Okay, okay, I'll come back later," he couldn't get away fast enough.

"Excuse me, sir. Sir!" Nix called after him.

"What did I do?"

"Nothing, so far, but would you please bring my friend a glass of water? She's feeling faint."

"Of course, I'll be right back. And a cold compress?"

"That would be sweet of you," Nix allowed, smiling.

He hurried off, happy to have a mission and a compliment.

"Honey," the woman in front of her said, "that was the quickest disassembly of a man and reconstruction into something useful I've ever seen. Did you know Andrei?"

"I did, but not for long. It wasn't that way."

"If you say so."

"I do," said Nix.

"Okay."

"But can you tell me which daughter is which?"

"I can."

"You've got a glass of water and a cold compress coming because of me."

"You're right, sorry, right is right. The one closest to us is Giuseppina, the eldest.

"Giuseppina?"

"I know."

"What do I call her?"

"Giuseppina. It means God-given daughter, after our mother."

"Our mother?"

"Andrei's and mine, God rest her soul. Then there's Francesca, in the middle, after her mother. We don't talk, her mother and I, don't ask. The last one is Margherita, after me. What do you want with them?"

Nix extended her hand and tried to smile, "How are you, Margherita? My name is Nix. I met Andrei a few days ago, but we got along well. He said if anything happened to him I should tell his daughters that I will look out for them. That's it."

"So, you're one of his, let's call them friends?"

"Ahh, well, actually, yeah, I suppose so."

"Nice to meet you, Nix. At least you're not covered in tattoos."

"How do you know?"

"The rain. Why don't you put that coat back on unless you're trying to show everything you've got? What are you doing here? Why didn't you just send a card?"

"Andrei asked me to come to his funeral, so I'm here."

"You're not a gangster, Nix."

"No, I'm not but I'm not straight up either. It's a funny situation."

"Funny situation, eh? Come on, I'll introduce you."

"I'd appreciate that."

On her way back to Leo and Steiger, Nix felt all eyes on her. She said: "Hey, Leo, why do I feel like everyone is eyeballing me?"

"Everyone is, Nix," interrupted Steiger, "there's a huge grease spot on your raincoat. The rain beads up on it. It looks like motor oil. Where have you been where there's motor oil?"

"Nowhere," Nix was trying to look at the back of her raincoat while still wearing it, "I just picked this up from the dry cleaner this morning."

Steiger nodded understandingly, "Well, somehow you found some motor oil or they did that at the dry cleaner and didn't tell you. That happens all the time. It's happened to me twice."

"The only places I've been since I put on the raincoat is here and before that your car. What's in your car, Steiger?"

"In my car, Nix? Where were you sitting?"

"We only got here half an hour ago. You can't remember where I was sitting? Wow, I talked to you on the way."

"Sooo."

"In the front passenger seat, Steiger."

"You're sure?"

"Of course, I'm sure."

"Hmm, why'd you sit there? I had half a quart of oil on that seat. You see, I've been burning oil. You didn't loosen the cap, did you? Nix?"

"You're paying for this, Steiger."

"You still owe me a hundred dollars."

"Fine, give me another hundred and we'll call it square. I was never going to pay you back anyway. You get zero offset."

"Okay, can we go now, Nix?"

"Yeah, let's go. We have an early day tomorrow."

"C'mon, Nix," whined Leo, "it's Saturday."

"Yeah, come on, Nix," echoed Steiger, "where do we have to go?"

"Gloucester. Get some sleep and wear warm clothes. Be ready at four thirty."

LXI

The Plow swallowed a handful of narcotics and steadied himself against the van. It didn't seem to matter how many he took. The pain was stubbornly assertive. They were at a gas station convenience store outside of Stamford on 95 North. His brother Albin was filling the tank while his other brother, Janusz, went in to pay and get some snacks. It was a warm night and Gus shook a cigarette from a pack of Luckys. Two fell to the ground before he was able to fight off gravity and hold onto a third. Gus sighed angrily, ground his teeth, and set his jaw. Composing himself, he stuck the Lucky between his lips so he could get a lighter from his pocket. Nothing was simple any longer. He took a deep drag and breathed it out hard.

"Are you smoking?" Gus heard his brother Al say from the other side of the van.

He ignored him.

"This is a gas station, you fool. Do you want to blow us up?" Still pumping, Al looked over his shoulder for Jan. Sometimes Jan could calm Gus down, but Al had his doubts this time. It didn't matter because Jan was still in the convenience store chatting up the clerk.

"C'mon, Gus," asked Al, "put it out before someone calls the cops and we have to explain two trussed up Jersey brats in the back?"

Before this ember could grow into an argument there was a bang against a panel from inside the van. Gus flicked the butt away so he could investigate. Climbing into the passenger seat, Gus shut the door. One armed, he quietly checked the bindings of two young men on the van floor. They were trussed up with plastic tie tags and gags. Everything seemed to be fine but the Plow still reached for the cattle prod and held it to the temple of each of them for thirty seconds. That settled them down.

When Jan got back he bitched out Gus for smoking and said that if Gus didn't leave the brats alone he was going to kill them before they reached Bridgeport.

Once back in the van things settled down and before long they were on the car ferry to Orient Point, Long Island, where they met Gus' friend Emil, a fisherman, in the parking lot. The parking lot was unlighted and deserted but they drove off into deeper shadows and off loaded the brats into Emil's truck bed and covered them with fishing gear and tarp.

It was too frustrating for Gus to count cash so Jan paid Emil two thousand from Gus' wallet. Then Gus said to Emil, "Remember, fourteen miles out before you weigh them down and dump them. I want them alive while they sink. Don't forget to weigh them good. Fourteen miles out."

"Okay, okay," Emil was nervous, looking over his shoulder, "you can leave now. I gotta get to the boat before sunrise. I'll only call if something goes wrong."

"Nothing is gonna go wrong, Emil."

"Easy peazy, Gus, they always sink. Leave now and you'll be home for breakfast. We haven't seen each other since the ball game last summer."

"We still haven't."

"It's been too long. We'll have a cook-out one of these days."

The Plow didn't know how to shake hands anymore so he just said, "So long, Emil, and thanks for doing this on short notice."

"Anything for a friend, Gus."

LXII

Most of the pleasure boats had been hauled out of Gloucester Harbor by this time of year but there were always a stubborn few still bobbing in the chop. Nix trained her glasses west of Smith Cove near the Federal Mooring Field.

"That's the 'Squam' sitting out there. Want to have a look, any of you?"

Sava said, "I'll have a look, if you please."

Neither Steiger nor Leo said a word. Neither had said ten words since Nix picked them up an hour ago.

"Looks like a boat, Nix," nodded Sava.

"Back in the car, Sava. We've got to get to a bar called The Yardarm before six."

Nix rapped on the back door until she was about to give up, then it opened a crack.

"What you want?"

"Open the door," Nix demanded, "Andrei sent me."

The voice behind the door said, "Oh, okay, if Andrei sent you...."

"Don't shut the door. I was at Andrei's wake last night, but he did send me."

"Yeah?"

"Do you know Andrei's sister, Margherita?"

"Why you wanna know what I know? I'm not knocking on your door."

"Call her and ask her if she knows Nix."

"You don't tell me what to do."

"You have a spider tattooed on the head of your dick."

"How would you know?"

"You got it in the Village in New York City. Andrei was with you."

"He told you?"

"Margherita told me last night, but Andrei called me the night he... died and told me about the Squam. He said you have the keys."

"Here you go. I don't know you and I don't know anything, but if you want to get rid of the boat I can fetch you a fair price, considering, of course, considering."

Nix and company waited until seven when launch service started. It was cold and choppy on the water so there was no chit chat with the operator. None of them brought gloves and their hands were crampy with the cold. Nix had trouble with the cabin door but finally they all got inside and out of the wind. Nix turned the engine over and, to everyone's surprise, it started. Nix got the cabin heater going and turned on the running lights. Leo cranked open the lee windows to get rid of the stuffy air. They all sat on boat cushions breathing fog and staring at one another until Nix spoke up.

"Okay, it's time for you two," indicating Leo and Steiger, "to stop sulking. You're lucky I don't take an ear from both of you. When did you learn about 'The Girls' Room' live stream?"

The engine idled. The boat rocked at its cable, going nowhere.

"An ear?" Leo's mouth opened and eyes widened.

"When did you learn about the bathroom feed, Steiger?"

"I swear to God, Nix, I only learned about it from Sava," Steiger belched and held his stomach, "Sava told Leo and Leo told me, I think that's how it went. So much has happened, Nix. I can't keep anything straight."

"Why didn't either of you tell me?"

"Is that a serious question," asked Leo, "after you've just threatened to take off our ears?"

"One ear a piece."

"Whatever," added Leo, "if we told you about it we were afraid you'd hunt down Buffum and execute him right then and there."

"That'd be Felony Murder, Nix," Steiger interjected, "I read up on it. I'd go to prison too, not just you."

"For what? For that? Why would I kill him? By the way, how do I get two of those Ramrod tee shirts? Andrei was supposed to get them for me but somebody killed him before he could."

"You're not mad?" asked Leo and Steiger.

"Why should I be mad? Because of that live stream and those tee shirts I'm going to be rich, excuse me, wealthy."

"Yeah?" they asked, relieved.

"Yeah, I'm going to sue the IRS, the Department of the Treasury and the United States of America for violations of my civil rights. The other ladies and I will make a shit ton of money. That's what it'll take to keep a jury from hearing our story, a solid ass shit ton of cash. I was thinking about it last night. As soon as we ladies file suit I'm going to hold a press conference telling whoever will listen that I'm writing a book about my experiences in government service at the IRS. The tentative title is 'Pissed Off, Pimped Out, and Fucked Hard By the IRS: Birth of Ramrod'. That should bring them to the table."

Leo chuckled, "I can't help myself, Nix. You make me laugh. You sound like some comic book superhero making declarations. I mean that in the nicest possible way. It's you at your cutest, if you'll forgive me. Anybody feeling seasick?"

"Yeah, Nix," added Steiger, "and now you've got pornography working for you too?"

"Yeah, you could say so. Anyway, boys, I won't be going back to work. I'll try and keep in touch but if I don't, you shouldn't take it personally. I may be working as a cop for the Horseshoe Falls PD."

"No shit!" chuckled Steiger.

"If I get the job," continued Nix, "I'll start as a lieutenant."

"You a cop, Nix? Doesn't seem right, does it?" offered Leo.

"It seems wrong, is what it seems," answered Steiger. "It's, I don't know, somehow criminal. It's ridiculous. You'd be such a bad cop, Nix."

"Want to hear something crazier?" added Nix, "This place has so many bad cops the Chief wants to hire me to straighten them out."

"Like two negatives equal a positive?" Leo tried to understand.

"Have you been to a psychiatrist yet?" asked Steiger.

"What kind of a question is that?" Nix turned on Steiger, "While you were in the hospital talking dirty with the nurses I was sleeping a couple hours a night, when I could. I did that for days on end and didn't eat regularly. I've been throwing my dirties in the trunk and buying cheap new. Who's had time for a shower, let alone a psychiatrist?"

Rolling his eyes, Steiger replied, "I don't need to know about your hygiene and diet issues, Nix. You have to make time for important things. You have to prioritize. Get to a psychiatrist before you start this new job or it might be too late. That's all I'm saying."

"I'm not going to need a psychiatrist, Steiger. This thing is nearly over and things are quiet in Horseshoe Falls. That's where I hope to work. It's a fresh start for me and I'll also be able to keep an eye on Charlie Aspirance and spend time with Lesous, a good cook and maybe a good man."

"Who's Charlie Aspirance?" asked Steiger.

"Who's Lesous?" Leo inquired.

"Part of this case you guys don't have to worry about. But what you should know is that Andrei talked to me privately and called just before he died. I could hear the thugs at his door. He asked me to look after his daughters. He said he had a half a million dollars. He offered me three hundred thousand to watch out for them. He asked me to hold onto two hundred thousand in the event an emergency came up and the ladies needed money fast."

"When did all this happen?" Leo wanted to know.

"Yeah, Nix, when was this?" Steiger chimed in.

"You're like Leo's monkey, Steiger. Andrei told me about the money when we walked out on the roof alone. He asked me to watch out for his daughters when we were there, okay? Anyway, I've been thinking about this because we've been in this together from the start, and that includes you, Sava."

"Da."

"So, we each walk out of this with seventy-five thousand, but there's a catch. If these women ever need me, they need you too. Is that understood?

"Seventy-five thousand each?" Leo asked with a big grin, "I'm in, Nix, and thanks."

"Yeah," said Steiger, "I don't know what to say, but we have to decide whether or not we're going to report this as income on our returns.

"No one is reporting anything, boys. Think of the source of the funds. Now listen, you're getting ahead of yourselves," Nix tried to get them grounded, "This money isn't free. Don't take it unless you agree to protect these women. If you do agree and you're ever needed, you have to make it your first priority. I hope that's understood because I'm not likely to get softer with age. Be careful what you agree to do."

They all agreed and Sava and Nix took turns unscrewing the alkalized head plate below the head until they found the gold, which was heavier than they imagined.

LXIII

Nix took an apartment in Horseshoe Falls where she works as a lieutenant on the police force. One Saturday morning Gus Miekewicz knocked on her door. Nix had been out late and had too much to drink so it took a moment for her to register who he was. She was only certain when she saw his eyes follow hers to the bulge in his right front coat pocket where his stump rested.

It was often this way, Gus wanted to tell her, but he didn't. There was a distant look in his eyes. Nix speculated that he wasn't whole and never would be. It brought tears to her eyes and she turned away and said, "It's good to see you up and out of the hospital, Gus. Where are my manners, come on in. Grab the chair."

"It's good to see you, Nix. I'll come in for a moment, but I'll stand," Gus made a show of wiping his feet even though it was dry as dust outside, "I left a message on your phone that I'd be by this morning."

"Sorry, Gus, I got in late and didn't check. Please have a seat. I'll make coffee. Just clear that chair off. And I have Pop Tarts."

"Just coffee. Black. Agent Nix?"

"It's not that anymore, Gus. I'm a local cop with Horseshoe Falls. I'm a lieutenant. It's just Nix now."

"Aww, that's great, Nix. Did you get kicked out of the IRS because...."

"No, Gus, I chose to leave."

"If you say so."

"I do."

"The Boss really liked you."

"I liked him, Gus. What can I do for you?"

"After I got out of the hospital me and my brothers found the three guys who took my hand. They weren't hard to find. They were vicious little bastards, but amateurs. Anyway, I have something to show you."

"Yeah, what's that?"

"The Polaroids of their heads."

"You have pictures of their heads?"

"Yeah. The heads are in the van if you need to see them."

"No, no thanks, Gus. The pictures are fine."

"Okay, Nix, I just have a little more. We found who they worked for, two punk cousins from Morristown, New Jersey, in their twenties. Spoiled brats. Their fathers are brothers and have a successful, ahhh, obstetrics and gynecology practice. The kids are fuck ups but they've been living large. They were making bank somehow and now we know they ran a pornography racket."

"Where, Gus? Where are they now?"

"Now? They're fourteen miles out to sea, cold, wet, and weighted down, never to be seen again."

"Oh, Gus, you wonderful man, thank you, Gus, thank you. You don't know what a relief it is to hear this. I was afraid those guys wouldn't stop coming, with what they did to you. Let me top off your coffee. Gus? Are you okay, Gus?"

"I miss him, Nix. I miss my hand too. I miss me. This isn't who I was. It sure is who I am. I'm sorry, I don't mean to go on." Gus shook his head and said, "Good coffee, strong. One last thing. The Boss wanted me to give this to you and I promised I would, so here."

With great ceremony he handed her a small bag with a wrapped package in it.

Stomach churning, Nix feared the package may contain penises or scalps. As she unwrapped the package, Gus unfolded a piece of paper with his left hand and tongue and read, 'He was a man of his word. He said that as a woman of honor, you'd understand that if he had to come back to give this to you himself, he would have found a way.'

There were two folded Army green Ramrod tee shirts. Nix held one up. It seemed like a perfect fit.

"Aww, Gus, you are gracious and such a loyal man. Andrei would be so proud. I'm going to wear this one and when I do I'll think of you and Andrei. The other tee shirt, well. I've got plans for that. You're a friend, Gus, a real friend. You didn't lose your hand. You gave it to me. I'll owe you a hand for the rest of my life. You wouldn't want to deliver pizzas for a while, would you?"

ACKNOWLEDGEMENTS

I would like to thank Susan Oleksiw, the author of several mystery novels, short stories, articles, and reviews, and the editor of several anthologies.

I would like to thank Brianna Denette, an accomplished graphic artist in Boston, as well as my daughter, Cal Shusta, for the thoughtfully designed cover.

Without the support, encouragement, and editorial eye of Joanna Mulkern, my partner and fellow writer, I would not have been able to complete this book.

ABOUT THE AUTHOR

This is Bill Scannell's debut novel, and the first of three works featuring the investigations and misadventures of Gwendolyn Nix.
He lives with his family in Rockport, MA.

NOTE FROM THE AUTHOR

Word-of-mouth is crucial for any author to succeed. If you enjoyed *The Last Taxpayer at King Henry's Faire*, please leave a review online—anywhere you are able. Even if it's just a sentence or two. It would make all the difference and would be very much appreciated.

Thanks!
Bill Scannell

CPSIA information can be obtained
at www.ICGtesting.com
Printed in the USA
LVHW041733130522
718403LV00004B/7